ARTIFACTS

of

an

EX

JENNIFER CHEN

W

WEDNESDAY BOOKS
NEW YORK

First published in the United States by Wednesday Books, an imprint of St. Martin's Publishing Group

ARTIFACTS OF AN EX. Copyright © 2023 by Jennifer Chen. All rights reserved. Printed in the United States of America. For information, address St. Martin's Publishing Group, 120 Broadway, New York, NY 10271.

www.wednesdaybooks.com

The Library of Congress Cataloging-in-Publication Data is available upon request.

ISBN 978-1-250-86566-3 (hardcover)
ISBN 978-1-250-86567-0 (ebook)

Our books may be purchased in bulk for promotional, educational, or business use. Please contact your local bookseller or the Macmillan Corporate and Premium Sales Department at 1-800-221-7945, extension 5442, or by email at MacmillanSpecialMarkets@macmillan.com.

First Edition: 2023

10 9 8 7 6 5 4 3 2 1

To Brendan Hay, everything I know about romance is because of you.

ARTIFACTS

of

an

EX

Los Angeles is disgustingly hot in October. I lug two large pink boxes full of egg tarts and sesame balls as a river of sweat snakes down my back. Pressing my pink-and-white sequin sneakers against the front doors of this random church, I step inside, carefully putting down the boxes when I notice the stained-glass windows.

Sunlight streams in—a rainbow of blood red, royal blue, and succulent green on the blond-gray hardwood floor. I marvel at this perfect potential gallery space with its wide-open layout, bare white walls, and mid-century boho chic furniture. I shake my head. No. I'm done with curating.

"Chloe?" a Latina woman asks.

Her brown curly locks bounce as she shakes my hand. I admire her flowy floral dress and the jangle of crystal bracelets along her bronze arms. She's got a very relaxed LA style—a mood I still haven't figured out.

"I brought the samples."

"Perfect." She extends a hand. "I'm Lourdes Hernandez, the owner of Ruby Street." She opens the lid of one box. "Ooh, these egg tarts smell divine."

"My mom made them this morning."

Lourdes lifts one out and cups it in her palms. Taking a big bite, she smiles wide. I know the feeling. The combination of the buttery tart crust and the smooth yellow custard is like eating sunshine for breakfast.

"Divine!" She wipes crumbs from her mouth. "Come."

I follow her. She smells like oranges and sandalwood. I've decided sandalwood and pot are the official scents of Los Angeles. I gawk at this church that's not a church. The interior is more coffee shop/fancy workspace, but the exterior has a church steeple, pointed roofs, and marine-blue paint. The way the sunlight streams in is ideal for art. Not that I'm interested. I'm just impressed. She stops in front of a corner area with a smooth white marble counter, an empty pastry display case, and a black espresso machine.

"This is where we envision the pop-up café. My idea is that different local vendors rotate on a monthly basis. The moment I tasted your dad's coffee, I knew we had to have Sweet Yen represented. Now that I've tasted the pastries, I know our clientele will love it."

I snap photos for my dad and mom. Dad will be thrilled. He's been wanting to expand the café beyond the storefront.

I turn around from the coffee counter and stare at the sea of white tables with clear rolling chairs. A coffee table that looks like a slab of wood from a tree. White and gold orbs hang from the ceiling to illuminate the space.

"What is this place? A tech start-up?"

Lourdes laughs. Her jewelry jangles too. "We're an event space, wedding venue, co-op workspace, and, soon, an art gallery."

My eyes widen. "This place is my heaven," I accidentally say out loud.

"We're going to have a teen night too. You should come." A buzz sounds from her back pocket. She pulls out her phone. "I gotta take this. Thanks, Chloe!"

I slowly stroll through the different rooms. My mind fills with ideas of what I could do with this sprawling space. In New York City, galleries are closet-sized, but here, there's so much open area. Sculptures, black-and-white photography, even a light show like James Turrell. Imagine what I could do with a fiber artist like Jake, my handsome, long-distance New York boyfriend, who was called "an eighteen-year-old art phenom" by *The New York Times*. Thinking of Jake while I'm stuck in still-eighty-five-in-October Los Angeles creates a dull ache in my stomach. I click on my phone's lock screen to stare at his sparkling sepia eyes, his broad brown nose, and a smile that instantly makes me weak.

I take a few pics, buzzing with the beginnings of several ideas. I bite my lip. I'm getting carried away. I rush out of the not-a-church and hope my buzz disappears as I step outside, cringing at another walk as a total tourist.

No one walks in Los Angeles, and anyone who does moves like a snail in mud. My internal monologue behind each person is: *Hurry up!*

As I walk back to my parents' café, I text Jake pics of the space.

Me: Look at this undiscovered gallery space!
Jake: Did you get my package?

I smirk and send him an eggplant and peach emoji. Ever

since we had sex six months ago on my sixteenth birthday, it's all he thinks about. Who am I kidding? It's on my mind too. But we usually trade texts like these at night under the cover of bedsheets, not in broad daylight. He doesn't respond.

Before I walk into the café, I decide to send him a selfie. I pose in front, whisking my black bangs into submission. I take seven shots before I'm satisfied. The photo pops up in our long-running text chain. Me: pink V-neck tank top to show off my fantastic bust, a mid-length rainbow skirt that I altered for my petite legs, and a perfect pink lipstick pout that pops against my olive cheeks.

I have a ridiculous smile on my face, thinking of Jake sending back a selfie. At 4 P.M. on a Tuesday, the café is filled with screenwriters typing away on laptops and a few students from my new public school. I'm not in any school clubs yet, so I've been helping out. When we arrived, Sweet Yen needed a major makeover. Mom and I took three weeks to clean and spruce it up. I credit my many hours binge-watching *Queer Eye* (thanks, Bobby Berk!) and my artistic eye for the upgrade in my ahma's café. It went from functional to modern indoor oasis for creative types. We've lived with my ahma Yen ever since a neighbor called my mom at 8 A.M. East Coast time, 5 A.M. here, to tell her that Ahma was in the street in her pajamas. The only person I'd leave NYC for is my ahma. So here I am.

I spot a customer's cup flipped down on its saucer. I grab the coffee pot to refill it and hustle over. My ahma started one-dollar refills for her regulars, and Dad keeps it going.

"Thanks," says one. "I need a serious sugar fix to get through this next scene."

"I highly recommend the taro buns with the custard filling," I say. "It's a sugar bomb stuffed inside a carb explosion."

He nods and I go behind the counter to grab one. The purple bun is bursting with fresh white cream and topped with coconut shreds. It has the perfect squish as I snatch it with tongs. I plate and present it.

"Chloe, mail for you," says my dad. He wiggles his eyebrows as he froths milk for a cappuccino. "It's from Jake," he says all singsongy. "Go ahead and take your break now."

Oh! Jake meant an actual package. Now I feel like a total perv. I rush toward the back room and push through the cardboard boxes, sacks of sugar, and towers of coffee beans. There it is. Swoon. Like real snail mail. I rip open the brown craft paper to reveal an Adidas shoebox. I slip off the lid. Nestled on top of white tissue paper is a note.

For C-Lo

In his black pen scribble. I bring the notebook paper to my face. It smells just like him. I inhale like it's his T-shirt after I've snugged into him during a scary movie. I close my eyes and picture his strong bronze arms around me. I let myself think of his thick lips on the inside of my neck. I open the letter with a stupid grin on my face.

Hey C-Lo:
I've had some time to think since everything happened at my exhibit. Then you and your family had to jet so quickly. To be real with you, I think it's for the

best you left. Your move is a good reason for us to
end things.

Hold up. WHAT. I reread the last sentence several times.
My vision blurs as I read the rest.

I care about you, you know that. But things got off
track in the last few months. You pushed me to do
the exhibit, even when I said I wasn't ready. None
of us were, but you were dead set on it. I respect
your drive and vision. Hell, you've got your whole life
planned. Anyway, I'm sending back some of your
things that you left behind. Please hug your ahma
for me.
    I'll always care about you,
    Jake

I riffle through the shoebox. A yellow and black Metro-
Card from our first date. The three-dollar black umbrella I
bought on the street when it downpoured on us, and when
Jake kissed me for the first time. The takeout menu from Ma-
moun's Falafel where he drew a cartoon version of me with
flames coming out of my mouth after I asked for the ghost
pepper hot sauce that set my tongue on fire for the entire
night. My heart stops at my Met ID pass. The one that Jake
doodled all over after my student internship was up. He hid
hearts and our initials throughout. His signature style. My
heart cracks open when I see the misshapen black and gray
knit hat I made for Jake after he taught me how to stitch.

I wipe my tears with the back of my hand and grab the box, heading for the dumpster outside the back of the shop. I can't believe I lost my virginity to a guy who would dump me through an Adidas shoebox. Seriously. How messed up is that?

Before I chuck the box, I grab my phone to FaceTime my best friend, Selena. I instruct Siri to call Selena, but instead it says, "Here's what I found. Serena Jameka Williams is an American professional tennis player."

"Oh my god, phone! I hate you!"

Then, the box slips out of my hands, the contents spilling out onto the black concrete. The flimsy umbrella is splayed out like an octopus. Great. I'm so frustrated that I stomp on the ground like a toddler having a tantrum.

This is the worst day ever.

"Hey," says a Latina girl. "You okay?"

Oh great. Somebody was watching me. She looks vaguely familiar. Her long brown hair is pulled into a ponytail sticking out of her blue LA Dodgers hat. A sticker-covered skateboard waits like a dog by her feet.

I attempt to appear together by blinking away my tears and smoothing my hair.

"Totally," I mutter.

"Claire, right? You're in my AP chem class."

"Chloe, actually."

Her name escapes my memory. Jake was always a whiz at remembering names. He'd come up with clever tricks, like calling someone *Cat* because she wears a cat bracelet and her name is Cathy. We were a good team, we could work a crowd. He'd charm them and I'd figure out exactly what they liked.

"I'm Francesca."

Francesca surveys the scene. I am embarrassed that all my stuff is on the ground, like the world's worst stoop sale.

When she turns back to me, she smiles. "Let me guess. You're throwing your ex's things in the dumpster."

I cover my face. "Is it that obvious?"

An ice cream truck's off-kilter jingle rings behind us.

"I understand what you're going through." She wiggles her phone out of the back pocket of her black skinny jeans. "Angela Alvarez."

I see a gorgeous tattooed Latina smushed against Francesca. Angela's bright red lipstick is imprinted on Francesca's left cheek.

Francesca slides through more photos of the two of them together: beach sunsets, taco trucks, on top of a cliff. Francesca laying in grass covered in bright neon pink . . . silly string.

"Is that silly string?"

"Yeah. She used to prank me with it. That stuff gets everywhere."

I point to a picture of a car's glove compartment filled with brown sugar packets. "Is this another prank?"

"I've got a crazy sweet tooth," says Francesca. She smiles, crooked teeth showing. "I stashed sugar packets all over the place. In her car. In her purse. Not anymore." Her smile fades.

She gestures to my random objects. "Want some help?"

I nod. When we finish putting my failed relationship back into the shoebox, she holds up my yellow MetroCard. She pulls out something in her phone case. It says *TAP* on the light blue plastic card.

"Our shared TAP card."

"La La Land has a metro system? For real?"

"Angela and I took it everywhere. Down to the beach. Downtown. Santa Monica. You name it, we've been there. We were making our way through the map until she dumped me for Emily. A UCLA freshman. If you're gonna dump me, at least let it be for a USC frosh. Come on, everyone knows that."

I shrug my shoulders. I have no idea what Francesca is talking about. Now it's my turn for this bizarre show-and-tell.

"My guy dumped me from New York with this box."

"Oof. That's harsh!"

"Right?" I say.

"At least call a girl."

"Thank you!"

I tell her about each item. Francesca winces and groans. In a weird way, it's a relief to know that someone else gets it. I hand over the letter. She reads it. Her brown eyes go wide.

"Yikes!"

It's the way she says *yikes* that hits me this is real. Jake, my first boyfriend, has broken up with me. I knew I'd messed up Jake's last art show, but this stupid shoebox confirms it all. I'm a failure as a girlfriend *and* as an art curator.

"Hey," says Francesca. She taps her black high-tops against my white-and-pink sneakers. "We're better off."

She presses her blue TAP card against the edge of the café's green dumpster bin. "On the count of three, let's toss this crap together."

I don't know what possesses me, but I grab the plastic card, catching the edge before it falls over into the pile of coffee grinds and empty sugar sacks.

"I'll give you twenty bucks for the card."

Francesca's well-shaped eyebrows shoot up. "You're serious? It's got five bucks on it."

"I want to buy it and other stuff you have too. Venmo?"

"Deal."

I scan her code and within seconds, Francesca's breakup TAP card is now mine. She tips her Dodgers hat at me.

"Nice doing business with you." Francesca grabs her skateboard and hops on. She turns back. "For what it's worth, that Jake guy is making a big mistake."

I finally smile.

"Angela too."

She gives me a salute and skateboards away.

And now, I possess someone else's random relationship item. If Selena were here, she'd say, *Girl, what are you doing?*

I rush into the back room with my shoebox and Francesca's card. It's a tiny closet, but it has a door that shuts. I told myself that I was done with art curating, but the idea forms fast.

Shoot. I don't have my Happy Planner Yes You Can notebook. It's at home on my desk with my colored markers and matching stickers.

I have to get this down and the house is too far. I desperately search for paper and a pen. Any pen will do, though it pains me not to have my Pilot G2 blue ink pen.

I turn over some old café menus and write with a black pen. It's like scratching words with a stewed Taiwanese-style chicken foot, but I eek out what I need to write down.

> *A gallery show of break-up boxes. Anonymous.*
>   *Teenagers only. The exhibit would be a list of what's*
>   *in the box and a short statement from the person*
>   *submitting.*
> *Music: breakup songs. On a loop.*
> *Food: Ooh, pints of ice cream? No, it'll all melt.*
>   *Something that's a universal break-up food. What*
>   *could that be? I've never been dumped before. Sad*
>   *face. Sad face.*
> *Title of the exhibit: Heartifacts (!!!). Too much?*
> *Venue: Ruby Street. That place is so gorgeous. Ask*
>   *Lourdes Hernandez.*
> *Guest list: ???*

I stop scribbling with the nearly dead black pen. Right. I'm one month in to Los Angeles, which means I have zero friends and zero connections. It's not like Selena and my crew are going to fly cross-country for a bunch of rando shoeboxes. And definitely not Jake. Maybe this is a stupid idea. Do I want to be a failure on another coast?

But I post the ad on my @PlanItGirl Instagram anyway. Just to see.

BEEN DUMPED?

For a possible art show, I'll pay $20 for your break-up objects for anyone ages 13–18. To apply, click the link in my bio and fill out the form. Must share details about what's in your box, why it matters to you, and why you broke up.

Ship to Sweet Yen Café, 5818 York Blvd., Los Angeles, CA 90042. Privacy will be protected and full names will not be listed in the exhibit.

I upload a pic of my Jake box with the personal details blurred out. I quickly create a Google Form. I review it three times for typos, then post a link in my Insta bio.

If no one responds, it'll be a funny story to tell Selena and only twenty bucks wasted on Francesca's TAP card. No big deal.

Chapter 2

On Sundays, I always answer three questions from my @PlanItGirl Instagram DMs. I haven't responded since we moved because it took me a hot minute to get my video equipment set up the way I like. My sticker stash alone took me an entire Saturday to organize by theme and size.

At my white desk in the corner of my bedroom, I double-check that my two soft box lights, ring light, and iPad mount are at the right angles. I place my Happy Planner products in order of each question. The only good thing about living in Los Angeles is that my bedroom in Ahma's house is way bigger than my parents' two-bedroom Flushing apartment.

Before I shoot today's video, I pluck Sesame, my black cat, from my desk. She meows loudly, then retreats into the empty box at my feet. In her first weeks in LA, Sesame hid under a mountain of bubble wrap. She is rejecting the move too.

"Sesame, you can't sleep there. Your bed is over there."

I point to her gray Pusheen the cat bed. She hops on my bed, ignoring me.

I review my manicure and notice that my right pointer fingernail is smudged. I carefully remove the polish and repaint with my JINsoon Dolly Pink color and a glossy topcoat for the ultimate shine.

I pull out the index cards I've prepped with today's questions.

Question #1: How do I plan the perfect promposal?

Crap. Normally I'd love this question, but after my less-than-stellar breakup, the thought of promposals makes my stomach queasy. I could skip it, but I already pulled out my Happy Planner supplies that I matched for my answer. Also, the natural light flooding onto my white desk is gorgeous. Perfect for shooting. Plus, this question is great content. *It's now or never, Chloe.*

Hi there! Today I'm answering a Plan It Girl question from Instagrammer @melodymakes who asked: How do you plan the perfect promposal? I pulled together my Happy Memory Keeping Kit just for this. It has everything you'll need to start planning. Stickers, washi tape, and memory pages with weekly and monthly options. I also grabbed my Mambi Everyday Memories value pack stickers because you can never have enough stickers.

@melodymakes, I'd start with the month that you want to ask your date, let's say Valentine's Day. I'd give yourself three months to plan. Start with November, looking at the whole month first. Block out the holidays, then proceed to the weekly

vertical spreads. Give yourself one manageable
task per week. For the first month, I'd schedule
three mood board sessions for inspiration and a
color scheme. Focus on what your date loves and
how you can incorporate their personality into your
promposal. My go-to filler paper for mood boards
are the Big Ideas dot grid sheets. Plenty of room
to play.

   I love these clear gold hearts on the Celebrate
sticker sheet. The sheen on these stickers is just so
pretty. I'll place them along the edges in a cluster
pattern . . .

When I'm done with the questions, it's dinner time. I
haven't even gotten to the four *Heartifacts* boxes that arrived at
Sweet Yen since I posted three days ago. I rush downstairs and
grab my half-eaten burrito from yesterday. My ahma watches
her current favorite Taiwanese soap, *Single Ladies Senior,* at
top volume so the characters seem like they're shouting their
lines. I kiss her pale pink cheek before I head back to my
room. Between bites, I spread out five shoeboxes and place a
printed sheet on top, matching the box to the name on the
application form.

   I grab my Still I Rise spiral-bound notebook and line up
my color-coded markers. Pink is for content. Turquoise is
for marketing/web/social. Dark purple is for brainstorming.
Light green is for $$$.

   I flip open my notebook to a fresh lined page. Starting

a new notebook is like the first bite of a taro bun. The first delicious sip of my dad's matcha latte. Like when Jake first wrapped his arms around me. I shake my head. Jake isn't my boyfriend anymore.

I open the shoebox Francesca gave me at school today. Nestled inside are a bottle of neon-pink silly string, brown sugar packets, and a blue TAP card. One sugar packet has hand-drawn, blue-inked hearts around the edge. I touch my own heart as a reflex. Now I understand why Francesca had trouble handing me the box in the cafeteria. I sigh, then move on to the other boxes.

Box #1: Connor and Vincent

Inside: a tiny black Moleskine notebook (my personal fave for on-the-go note-taking), movie tickets with *ArcLight* printed across the top, a red plastic guitar pick, and a black-and-white photo booth strip of two boys: one Asian American, the other white. They pose with tongues out, then a kissing shot, and the last where their cheeks are smushed together. It feels too intimate to see their happiness, especially since I know their fate, so I set the photo aside. I crack open the Moleskine. The pages are glued with coffee stains. I gently pry the paper apart. I read the words. A poem.

For V, you are the moon. You light the way for me. Our nights held by her light. Under the perch of stars, you touch my cheek and like the ocean I am pulled to you. Swept away tides.

I shut the Moleskine and rest it against my heart. I remember when Jake knitted words into the soft blanket he gave me: *To the moon and back.* I'm getting sidetracked. *Focus on the task at hand.* I can't get moon-eyed over every single box. It'll take me forever to finish.

Box #2: Andy and Aimee

An In-and-Out burger box with *For finals* written in Sharpie on it. Dodgers tickets. A glossy photo of a beach with palm trees. I squint and see a giant Ferris wheel and an endless boardwalk. I flip over the photo and on the back there's a note in blue pen: *Our last date.* A signed copy of *Wow, No Thank You.* by Samantha Irby. I read over the application that Aimee sent.

Andy and I met at this Sam Irby event. He wrote his number in the book, next to Sam's signature. We talked for hours until Chevalier's Books closed. The manager ushered us out. Why we broke up: I'm still not sure. He stopped responding to my texts. He deleted our chats. He disappeared. I'm hoping that Andy somehow sees this. Maybe he'll remember why we were so good together. Maybe he'll text me back.

I wander to my bed with Aimee's application clutched in my hands. This poor girl! She doesn't even know. How heartbreaking.

Hell, I don't even know. I keep tracing back in my relationship. I know I messed up Jake's first solo show. I apologized fifty times that night. He'd texted *It's fine* and I stared at those two words the entire five-hour flight from JFK to LAX. I thought we were fine. He said so. But here I am, weepy over strangers' breakup objects and my first real breakup. Selena says that it was a jerk move for sure, but I'll meet someone way hotter in Los Angeles. I don't want to meet anyone in Los Angeles. I want my handsome knitter artist boyfriend back!

I haven't told Selena that I transformed my relationship memory planner into Operation Get Back Together with Jake. A simple five-step approach to win him back from three thousand miles away.

> Step 1: Get Jake to visit LA.
> Step 2: Act totally cool around him.
> Step 3: Invite him to Heartifacts.
> Step 4: Remind him why we were so good together.
> Step 5: Kiss him.

Somewhere, Selena is rolling her eyes at my meticulous plans. She'd tell me to hook up with some surfer hottie instead.

Box #3: James and El

Neatly folded navy blue socks with *Vegan AF* in yellow text. A vinyl sticker with a smiling white dog and *Monty's Good Burger* at the top in a red cursive font. A book of matches with *Crossroads Kitchen* on it. A cookbook with a brown-haired girl holding a tray of cupcakes: *Chloe's Vegan Desserts*. The application, written by James, is sparse.

The socks were a gift from El on my one-year veganversary. The sticker is from where we shared burgers and milkshakes in K-town. The matches were from our Valentine's Day prix fixe dinner. I bought this cookbook to make El a birthday cake. Why we broke up: we met at Pride in WeHo. My friends said post-Pride dates have an expiration date. But we dated for 1+ years, even though El didn't want to be serious. They wanted to "dance the life out of this party." Well, now they can.

Ugh. Valentine's Day! Jake is the best Valentine's Day planner. I toss the matchbook back into the box like it's on fire.

Selena is right. Breakups are the freaking worst. She's been through, like, five since middle school. Our regular ritual involved me bringing over an obscene amount of Japanese salt lychee Kit Kats and a stack of lesbian romance novels, and lying on the floor of her room with a tissue box. The real truth is I faked it the whole time. Heartbreak didn't seem that bad to me. Almost fun. I got to steal moments with my best friend back.

But, of course, now that I'm going through an actual breakup, Selena is far away. I flop on my bed, snuggle Sesame, and call her instead.

'm in charge of carrying our best-selling pastries—black sesame mochi, egg tarts, and cream-filled taro buns—on giant silver trays wrapped in plastic wrap. Dad won't let me anywhere near his coffee equipment. He carries each item, like his portable Nespresso milk foamer, as if it were a teacup pig. I dropped his glass teapot one time and, even though I paid for a new one, I'm Judas forever. As I unwrap each tray and place each doughy dessert into the display case, Dad sets up his to-go gear.

"You okay working an entire weekend shift with me?" asks Dad.

I shrug. My social life in LA is less than thrilling. In NYC, my weekends were staged readings at New York Theatre Workshop, traipsing through exhibits in Chelsea galleries, or reading on Jake's couch as he mapped out his latest knit mural. My high school was across the street from Lincoln Center, so we'd get to attend special dance dress rehearsals. Here, I feel like a freshman getting lost in my new school and not knowing anyone. Skinny people take selfies while eating fancy doughnuts and wear sweaters when it's sixty-five degrees out. If there's an art culture here, I haven't seen it. I went to one *book* reading and it was an anthology of people's love letters to their plastic surgeons, personal trainers, and hair stylists. No joke. You can't make this stuff up. I texted Selena and she'd said, Fly home immediately.

I wished.

"I like hanging out with my old man."

"Oof. I felt a gray hair sprout just now." He pats his boyish black hair. I pinch his golden cheeks.

"Please. People think you're my older brother."

Dad beams. His tawny brown eyes crinkle. He's easily pleased. He stands in front of the bakery case.

"Today's drink special is a black sesame latte. Let's put the black sesame mochi up front in the display and move the taro to the back."

I put on plastic gloves and silently rearrange the soft circles of sweet rice dough with the squishy black centers. A dusting of potato starch covers my gloves. When it's all done, I work on the white placards that I'll place in front of the desserts. I'm not an artist, but I can trick out a font. I add a smiling kitty face, which looks just like Sesame, to each sign.

"Good job, kiddo."

"Thanks."

He stands closer to me, wiping white flour off my forehead. "Your mom broke up with me once."

"I know. Ahma set you back up. And that's why you hate mochi."

"I don't hate mochi."

I raise my eyebrows in protest.

"Your mom's summer abroad in Tokyo studying with that pastry chef was her time to explore."

I cover my ears. "Ew, Dad. Please don't."

"All I'm saying is that breakups aren't all bad."

"Says the guy who only had one girlfriend ever."

"When you know, you know." He pats my back. "Give it time."

We finish cleaning up before Ruby Street opens at 10 A.M. I slip on my white Sweet Yen baseball cap (Dad's idea) and secure my matching apron. There's a steady stream of people who slip behind the white desks and flip open their laptops. I watch as Francesca, with splatters of oil paints on her white overalls, wrestles with three canvas paintings while speaking Spanish with Lourdes. She lugs more art into a closet. The line in front of our pop-up grows.

"No offense, Chlo, but you gotta move quicker."

Shoot.

"Sorry."

I focus and plate the orders as they come in. The case empties as Dad whips up cappuccinos, espressos, and iced lattes in expert time. I credit us working in Chinatown for our fast-paced work ethic. Soon, the line settles down enough that I can steal another glance at Francesca.

When there's a pause in the action, I ask Dad if I can take a ten-minute break. Dad nods, deep into cleaning his equipment with the thoroughness of a surgeon. I head to the closet and peek in. Francesca rearranges different pieces.

"Wow!"

"Holy crap!" She clutches her heart.

"Sorry! I didn't mean to scare you. What are you doing with all this art? Is it yours?"

"Some of it is. Are you interested in buying?"

I laugh. "No. Not yet anyway. I'm working on an idea."

Lourdes comes into the closet. "Hey, Franny." She looks at

me. "Oh, hi, Chloe. Your dad's pop-up is going so well. My clients are asking for a repeat visit next week."

I smile. "My dad will agree to that in a heartbeat. Any chance to rep Sweet Yen."

"Perfect." Lourdes turns to face Francesca. "Is there more?"

Francesca shakes her head. "That's it."

"Great. I can't wait to see you get some art on the walls. This place is too bare," says Lourdes. "You have any friends who want to produce something for next week's teen night? The DJ I booked dropped out. He got a more lucrative gig."

Francesca rolls her hazel brown eyes. "Awful. Yeah, let me text my friends. We can rally something up."

"Actually, I have an idea," I say.

All eyes are on me. I'm used to this. I've presented in front of school principals, art gallery owners, and the entire curator team at The Met, but I usually prep for those meetings weeks in advance. I try to form a thought.

"For teen night, I'd love to do a curated exhibit of original found objects."

Lourdes crinkles her forehead. She taps her pointer finger to her lips.

"Tell me more."

I have zero notes prepared. My tongue turns into sandpaper, but I continue anyway.

"It's based on a Danish museum called the Museum of Broken Relationships. People submit the objects that they owned during and are done with after a breakup. I collect them. Each person submits a short essay about their found objects and why they broke up. It's all anonymous. I want my version to be by teens, for teens."

"I love it," exclaims Lourdes. "I've got a wide-open space for the next teen night."

"Great! I'll fill it. When?"

"A week from today. October nineteenth."

"Fantastic," I say.

Inside, I am crumbling. I have seven days to pull this off and I have five boxes. I have zero friends or art contacts here. But this is my chance.

"Ping me with more details, Chloe. You too, Franny."

I have a regrettable trait that involves profuse body sweat the moment that I panic. Like, it looks like my armpits are Lake George. Or like I've peed through my white Sweet Yen apron.

"That's a genius idea. Your exhibit, I mean. Do you need more found objects?"

Francesca grabs her phone out of the front pocket of her overalls and scrolls through.

"It's like breakup city over at Highland High. People want new people to make out with in the fall."

I laugh. "This is fall?"

She sighs. "You're one of those."

"One of what?"

"New York transplants."

"Guilty."

"I won't hold it against you, but I'll have you know that October does have some chilly nights, especially near the Valley."

I nod like I know what she's talking about, but I don't.

"What's your number?"

I read out my 917 number and she taps it into her phone.

"I'll ask around and get back to you."

"Actually, I have a form anyone can fill out. It asks for basic information, a short form essay about each object's sentimental value, and their permission to use the objects for public display. On the back end, it keeps everything neat in a spreadsheet."

Francesca's green eyes widen like my cat Sesame's when she hears a loud sound.

"You're no joke."

"It's easier."

My phone buzzes in the back pocket of my jeans.

"Send me the form link. I'll pass it around. Twenty bucks, right?"

"Yup. Venmo. They drop their Venmo username in the form to get prompt payment."

Francesca laughs. "Girl, you're the real deal. I need you to organize my life."

"I can help you with that. I have this YouTube channel called *Plan It Girl*. I've helped seniors get into their dream colleges and move cross-country. I even helped an adoptee find her birth mother."

"Dang. You're a boss. Come to my next meeting."

"What exactly is your group?"

She motions to the art around her. "Arte Para La Gente. A diverse collective of artists of all different disciplines.

Sculpture, clay, fiber arts, paintings. Heck, one of us makes these badass porcelain dumplings with hidden fortunes in them."

I walk through the closet.

"Is it okay if I look?"

"Please don't post anything on social. We're debuting it here in two weeks."

I nod, lifting a white sheet. "I get it. I've worked with artists. I had a student internship at The Met and curated the first-ever young artists exhibit with my supervisor. I landed Jake Miller for the show."

Francesca's red lipsticked mouth drops open. "Holy shit."

I neglect to tell her that Jake Miller is my boyfriend. My ex-boyfriend. I can't even say it in my head. If I say it, it's real.

"If you get me ten people to commit to being in the show, I'll come to your meeting."

"Deal," says Francesca. "We are in desperate need of organization. Right now, it's just me and my art teacher."

"Your group is all students?"

"Technically, we're an after-school art club, but I consider us a forward-thinking collective that will change the world."

I smile widely. "I like the way you think."

We shake hands.

"Sorry about the sugar. Mochi dust. I'm working the café pop-up with my pops."

"O-m-g. You sell mochi? It's my perfect post-painting snack."

She follows me back to the counter. The line is a snake. Dad raises his black eyebrows at me. His distress signal. I dutifully swoop behind the counter and quickly put on my Sweet Yen hat. I take out one mochi, stick it in a bag, and wave Francesca over. She slips away with a smile. I focus on taking each customer's order and not on the impending panic over organizing an art show in a new-to-me city in less than a week.

Our tiny kitchen looks like the aftermath of an episode of a baking show. The countertop is littered with pineapple rinds, chunks of fresh pineapple, and flour. So much flour. Powdered sugar perfumes the air. Several baking sheets, including one that fell on the floor, cover every available space. The citrus scent of pineapple is embedded in my fingernails.

My mom, who truly loves baking, is curse-whispering at the misshapen pineapple cakes whose insides have burst open. They are supposed to be rectangular, but we cannot find my ahma's pineapple cake tins, so my mom and I free-form-shaped them, and they look hideous.

Ahma sits at the kitchen table with her favorite teapot with the blue painted crane on it and sips her oolong tea. She's wearing her favorite purple floral shirt and matching pants, not a speck of flour on her. Meanwhile, Mom and I look like two Mexican wedding cookies, powdered from top to bottom. I swear there is flour in my toes.

"I cannot serve these to your grandmother," whispers my mom.

Her brown eyes silently convey her desperation. She holds a plate with the saddest explosion of sugared pineapple. It smells as appetizing as burnt coffee.

I whisper back, "Well, I am not going to put a packaged pineapple cake from 99 Ranch in front of her."

"Maybe she won't know?"

I take the plate from my mom and gingerly place it in front of my ahma. Ahma pats my hand. She reviews the small tart with such silent precision that I don't need to see my mom's face to know she is sweating profusely.

Ahma shakes her head, pushing the plate away. She goes back to sipping her tea.

I carry the plate to the trash can and dump the cake remains into it. My mom is near tears. I touch her shoulder, then kiss her all-purpose-floured cheek.

This is her eighth attempt to nail my ahma's signature recipe. It was a customer favorite. Lines formed on Sunday when she churned out fresh batches. Whenever Ahma sent us a box, we all staked claims on which one was ours.

And now, neither my mom nor I can figure out the recipe. We have tried countless ones on YouTube, and none have been right. Nothing tastes the same.

I grab my Recipe Planning notebook with tiny pink whisks on the cover and write: *October 16. Another failed batch.* I flip through the pages to my ingredients list, reading them over again.

Ahma fills two teacups for us. Swirls of heat rise from the cups. She gestures for us to sit. I bring my notebook.

"We have to be getting the ingredients wrong," I say to my mom, passing her the notebook.

She reviews it, then my mom speaks in Hokkien, her native

Taiwanese dialect, with Ahma. Ahma shakes her head. I'm not certain what they are saying, but I know the look in my ahma's eyes when she's getting overwhelmed. Her eyes turn glassy like the whole fish we eat on Lunar New Year.

"Mom, stop. She doesn't know."

My mom sighs loudly. "I feel like a failure, Chloe."

"It's not your fault that Ahma has trouble remembering."

I look through my notebook again like I can somehow solve this mystery.

"What if I take Ahma to 99 Ranch and see if she remembers? She's always better when she holds something."

My mom hugs me. "That's a great idea, sweetheart."

"I'll clean up the kitchen," I say. "You go and take a shower."

She clasps her hands together and mouths *Thank you* as she hurries out of the kitchen.

As I scrub a caked-on baking sheet clean, I remember the days when I was a little kid and I would flip through my sticker book collection while Ahma baked. The kitchen would be filled with the warm scent of buttered baking. When the pineapple cakes were ready, we sat together secretly devouring one batch that Ahma had made just for us.

I wish I had observed her more.

I kiss the top of her cropped gray hair, then take her teacups to hand wash. Ahma shuffles out of the kitchen at her slow pace. I follow, just in case. She waves me off, so I linger in the hallway as she shuts her bedroom door.

I wish she could remember.

I t wasn't the brightest idea to shoot my first Happy Planner Squad Box video on the same night that *Heartifacts* opens. In my weekly planning, it seemed totally doable. As a brand-new squad member, I have to release unboxing content at the same time as my fellow #PlanWithMe squad. But I didn't realize how many products were inside until I started shooting. Also, I may have gone hardcore into the Brights sticker packs Happy Planner sent me. I couldn't help myself.

I arrive at Ruby Street twenty minutes later than I wanted. Luckily, Francesca and my parents are already setting up the breakup boxes. Dad handles each box like he's carrying his Nespresso milk frother. Francesca arranges the contents on the tables.

I snap a photo for my Insta with the caption *Huge thanks to my @PlanItGirl team and @FrancescArte! With your help, I got ten boxes for opening night. Phew!*

Francesca rallied her crew to bring at least two people each, so we'll have some sort of crowd. But it freaks me out that I know no one, except Francesca and my parents. I sent out invites to each person who sent a box and asked if they wanted to invite their ex. It seemed risky, but I sent along a form letter that they could forward. Maybe they'd realize how much they missed each other and that it was a stupid fight or something else not as important as they are to each other and get back together.

I find myself in front of my breakup box. As I hold the knit hat Jake sent back, I think maybe he'll see the knit hat I fumbled to make, and how I tried to follow along but stayed up until midnight with YouTube tutorials and still couldn't master intarsia, let alone say it out loud. The yarn is stiff and heavy because I accidentally washed it in hot water, and it shrank so it could only fit a baby. He kept it in his studio, placed on the head of a childhood stuffed animal, Ducky, that his grandma gave him. It was our inside joke. *Ducky's hat* was our code for something ugly that we just had to keep.

I look down at Ducky's hat. Clearly, our relationship was too ugly for Jake to keep. I put it down, laid out next to the other items in Jake's box. I don't normally contribute to exhibits. I'm not really an artist, but in my gallery statement I included my inspiration. My own heartbreak. For everyone to see. And by everyone, I mean the small crowd gathered here.

I still get pre-opening jitters. It starts with my palms turning slippery. Then, my feet can't be still, like I'm on a moving walkway. Tonight, it's like I'm standing at the edge of the subway platform, waiting for the two beaming headlights.

My thoughts are train cars: *No one is coming. No one cares. You don't know anyone in Los Angeles. Your last show was a disaster.*

"What do you think?" Mom asks.

She shows me a platter of pink mochi with strawberry hearts in the centers. Some of the fruit hearts have zigzags in the middle. Some are kept whole.

"It's perfect, Mom," I say.

"Let me get in on that action. What if those mochi are accidentally poisonous?" says my dad.

My married-forever parents giggle like newlyweds. Mom feeds him one. He nibbles her fingers. Normally, their displays of affection don't annoy me. I used to think it was sweet, but tonight, I'd rather focus on making sure each station is set.

I review the flow one more time by pretending to be a viewer seeing it with fresh eyes. I start at the entrance where I've placed my mission statement—triple-checked for typos.

Welcome to Heartifacts. *I didn't intend to start an exhibit of my ex-boyfriend's objects, but when we broke up, it inspired me to find out what other people saved from the ruins of their relationships. Like fossil excavating, but for the lost bones of love. Each box is anonymous with a short explanation from the contributor about the meaning of the objects and why the breakup happened. In respect to the contributors' privacy, photography and videos are strictly prohibited.*

I start at box number one. The initials of the couple are on the lid of the shoebox. I read the small placard about why they broke up and what the objects meant to them. As I move through the U-shaped gallery display, I jot down notes about which objects are hard to see from my viewpoint. I move the shoeboxes embellished with sequins or graffiti to the front. Francesca gave me one from her art club. The artist created an epic photo collage of the couple on the shoebox lid. The collage is separated in the middle like two islands with an ocean between them. I lean the lid against the box and step back. It's much easier to see now. When I reach the last table, I review the food labels to make sure everything is readable and labeled with allergens.

During my second lap around the space, I follow my checklist and adjust each item, so all are in view. On my third lap, I glance around the entire room. I love it.

"Hey, kiddo, sample this. I call it the Taste of Heartache," says my dad.

He hands me a plastic cup. I sip. It's fizzy. Somehow, my dad made this drink taste sweet and sad at the same time.

"It's grapefruit LaCroix," he says.

"If anything tastes like a breakup, it's grapefruit."

"Definitely. It's grenadine syrup, fizzy grapefruit LaCroix, and a maraschino cherry."

"Did you drink this when Mom broke up with you?"

"Us old-timers didn't have grapefruit LaCroix back then. Only grapefruit juice." He laughs and walks away.

"I take that as a yes!"

I made a playlist mostly of breakup songs but mixed in with some Beyoncé. The mood can't get too dark. It's all about creating the right environment. Create a list of Adele and everyone will be eating pints of Ben & Jerry's in the corner. But sprinkle in something danceable and add a dash of revenge energy like "Irreplaceable," then you've got an event.

The runaway train of thoughts slows down when I look

over the details. I make sure each box is properly lit. I check the room temperature. Pop into each bathroom to see that all supplies are stocked. Nothing dampens an event more than no toilet paper. Everything is in order. All I have to do is wait for the doors to open and everyone to show up.

They'll show up, right?

The show opened at 8 P.M. It's 8:31 P.M. and three people are here. Two of them are my parents. The one person who isn't related to me walks through and when I approach with a friendly smile, she asks, "Where's the bathroom?"

My parents hold hands as they walk through the exhibit, *ooh*ing and *aah*ing and talking about each piece. It's really sweet, but also embarrassing. Even art shows I organized in eighth grade were better attended than this disaster. Lourdes gave me the space from 8 P.M. to 10 P.M. so I have to endure ninety more minutes before I can turn out the lights.

I'm drowning my sorrows in my third Taste of Heartache so, bladder full, I slip into the bathroom. I look up at the small window at the top of the wall. If I suck in my stomach and wiggle, I can crawl through that opening and escape my personal hell.

"Chloe?"

"Mom?"

She sticks a Post-it Note under the stall door. *Your work matters.* I unlock the stall and go wash my hands.

"This is humiliating."

Mom wraps me in her arms. I sink into her chest like I

did when I was a kid. She kisses the top of my head. I stare at her curled black lashes, strong jawline, and golden cheeks, and instantly feel better.

"It takes time," she says, rubbing her hand on my back.

A knock.

"You two coming out?" asks Dad. "People are asking questions."

People? I rush out to the gallery space. Francesca waves enthusiastically at me with a crew of eleven people. A few other people I recognize from Highland Park High are milling about with cups of Dad's mocktail. There are two attractive Asian guys side by side. One has perfect pomade hair, black jeans, and a tight white T-shirt. The other has darker skin and is dressed entirely in black. How adorbs that a couple came together! I do a quick head count—there are eighteen people not related to me.

Francesca comes closer and her posse gives me a head nod when she introduces us. They disperse to check out their boxes.

"Dude, nice. The food is killer," she says.

"Thanks," I whisper. "I thought no one was coming. It was a ghost town here."

Francesca cracks up. "No one in LA gets anywhere on time. Tack on thirty to forty-five minutes to any event start time. And if there's an accident on a freeway, clock it at one hour late."

"Seriously?"

She pats my shoulder. "You New Yorkers gotta take it down a notch."

I shake my shoulders loose like I'm suddenly a super-chill surfboard chick. "I'm at ease."

"Sure," she says, smiling. She gives a nod to the gay Asian couple. "I heard Vincent's boyfriend cheated on him. Like, for months."

"Ouch," I say.

"I'm gonna snag another strawberry mochi ASAP before my friends gobble them all up." She gives me a peace sign with her right hand.

I eye the couple. My greatest fear was Jake cheating on me. Girls and guys were always all over him. The guy dressed in all black hugs white T-shirt tightly. Maybe cheating is totally normal here? I have so much to learn about La La Land.

I move through the crowd. I chat it up with some of Francesca's friends. I sneak a glance at All-Black. It's totally silly because he's taken, but a girl can look. The sides of his head are shaved so there's a single ocean wave of inky black hair. All-Black is not as fit as his ex-boyfriend who is all muscles, but he's got broad shoulders and the cutest face. Cheeks for days. Selena would scold me for crushing on gay boys, which was how I spent most of freshman year. But she's not here so I sneak another glance at All-Black's fitted jeans, specifically his butt. My eyes wander up, and I spy All-Black whipping out his phone to record White T-Shirt. What the hell?

White T-Shirt stands in front of one box. His back is facing me, but it's clear he's upset from how his shoulders sag.

I move toward the couple. The buzz of conversation dulls the sound of heartbreak songs.

"Hi! I'm Chloe, the curator of this exhibit. I'd appreciate

you not filming. There's a sign at the entrance about video and photography being strictly prohibited," I say.

All-Black keeps his eyes focused on his phone. I can't help but notice his gorgeous brown eyes, long eyelashes, and serious stare. All-Black continues to point his phone at White T-Shirt who I now notice is silently crying. White T-Shirt has pulled out a photo booth strip. He places it alongside the one on the table.

"I told you it was here, Daniel," says White T-Shirt.

The side-by-side photo strips match. This is incredibly awkward to be sandwiched between a broken-up couple, but rules are rules.

"Daniel, is it?" I ask.

Daniel nods.

"Please stop filming. Also, it feels especially cruel to record your ex crying over your photos," I say.

White T-Shirt bursts into a laugh with tears on his structured cheekbones. "Daniel's not my ex."

Wait. What? Then, I peek at the photo strip and see that White T-Shirt is making out with a white guy. Daniel and him are not a couple. I hold my hand over Daniel's phone, blocking the lens.

"Hey!" exclaims Daniel.

He tries to dodge me, but I honed my skills in New York City. I'm a shadow boxer. Artists are sensitive about their work being recorded without their permission and it's my job to protect the work. With my palm on the lens, I swiftly wrestle the phone out of Daniel's hand. I tuck it behind my back.

"Vincent was having a moment and you ruined it."

A few people have started staring at us. Great. Just what I need for my first West Coast show. Some jerk thinking he's the next Jon M. Chu.

"Listen, Daniel, I don't know what you think you're doing here, but there's no recording whatsoever."

"D, let it go," says Vincent. "I've got enough heartbreak to re-create that scene."

"Cinema vérité documentary is about capturing the moment. Not dramatic re-creations. Real life is the moment."

I roll my eyes. Great. I'm dealing with a pompous know-it-all film geek. An attractive, pompous know-it-all, but still annoying AF.

"Come on, Spielberg. We can chat over here," I say.

Vincent stays while Daniel follows me. I don't want anyone thinking anything's wrong, so I duck into a small office away from the exhibit. I flick on a light.

"You can have your phone back if you agree to stop filming."

"The correct term is *shooting,* not *filming,*" says Daniel.

I eye-roll so hard that I probably pop a blood vessel.

He throws his hands up in the air. "The moment is ruined anyway."

"Shake on it before I hand your phone over," I say.

I stick out my hand, keeping Daniel's phone behind my back. He sighs and shakes my hand.

"Here you go."

"Thanks." He reviews the footage on his phone. "You're wrong. Spielberg is a Hollywood director. What I'm doing is entirely different."

I put my hands on my hips. Do I want to waste my time

listening to Daniel's explanation of why what he does is so magically different? I have a gallery with patrons. I turn to leave. I learned after one unsuccessful date with a future wannabe filmmaker to never get into it with them. It's a useless tirade of verbal nonsense.

"Your exhibit needs video," says Daniel.

I stop immediately and turn to face him. He steps closer. Why does a jerk need deep dimples and an arresting smile? Seems like a waste to me.

"What you're doing here is really fascinating, but it's missing moving images."

"The objects are the art," I say, folding my arms across my chest.

"Yes. Vee and I loved looking at each one. But if the purpose of the exhibit is to feel each person's heartbreak, then video is the way to take it to the next level."

The nerve of this guy! Just because he can point a phone in one direction doesn't make him a filmmaker. It makes him every other person on the planet.

"Look at this."

He turns his phone to me. We are super close. He smells like a day at the beach. Coconutty. I move closer for the video. He hits play and I watch Vincent as he approaches his ex's box. Vincent touches his heart first as if he's catching it. Then Vincent reads the words that Connor has written about their breakup. Vincent bites his lip, and his fingers linger on the words on the white placard.

"I can't believe he did this," says on-camera Vincent. "I

thought he didn't care about me. I didn't know he saved any of this stuff."

Tears well up in my eyes. That's when Vincent pulls out the matching photo booth strip like two parts of a heart-shaped necklace and puts them next to each other. My vision blurs, then I hear my voice barging in. Our argument. Does my voice sound that pitchy when I get angry? The video stops. A few minutes of silence between us. Daniel pulls a tissue out of his pocket.

"It's clean, I swear," he says.

He smiles at me. I get lost in his dimples. For a few seconds, I'm awkwardly staring at him. Come on, Chloe. Say something!

"You might have a point," I say finally. "That was incredible."

"I'm not Spielberg, but I don't want to be. I want to be Daniel Kwak. I really like what you're doing here. It's intimate, intriguing, and it helped my best friend so that's saying something."

"What do you mean?"

"Vee's been in a funk after his breakup. My extrovert best friend who is out every night of the week was a hermit for two months. He asked me to come with him to this exhibit after Connor sent him an email about it. It gave him closure."

I smile. "I'm glad. You're a good friend."

"Vee's like a brother to me. It's the least I could do."

It dawns on me that maybe having a video component *could* be interesting. Different. I've tried to play with tech in my exhibits, but after Jake's big disaster, I stayed the hell away.

But this fine pompous filmmaker has a point. Videos can add
more depth to *Heartifacts*.

"Maybe we could meet for coffee. Discuss video ideas?"

"Sounds good."

"I know a great shop," I say. "I'm Chloe, by the way."

We exchange phone numbers, and he follows me out.

"I should get back to Vee before he melts into a puddle of
tears. Thanks for this, Chloe."

I wave goodbye to Daniel, sneaking in one last look at his
dimples. I join the small group milling around the space. My
first West Coast show isn't the huge splash I wanted, but the
modest size is a start. Besides, I can plan the hell out of scaling
up. This is only the beginning.

Sweet Yen is packed. Luckily I reserved a table in the back. The ones in front and by the coffee bar go the fastest, so I save those for the regulars. At 4 P.M. on the dot, I place two egg tarts on the table. Dad winks at me as he whips up two black sesame lattes.

"It's not a date, Dad."

"I know! He's a friend from school. Your mom and I started out as friends."

"We're hardly friends. He sabotaged my opening night."

Dad hands me the mugs. He's foamed two black hearts in the middle. I grab a wooden stirrer and swirl away both hearts. Jake and I have been barely broken up for a second, and Dad's already planning my next date.

"Yet you invited him here."

"For a brainstorm session. To help the exhibit. That's all."

I take the mugs to the table and see Daniel is already there. My cheeks burn red. Did he overhear what my dad said? I stare down at the mugs that look like a swirl of black and white now. Thank god I fixed the foam.

"I didn't expect you on time."

Daniel smiles. "I'm usually late." He glances around. "I love this place. Yen, the owner, always gave me a free pineapple cake. It hasn't been the same without her here."

The mention of the Taiwanese pineapple tart sinks my

stomach. My ahma's signature dessert that we still haven't figured out how to make. The perfect tiny square of pastry with a flaky, milky crust and sweet, chewy pineapple filling. As a kid, I nibbled the corners so that all I had left was the center. The tan-yellow rectangle. The last time my ahma made them, she burnt the pineapple cakes. She had forgotten how long she left them in the oven. The edges were blackened. The inside had the consistency of a hard yellow Starburst forgotten in my Halloween bucket until Thanksgiving.

"Hey," says Daniel. "You okay?"

"Yen is my ahma. She's home now. My parents and I took over, and we have no idea how to make her pineapple tarts. My mom and I have been trying to crack the recipe since we arrived a month ago."

"I'm sorry. She's a firecracker. Someone tried to steal my laptop once and she cracked his knuckles with a ruler and made him work behind the counter with her."

"That ruler!" I burst out laughing. "She used it for everything."

He digs through his black messenger bag and fishes out a Polaroid photo. "Give her this from me."

I examine the photo, taken right here in the shop before we came to LA. When the walls were still red and fading white and the tables and chairs cracked from age. Ahma smiles wide with her arms crossed. The tan ruler is in her wrinkled hands. Next to her is a white guy in a black beanie hat with his arm around her. He towers over her petite body.

"Is this the thief?"

"She gave him a part-time job."

"Of course she did."

I tuck the photo in my notebook to give to Ahma later. Maybe she'll remember something if I give her this with her ruler. She tossed it in the garbage last week and I dug it out from under fish bones. I had to soak it in Febreze, but I saved it.

"You have a lot of notebooks," says Daniel.

He gestures to my stash of supplies—markers, a pouch for stickers, Post-its, highlighters, index cards, and three planners.

"Three notebooks are nothing. I have an entire bookshelf full of them. They are part of my YouTube planner channel."

"I know. *Plan It Girl.*"

Now it's my turn to be shocked. My followers are mostly female-identifying.

"Vincent is a fan. He's a dancer and uses your calendar system to organize all his rehearsals, events, and stuff. He sent me a link to your index card video."

"Color me impressed," I say.

"I think you mean *color-code me impressed.*"

He grins at me.

"I'm surprised you use three-by-five index cards. I tend to work with five-by-seven, color-coded by writing stage. Blue for first draft, red for revision, and green for entirely new scene," says Daniel.

To anyone else, this sounds like two nerds geeking out over office supplies, but his attention to detail wins me over immediately.

"Three-by-five index cards fit my corkboard best. Besides, everything that needs to be said should be short and simple anyway," I say.

He cracks a smile and taps his finger on my stack of index cards.

"True, but could we use mine instead?"

And then this boy pulls out a tan Smoko pearl boba tea storage box with its signature cute *kawaii* smile and tiny black tapioca balls floating at the bottom. I can't help but gawk.

"Is that a Smoko boba box? I thought they were all sold out."

"They were. I have a friend who works at Smoko and got me one before they disappeared. I hate when my index cards are bent."

Daniel opens the box and pulls out perfectly neat index cards.

"Exactly."

Dad chooses this precise moment to come over and check on us. He winks at me.

"How are you all doing? Isn't that the boba tea box you've been hunting down, sweetheart?"

"Dad!"

Daniel reaches out to shake my dad's hand. "Nice to meet you. I'm Daniel Kwak. Chloe and I go to school together. Please give my best to your mother. She's been feeding me since I could walk. We don't have sweet Korean desserts at home, so she pitied me and gave me my first pineapple cake."

Dad's smile is so wide that he looks like a cat that ate an entire fish. "Ah, an old customer! Her loyal ones still come almost every day. My daughter helped give the shop a makeover."

"Gosh, the line is getting long, Dad."

He finally gets the hint, but not before he winks at me again and nudges my arm. How embarrassing.

Luckily, Daniel doesn't notice my red cheeks. He lays out his index cards. All blue in a line of five.

"Unlined index cards?" I ask. I raise my eyebrows.

"I storyboard my scenes."

"What's that?"

"A fancy way of saying that I doodle out what I think the scenes might look like. A snapshot," says Daniel. "The blue lines on index cards get in the way."

Then, be still my heart. He pulls out a Pentel GraphGear 1000 mechanical pencil and clicks it until the lead comes out. I watch in amazement as he sketches in front of me. I study what he's doing, sipping my latte. A story comes together as I eat my egg tart.

"This is what I had in mind. After the exhibit, I got home and had this thought. The walls are blank. We could project a story. A short film that repeats as your audience walks through."

As Daniel talks, I grab my Goal Setting journal and open it to a fresh page, taking notes as he speaks.

"A two-minute film of a teenage couple that goes through the course of their relationship from meet-cute until the breakup. Then the film repeats so that you're in it. Here are my ideas for the five scenes, twenty-four seconds for each one. A portrait of a relationship."

He nudges the index cards closer to me and I see his vision.

Five scenes:

1) *The meet-cute*
2) *First kiss*
3) *Problems!*
4) *Questioning*
5) *Breakup*

His notes include possible locations and what the mood of each scene should be. I look up at him. He has an impossibly charming smile on his face as he holds his palms up like his hands are a camera lens.

"Imagine your viewer is walking through and seeing each object, then they look up and see this film. It's silent. Just a visual story. And they get lost in the couple and think about their own relationship. Or how they miss their person. The film should be a visual representation of what your exhibit is all about."

I clap my hands. "I see it entirely in black and white."

"Yes! That's great. Like a silent film with captions below."

"A minimal number of captions."

"A three-by-five index card's worth of words?" Daniel asks. His eyes crinkle when he says it.

"It's simple," I say.

"Who should the couple be?" Daniel asks.

I shrug my shoulders. "I don't know a soul here. Surely you have actor friends."

He laughs. Egg tart crumbs fly out of his mouth. He clamps his hand over it.

"Sorry!"

I hand him a napkin. "I didn't know there's a film program at Highland High. Or is it a club?"

"It's just me. I mostly shoot documentary style. I'm more interested in random, everyday people than actors and performance."

"Maybe we could put an ad out?"

"Do you have a budget?"

I tap my Goal Setting journal. "Since *Heartifacts* is free, my current budget is zero dollars."

"How about us?" asks Daniel.

It's my turn to spit out my tart crumbs on the table. I wipe my mouth with a napkin.

"I'm not an actor. I chose non-speaking roles for all my class plays," I say.

"It's a silent film," says Daniel. "And there's no script to memorize. Besides, I don't think it's fair to ask an actor to work for free, and I need a short, two-minute film in my creative portfolio for my film school application anyway."

"You're going to film school?"

"Applying for next year. Big difference. But yeah."

"And your parents are cool with that?"

"My parents split when I was three. My umma and halmeoni would prefer if I were a K-pop star, but since my singing voice is similar to a howling werewolf, they think I'll be the next Bong Joon-ho." Daniel laughs. "I'd like to be the Asian Werner Herzog."

"Who?"

Daniel's jaw drops open. *"Encounters at the End of the World, Cave of Forgotten Dreams, Grizzly Man . . ."*

I shake my head.

"You have to watch *Cave of Forgotten Dreams*. Please, I beg you. As payment for making this film pro bono."

"I thought this creative project was for your college application. Seems like I'm doing you a favor," I say.

"So you'll be in it then?"

I consider saying no. It's one thing to shoot my *Plan It Girl* videos in my studio setup. It's another to be an actress in a film. Sure, I'm comfortable on camera, but it's super easy for me to talk planning and organization. I could do that in my sleep. Plus, I've had my channel since eighth grade. My followers and I are tight. This is way different.

"Consider it a creative challenge. Putting yourself in the heart of a breakup. It's real. People will see it and recognize themselves in it. It adds a whole new dimension to the exhibit," says Daniel.

"I don't know."

I look at my planner. The next big goal is: *secure bigger audience for* Heartifacts. I plotted out a social media marketing plan. I know that videos get views, especially to my sixty-three thousand (and counting) subscribers.

"To be honest, the last time I did a tech thing at an art exhibit, it failed spectacularly. Like, created another dimension," I say.

Daniel laughs and thumps the table with his hand.

"Okay. I promise I'll run all the tech. You just have to show up to my shoot dates. I'll arrange all the locations, equipment, and schedule," says Daniel.

This is the first time anyone has ever volunteered to help me plan out a creative endeavor. I know from tracking my website statistics that videos boost my viewership every single time. All I have to do is show up. It's basically a free commercial for the exhibit.

"I'm in."

We shake hands to seal the deal. Daniel and I spend the rest of the time discussing the look for the film. What I'll wear and what he'll wear. I don't know what time we end, but we finish our black sesame lattes and Dad brings over spicy ginger tea.

Daniel and I come up with the exact storyboard of our short film. I've never done anything like this before. I dictate how a show will go. I plan every single detail down to the invite, menu, guest list, and schedule. But there's something really exciting happening. We started out with a vague idea of a couple's evolution from hot and heavy to heartbroken. As we finish the final index card, I can't wait for our first shoot day. When we look up, the café has cleared. It's just us and my dad.

"I should let you go," I say.

Daniel glances at his watch. "I had no idea how late it had gotten. I should head out. Before I go, I want to apologize. I was a jerk at your exhibit. I get riled up when I'm filming."

I nod. "I believe you said: *The correct term is* shooting, *not* filming."

He hangs his head.

"I did call you Spielberg like it was an insult. Call it even on the jerk meter?"

I help him clean up his supplies. Our hands briefly brush against each other. I pull mine away quickly.

"Thanks for this. It's been fun. I'll text you the location details. See you Wednesday," says Daniel.

As Daniel leaves, I lock up the front door. I turn back, smiling to myself. Dad whistles loudly. I ignore his gaze as I gather my planners.

I might actually make my next big goal happen by November.

D aniel texted me a Google pin. So, on Friday night, I walk to the location, Mac & Cheese Rebel, while marveling at Highland Park. There are rows of food trucks and lines at each: Cena Vegan, Vivo Tacos Azteca, and Bang Bang Noodles. Usually, when it's this close to Halloween, my friends and I hung out in each other's apartments, ordering takeout and binge-watching whatever show everyone was talking about. But here, it's sixty-five degrees at night. This is not normal. I pass people bundled in scarves and puffy jackets and snap pics to send to Selena.

Selena: Ridiculous! 65 is hot.
Me: I know. I'm wearing a skirt.

I don't mention that I'm meeting a guy on this food truck adventure. It's a creative project, but still. Selena and I trade pics back and forth. She shares possible Halloween costumes: sexy cat, sexy dragon, sexy vampire. Everything looks amazing on her curvy body.

Me: You are a Filipina goddess. You could wear the Jollibee mascot costume and look hot.
Selena: Stop! You know I'm scared of that red bee with his blinking humanoid eyes.

Me: Fine. The sexy cat.
Selena: Predictable.

Just as predictable, Selena texts me photos of three hot artist types she swears are *perfect for me,* and five fire emojis.

Selena: Dude #1: Lives in LA. Dude #2: Sexy Spanish accent. Dude #3: Ripped.
Me: Girl, no.
Selena: You are no fun.
Me: If you must know, I'm hanging out with a guy tonight.
Selena: Name. Picture.
Me: Daniel. That's all for now.
Selena: Get it, girl.

I laugh, shaking my head before stuffing my phone into my purse. From across the street, I spot the truck I'm looking for. It's hard to miss. Bright yellow with a red logo and an Aladdin Sane–style red lightning bolt for the *L* in *Rebel.* Daniel is already there, chatting it up with people on the line. He's holding a black tripod and a glowing white paper lantern. I jog across the crosswalk. He spots me and waves, continuing his conversation. I ignore the thump in my heart at seeing him and instead inhale deeply. The wafting smells of sizzling onions and cheese are enough to distract me from Daniel's divine dimples.

"Hey," says Daniel. He hugs me. He turns to the people he was chatting with and says, "Have a good night!"

"Thanks for the rec, man," says a white guy who fist-bumps Daniel.

Daniel waves at the people in the truck.

"She's here!"

Suddenly, the line of people and the chefs inside the truck clap. I blush. Daniel sets up his iPhone on the tripod that has a tiny LED light attached. He asks if anyone is using the tiny folding table to eat. No one claims it. Daniel places his iPhone on it. He hands off the paper lantern to a young Latina woman on the line. She holds it up.

"A little bit higher. Perfect!"

He turns to me. "Ready to do this?"

"Right now? I thought I'd have a moment to prep or fix my makeup. Don't you need a microphone?"

"Your makeup looks perfect. The Mac & Cheese Rebel owners said I could use this exact locale as long as the line wasn't interrupted. No need for a microphone. It's a silent film, remember? Come," he says.

He leads me by the hand. A few people part so that Daniel and I are at the front of the line. He whispers and his full lips graze the edge of my ear. I shut my eyes briefly.

"This is our meet-cute moment. Think about your perfect first date and we'll let the camera capture it."

He runs and hits the record button on his iPhone. Everyone on the line watches us as the chefs call out order names. Daniel's name is called. He dashes off to retrieve our orders. I am frozen. My perfect first date hasn't happened yet. Technically, Jake and I never even went on a real date. I hung out in his studio. He knitted. I planned, did homework, watched TV on my laptop. We went to art openings with his friends. We lounged in Washington Square Park, checking out the dogs in the fenced-in area. But dinner and a movie? Nope.

"Hey. Just smile at me," says Daniel, returning with two plastic containers.

I focus on his brown eyes and thick black eyebrows.

"I've got an idea. You reach for the sriracha bottle. I'll reach for it at the same time. We smile at each other, then share the bottle at a table."

"Great. I can do that," I say.

I feel like I am weird and wooden, but we act out the mini scene. Our hands briefly touch around the red bottle of hot sauce. I smile instantly.

"Share it?" he asks.

I follow Daniel as he sits on a black folding chair that's right in front of the camera. The light operator (aka paper lantern holder) moves with him. He pops open the clear plastic lid. Steam rises from the cheesy pasta. On top, there's a pile of shiitake mushrooms, green onions, and oblong brown shapes.

"What's that?"

"Mock duck made out of vital wheat gluten."

"I thought no one in Los Angeles ate gluten."

Daniel holds a finger to his lips. "That's why it's on the secret menu."

I genuinely laugh. Daniel covers his mac with the red sauce, then offers me the bottle. I take it. I open my container. It smells garlicky and delicious, so I take a bite.

"That's actually really good."

"I don't steer anyone wrong when it comes to food," he says.

"I'll confess a secret too," I say.

Daniel touches my hand gently. My heart races.

I look around and lean extra close. My lips are on his ear lobe. He smells like a salty ocean wave. "I don't like food trucks. Well, until now."

"No!"

Daniel clutches his heart. I giggle. He stands still for a moment, then turns to face his phone.

"That's a wrap on this scene."

The line claps again. Daniel disassembles his iPhone from the tripod and light setup. He folds it all down compactly and stuffs it into a black messenger bag that he stowed by the truck's drinks station. He waves to the chefs.

"Thanks, guys! Another awesome meal."

They wave back. Daniel takes me to a small fake grass area lining the sidewalk and street. There are some built-in wooden park benches, dangling lights, and a few people milling about with takeout containers.

"It's called a parklet. The city built them around Highland Park for food truck nights."

We sit close together as we polish off the still-warm mac and cheese.

"It's weird eating dinner outside at the end of October." Off his look, I say, "In New York City, eating outside is more May through September."

"Ah, that explains everything," says Daniel.

"What does that mean?"

"You've got a look when you cross the street. Like this."

He scrunches his eyebrows and frowns slightly. I swat his arm.

"I want to get where I'm going quickly. What's wrong with that?"

"Here, we reserve that face for traffic."

"I wouldn't know. I don't have my license."

"What?"

"I took the subway everywhere. It didn't seem necessary. Now that I'm here, I walk from Ahma's house to the coffee shop and school. Easy enough."

"You haven't been anywhere else?"

I shake my head.

"Stop eating. I've got to take you on a proper Highland Park tour then. If I had known you were such a newbie, I would've picked Mac & Cheese Rebel as our last stop."

We place our lids on our containers. He places them in a plastic bag.

"Important questions first: How do you feel about spicy foods, mochi doughnuts, and ice cream?"

"I thought there were only green juice spots and weed shops in LA."

Daniel wags his finger at me. "That's the next tour. Don't ruin the agenda."

"In that case, I love all three."

"Then we'll go to Joy first. Hit up Mochinut, then a final stop at Magpies."

He offers me his arm. I slip my hand around it. We walk

until we hit a very long line outside of a small restaurant. I peek at the menu from my sidewalk view.

"Ooh, bao sandwiches," I say.

"The hot and sour soup is my personal favorite. And the wood ear mushroom salad with extra red chilies."

"Yes to all of that."

He raises his hand for a high five. We slap palms. The line moves steadily. Daniel tells me all about the neighborhood. How his mom manages an H Mart in Koreatown, and she bought a three-bedroom house in Highland Park, way back when it was just a few shops and the house prices were ridiculously low. He says hi to people, slapping a few high fives or showing off photos on his phone to other people he knows. For the first time since we moved here, I actually get to feel the rhythm of this block. I usually just hustle along, not noticing anyone's faces or even the storefronts, but suddenly, it feels a little more familiar.

We reach the counter and Daniel orders everything. We snag a table close to the street. The food comes and the bao sandwich is pillowy soft.

"This is heaven," I say.

He nudges the wood ear mushroom salad toward me. "If you dare, their crispy chili oil is awesome on top."

In response, I drizzle a healthy amount over my portion of the brown mushroom salad. It's crunchy and spicy with a nice tang of vinegar. The heat is intense, so I bite into my bao to soothe my taste buds.

"Want some?"

I nod. Daniel spoons half of his soup into a red bowl for me. I sip.

"You're right about this soup, but I'm going to admit something. I hope you don't hate me."

Daniel wiggles his eyebrows at me. I laugh and put my soup down.

"I hate Los Angeles."

He flops over the red table and feigns passing out. The silver metal water cups jostle. He lays there for a few seconds. A few people look over at our table. I nudge him. He pops up with a huge grin.

"My smog-filled heart is broken. Tell me what it is that you don't like," says Daniel.

"Everything."

"Way harsh."

I polish off my portion of the hot and sour soup. By now, my nose is running from the spice levels. I dab a napkin against it.

"I can't find a decent bagel. There's no art or culture. Theater here is popularized Broadway rip-offs, and the freeways are like NASCAR race tracks," I say.

"Is that it?"

"I have a longer list."

"Of course you do," says Daniel, grinning.

He has a bean sprout stuck in his front teeth. I reach for my phone in my purse and turn on the camera.

"You have a sprout."

He immediately covers his mouth. "Thanks. I'm glad this wasn't a real date, otherwise I'd be hella embarrassed."

I cringe at the *not a real date* part. This is the best non-date I've ever been on, but it's clear that he's not interested so I decide to focus on our agenda.

"Where to next?"

"Mochinut, which has these incredible doughnuts that are chewy, and Magpies for the best slice of soft-serve pie you've ever had. But before we depart for the dessert portion of the tour, there must be *something* you like about Los Angeles."

He stares at me. I want to say, *This moment is the first time I've liked LA since moving here and being dumped by my boyfriend,* but I can't. I shouldn't. This isn't a date. It's just pretend. A movie version of romance that he'll edit together later.

"We moved so quickly that I feel like I have no idea what I like here. There is one place I've been wanting to check out called Craft Contemporary. I follow their Insta and it looks up my alley."

I pull out my phone and show him the museum's website.

"Let's go there for scene two then."

"Great."

We stand close to each other. Close enough to kiss. Instead, Daniel smiles and we walk down York Boulevard at a snail's pace. I can't wait for our next not-a-date.

When I get home from school, I see my latest Happy Planner box waiting on the doorstep. I can't believe I get stickers, notebooks, *and* washi tape sent to me like it's Christmas. It's super heavy, so I drag it along the ground, using my butt to hold the door open. Phew. I pull up my jeans since they've slid down a little.

I head into the kitchen and Daniel is standing there with a pink box. Daniel, the best not-a-date I've had since the breakup, is here. I wasn't expecting him; otherwise I wouldn't have worn my one-size-too-big jeans and this ratty gray sweat-shirt that says *Booty Bootcamp* on it.

"Daniel, what are you doing in my house? Did I get the date wrong? I could've sworn I wrote in my planner that we're meeting tomorrow."

Daniel's dimpled smile makes me blush. Is it obvious I like him? He reaches for Ahma's blue crane teapot on the kitchen counter. Steam rises out of the spout. I smell the roasted sweet rice scent of Ahma's soba cha tea. My personal favorite.

I follow him as he walks to our dining table. Ahma sips her tea, wearing the maroon velvet pants I bought her last Christmas.

Daniel pours more soba cha into Ahma's cup. "We have tea together."

Ahma pats his hand gently.

"Oh my god." I perk up. "You're the boy. Ahma used to tell me about a boy in the neighborhood who kept her company."

"She taught me how to play mah-jong by beating me every single time."

At the words *mah-jong,* Ahma pokes Daniel's hand and chuckles. "She remembers the last time she trounced me. I learned to stop playing for actual money with her."

Ahma grins widely. I smile too. I remember her urging me to meet this nice neighborhood boy, even though I had a boyfriend. Well, now I don't, so it seems like perfect timing. I notice the bright blue and yellow Dole crushed pineapple can sitting between him and Ahma.

"Canned pineapple?"

Daniel taps the top of the silver can. "I thought it might be a clue. You said you're trying to figure out the pineapple cake recipe. Your ahma asked me to get this brand from the store once. I got a fresh batch of cakes in return."

I hold the can. "This entire time we've been using fresh pineapple and cutting it into chunks. No wonder it never turns into the jelly consistency we want. It's too thick."

Ahma tightly grips my arm. A light in her eyes. She inspects the can, then says, "*Ong-lâi-so.*" *Pineapple cake.* Her smile is huge. It matches mine.

I raise the can like it's an Olympic gold medal. Then, I hug Daniel. He's caught off guard and laughs.

"I could kiss you!" I say to Daniel.

Daniel turns red.

"I mean, I won't. But this is amazing. One piece of the puzzle."

My heart beats fast. I try to cover for my kiss declaration with a jumble of words, like I can filibuster him into forgetting. Ahma puts me out of my misery by grabbing Daniel's hand.

"TV," she says in English.

"Excuse me," says Daniel, "it's time for *Single Ladies Senior*. She's got me hooked."

They sit down together, and Daniel turns up the volume. I tap a text to Selena.

Me: I did the most embarrassing thing.

Selena: Do share.

Me: I just told Daniel that I could kiss him.

Selena: You're finally being direct. I like it.

Me: OMG. I need to hide. Has teleportation been
    invented yet?

Selena: Not since the last time I checked. Relax. Is he still
    around?

Me: He's watching TV with my ahma.

Selena: If he was really freaked out, he would've bounced
    already. Also, I was so right.

Me: We are friends with a capital F.

Selena: I'm sure you'd like to F him.

Me: Oh my god. What is wrong with you? BYE!

She sends me a dozen laughing sideways emojis and I toss my phone like it's a bomb. Instead of focusing on Selena's stupid text, I lug the Happy Planner box upstairs to my room.

I casually act like I need to do that, and then I can hide in my bedroom until next year.

"Do you want some help with that ginormous package?" asks Daniel.

Somewhere, Selena is dying with laughter and sending me eggplant emojis.

"I'm fine. Thanks though."

"It's no big deal," he says.

He grabs one side. Our fingertips graze under the box as we shuffle into my bedroom. I put down my side. When I stand up, his brown eyes are big.

"Um," he says. "Your pants."

Of course my jeans slid down. I yank them up. Cool. What's next? Will my ahma show him my naked baby photos?

"I'll come by tomorrow for our Craft Contemporary outing."

"Yes. Sounds great."

I go to shut my bedroom door to end my embarrassing streak, but Daniel stops in the doorway. "Your ahma's pineapple cakes are important to the neighborhood. Whenever she made them, it was someone's birthday, a baby was born, or somebody got married. She brought us together every Lunar New Year with a block party. We became a neighborhood because of her."

"Now I know why she refused to move to New York to live with us."

"We want to help."

I touch his shoulder. "Thank you."

"See you later, Chloe," he says.

A blush takes over my cheeks as I watch Daniel head downstairs. The loud chatter of *Single Ladies Senior* blares from the living room.

Me: Okay, fine. He's freaking adorable. You're right.
Selena: As always.
Me: We're going to an art museum tomorrow.
Selena: Girl, that's your Achilles heel.

I have made out in every major museum in New York City with Jake. I can't help myself. Whenever Jake talked about color theory or different artistic movements, I had to move closer to his lips.

Selena: You're thinking about Jake, aren't you?
Me: Stop reading my mind.
Selena: Too late. Have fun tomorrow! ;)

I can totally resist Daniel in an art museum. It's just a building and he's just a boy. I've got this. I unbox my Happy Planner box with a ridiculous smile on my face. Because I love stickers. That's all.

D aniel picks me up. As we drive to Craft Contemporary, I marvel at the palm trees that seem to touch
the endless blue sky. I hate to admit that I like how
it looks here. I remember when we flew into LAX, all I could
see from the airplane window were pools and mountains.
Where were the skyscrapers and the iconic bridges? Everything looked the same, but somehow, as Daniel hums along
to a song, I like it a tiny bit more. I also like that I can bust
out my favorite dresses, like tonight's strappy turquoise mini
dress, that I normally reserve for summer.

"I read that there's an exhibit in Craft Contemporary
called *Good Intentions* that's getting rave reviews from the *Los
Angeles Times* art critic," I say. "Artists took text messages that
they've gotten from well-meaning people and wove them into
murals. Some are paintings. Others are collage. Basically, they
were left to interpret the messages however they wanted."

"That's really cool. I had no idea this museum even existed. Look, I know you are Team New York, but if I may
enter some items in the Team Los Angeles column," he says.

"Like a Google spreadsheet," I offer.

"Is there any other kind?"

I laugh. "Continue."

"We do have some great museums here. The Broad downtown has free admission. It has this Kara Walker—"

"I adore her work!"

"The first time I saw her silhouettes, I was shook. And there's LACMA in Mid City. Vee and our friends bring a picnic basket in the summer and roam the late nights."

"Two viable entries into the Team Los Angeles column, but I could easily fill the Team New York column with dozens of museums," I say.

"Okay. I've got my work cut out for me," says Daniel.

When we walk into the museum, I am amazed at the vast open space and the fiber arts displayed. When Jake and I went to shows like these in the city, people were often crammed together. It was like seeing Monet in someone's closet. But here, we wander and gaze, walking around entire pieces and getting time to see everything up close. I like how Daniel stands in front of the art and studies it. He puts his hands up like he's holding a camera lens and looks at the work intently. It makes me swoon, but I clamp my heart shut. Remind myself that we are not on a date. We are making a movie. This is just a scene.

We finally get to the *Good Intentions* exhibit. There's text on the white wall at the entrance that explains what we're about to see. Daniel walks forward, but I stop him.

"We should read this. Most people glance over it and head straight toward the art, but after my Met internship, I know how hard curators work on perfecting each word. My supervisor used to say, 'These two hundred words should sum up what we want the viewers to consider as they view the work. We are not dictating what they should see. We are inviting them into a world that will change theirs. Choose your words wisely.'"

"I had no idea," says Daniel.

"The first exhibit where she let me write the initial copy, I had to rewrite it eleven times before she even considered it for the wall. It felt like torture at the time, but when she chose two sentences of mine for the final version, it felt like winning Olympic gold."

He and I move closer to the wall to read each word carefully.

Good Intentions *was conceived by Fiber Artists United as a response to text messages we have received as artists. Most are related to our racial identities; some are connected to awards we've gotten as artists; and others are from people in our art community who we think have good intentions, although misguided. We, as a collective, wrote down several messages, put them in a bowl, and picked randomly. The messages we chose were then left up to us to interpret in whatever medium we thought best for the text and for the emotional response that it elicited in us. We ask viewers to consider not only the words, but the way the words—out of context—make you feel. We hope that by highlighting the microaggressions artists receive we can all recognize our collective guilt in good intentions.*

"Wow," says Daniel. "I'm glad you told me to read that. It makes me excited to see the pieces."

"I used to think that art should speak for itself until my internship. It was clear to me that curators have a responsibility to the artists and viewers to invite deeper understanding and connection with these opening words," I say.

As the words come out, I feel a pang. This is exactly why I want to be an art curator. And until Jake's solo show disaster, I thought I could be.

"Come on," I say. "Let's check it out."

I am immediately drawn to the biggest woven mural in the room. It reminds me of Jake's work. I peer at the museum label on the piece.

ZOE NGUYEN

2018

People of Color

Hand-dyed wool and acrylic yarn

On loan courtesy of the artist

"I know this Vietnamese artist. She's an incredible knitter. She used to be known for knitting these giant pieces on the subway during her commute. People called her the Needle Lady. She was featured in a *New York* magazine photo essay about how she lugs her materials around with her on the seven train."

Daniel gets as close as he can.

"She made this entire thing?"

I nod. The message written into the navy-blue yarn reads, *Do you consider yourself a person of color?* The text is in a shocking neon yellow. It's almost too much because it's so bright. Like a yellow highlighter exploded on the yarn. Each letter is the size of my head. After the word *color,* the navy yarn transforms into an explosion of ombre colors. A rainbow of colors and skin tones. I always thought Zoe was talented, but this is extraordinary. It makes me consider every single woven word.

"What does this piece evoke in you?" asks Daniel.

I tilt my head. It's not an easy question to answer. I used to have conversations like these with Jake. Long, late-night talks over stale coffee at Georgio's Diner in Hell's Kitchen. We'd consider every brush stroke. What each color meant. Why the artist chose that particular medium to express themselves. Those were my favorite conversations. When Jake and I would argue until the waitress shoved the bill under our noses.

"Tightness in my chest. Like the shock of the words is one part. Then there's the colors she chose to use. They're bold, just like the question," I say.

"I didn't see that. Is that why this section of the mural is so tight?"

Daniel waves me over. He points at the section of yarn right after the question mark. The stitches are so close that the yarn folds in over itself. It almost looks like the physical representation of a stomach in knots.

"I didn't notice that, but you're right. It's like she's saying that the question itself tightened her up."

Daniel snaps his fingers. "Yes! I mean, I get it. If someone asked me that question, I'd feel all sorts of knotted up."

"Exactly."

We exchange a smile. I reach for Daniel's hand without realizing what I'm doing. I want to show him a particular part.

"Look at the section where she uses different color yarn. Even sparkly yarn. A mixture of textures. It feels like her response to the question is even more varied than she could've imagined."

He kneels down to see the yarn up close. A museum guard comes over.

"Sir, please step back."

Daniel nods and moves away from the piece, but his eyes are glued on it. He's got the look like I do. Like we're so mesmerized that we want to memorize what we're seeing to remember it later. I thought Jake was the only boy who ever got The Look, but watching Daniel, I see it in him too. My heart is saying *kiss him*. I mean, we're still holding hands. Then it occurs to me: the next scene he storyboarded is a kiss. The fictional couple's first kiss. If I suggest it in the context of the scene, then it's totally natural and has nothing to do with The Look.

"Maybe we could shoot scene two here and now," I say.

Daniel bites his lower lip. Maybe this was a stupid idea to suggest.

"I don't have any equipment and my phone is low on juice."

"I've got mine," I say. "We could use this bench as a tripod."

I offer him my phone. He takes it, then walks over to the guard. They chat for a moment. Daniel returns to me.

"I told him that we're shooting this for a high school art project," says Daniel.

"Technically, we are in high school. And it is for an art project."

"He said as long as we don't interfere with the exhibit or show any of the museum's signage, we have five minutes to shoot."

I am completely terrified and exhilarated at the same time.

"I think the backdrop of this knitted mural would look nice. It would add to the intimate feel of the scene."

I nod. My fingers sweat, but I keep up the act. It's just part of a scene. Not a real kiss. Just for the camera. He pops open my grip holder, steadies my phone on the bench, and hits record. For a second, I see us on the screen, close up. I turn away to look into Daniel's eyes. I haven't kissed another boy in a while. He moves closer to me.

"Can you come closer? I don't see you in frame."

I inch closer. His ocean scent is close.

"Is this good?"

He smiles at me in response. I am falling into his brown eyes. I dip into the edges of his dimples and am crushing so hard. I place a hand on his chest. His other hand is on my waist. I can do this.

"Ready?" he asks.

I lean in. Our lips tentatively touch. His breath is sweet like mints. Then, he kisses me deeper. I am falling even further. His lips are soft, warm, delicious. I curl my hand around his neck. Our breaths are intertwined. I move my hand along his back to press him closer to my body. I want to stay like this until the museum closes. Daniel pulls away first. He stares at my phone. He watches the replay. I glance over his shoulder. It's weird to watch yourself kiss on screen. As it plays, I feel my heart thump like it's going to leap out of my chest. It seems so natural how we move together. It's not until Daniel hits stop on the video that I remember that we're filming a scene in a movie. We're not an adorable couple on a date in a cool art museum. We're actors playing it up for the camera.

"Looks great. I think we got that one in the can," he says.

I watch him to see if there's more. Like he wants to continue the kiss, but he just hands my phone back to me like I'm a tourist and he took my photo with the Hollywood sign in the background. He moves to the next art piece. I put my phone in my purse and collect my heart. *It's not real, Chloe.* It's pretend. The sooner I can get that in my head, the better.

We've been here for more than two hours, and I could keep going, but my stomach rumbles.

"Can we grab a bite in the museum café?" I ask.

Daniel nods. The café has ceramic cups made by artists who've exhibited there, so our teacups are different. Mine is pink with etchings of anatomically correct hearts. Daniel's has the word *power* on it with streaks of black coming out of the center of the word.

"I've been thinking," I say. "How can I bring a social message to *Heartifacts*? I love what Zoe Nguyen did with that knit mural. I want to do something similar."

Daniel sips his tea. "Tell me more."

"I like the idea of artists responding to a theme and seeing how they interpret it."

"Why?"

I strum my fingers along my lips. "My favorite thing about art is how we can all see the same thing and yet interpret it so many different ways."

Daniel nods, leaning forward. He's close enough that I could reach out and touch his hand.

"Yes. Like people view the same movie. Some enjoy it. Some hate-watch it. Whatever book, movie, or show you worship, there's bound to be someone who despises it," says Daniel.

"Exactly." I pull out my Still I Rise notebook and turn to a fresh sheet of lined paper. "What if people sent in anonymous notes about love?"

"Why anonymous?"

"There's something fun about mystery. And it could also be universal. Like we all feel the same way."

"What are the notes about? Random love letters?"

I scribble his questions and my own on the page. This is my favorite part of an idea. The infancy. When it's just a jumble of random thoughts, then it slowly forms on the paper.

"A response to a question," I say. "What love is and what love isn't."

Daniel's black eyebrows shoot up, so I know I've got something. I write these two phrases over and over.

"It's open to interpretation," says Daniel.

"I could have artists take the messages and turn them into whatever they want. Like a pen pal who responds with art."

"Very cool," says Daniel.

I can't help myself. I squeeze his hand. He squeezes it back.

"You could reach out to an organization with *love* in their name and send images of the final pieces to people who can't attend in person. There's this org called Love for Our Elders. They send handwritten letters to elderly people in assisted living facilities. Vee and I usually spend some time every month writing out letters."

I don't remove my hand from his. I am swooning inside. Who is this amazing angel in front of me? No wonder my ahma likes him.

"That's a great idea."

"You should connect with Francesca Cruz. She's the head of Arte Para La Gente, and she can move mountains. You want any movement on something, you talk to Cruz," says Daniel.

"She mentioned her collective to me. It sounds amazing."

I continue writing as Daniel finishes his tea. My tea goes cold as I lay out the plans in front of me. Daniel doesn't push me to hurry up or finish. He pulls out his own notebook—plain black, unlined—and writes with a blue Pilot pen. The ideas flow and I see *Heartifacts* forming into something new. He taps his foot against mine.

"You're really something, you know that?"

I bring my teacup to my lips to hide my smile. To shield myself from his brightness.

"I'm serious. You've been in this city for a month, and you already have plans. Ideas. You're adding to the voice of our community. I know you think LA is devoid of actual art and culture, but you're now part of our community."

I can't help but shift closer to him. I want to kiss him for real. Not one for the camera, but for me. I don't move.

"Thanks for coming with me to this museum. It's beyond what I imagined," I say.

"Anytime, friend."

And that's the word that deflates my hopes for anything more with Daniel. *Friend.* I want to be more than friends with Daniel, but it's clear he doesn't. We still have more to shoot before the mini-film is done, so I'll stay his friend. At least we can hang out. I'll settle for the *F* word if it means I get to be around him. When Daniel looks at his phone, I slyly take the Craft Contemporary café napkin where he's doodled *power* a few times. I slip it into my purse before he can notice.

"Vee hit me up to hang with him. I should get going," says Daniel.

"How's he doing?"

"Better. Connor was his first boyfriend."

"Really?" Off Daniel's look, I add, "I mean, he's hot. I'm surprised."

"He's dated guys and girls. But this was his first serious boyfriend. When he introduced Connor to me as his boyfriend, I knew it was official."

"I'm completely prying into your best friend's love life, but what happened? I read Connor's note, but there's always two sides to the breakup story."

As I say this out loud, I remember my own side of my first real breakup.

"Connor always scoffed at Vee being bisexual. He'd call it a phase."

"Harsh," I say.

"And he cheated. A lot."

"That's awful."

As we pack up to go, I walk alongside Daniel. I brainstorm ways to keep talking to him. Keep him close to me.

"Can you drop me at the nearest Metro station?" I ask.

"Oh right, I forgot you don't drive. I'll text Vee that I'll drop you off first then head to his place. He'll understand. Besides, it's cold out. You'll freeze in that dress."

I touch Daniel's arm. "Thanks." I swallow my snarky remark about Angelenos being weather wusses.

He wraps his arm around my shoulders. An electric thrill runs through my body. Even if it's not real, pretending to be together feels almost as nice.

D aniel and I walk down an alley, alongside a black
dumpster bin filled with trash bags. It reminds me
of walking home from the subway late at night and
scurrying as fast as the rats on the street. I hold on to his arm.

"Where exactly are we going?" I say.

We are headed to film the third storyboard scene, the one
we titled "Problems." The cracks in the couple.

"I had a vision of us having a fight in a well-lit area. Some
place with less of a garbage smell and more of a white table-
cloth with a bread basket."

"Trust me," says Daniel.

He takes off his blue blazer and wraps it around my shoulders. I tell myself it's just part of the scene, even though we're
not filming yet.

"You're shivering."

"Thanks," I say.

I wrap his blazer tighter around me and inhale his warm,
breezy scent. He asked me to dress up so I'm wearing my royal
blue dress with gold constellation patterns and impossibly tall
heels. Normally, I'd never wear anything like this, but since
I had a ride here, I thought the heels would make my legs
look extra long. Instead, I am dodging random puddles, even
though it hasn't rained.

"We're here," says Daniel.

Here is a service elevator. No one is around. Daniel knocks on the metal. Suddenly, the elevator groans. Great. This is why I shouldn't have worn heels. I can't run away fast enough from whatever is coming off the elevator.

"I should warn you that my best friend Selena took me to a crazy corn maze in New Paltz and I straight-up bolted when someone tried to grab my ankle," I say.

Daniel laughs. Those dimples distract me a little. The elevator doors open. There's a Black guy in a full tuxedo. WTF.

"Name?" asks Tuxedo.

"Is this some secret society, Daniel?"

"Daniel Kwak plus one."

Tuxedo doesn't even look it up on an iPad or anything. He nods and moves aside. We step into the service elevator. I look over at Daniel who is wearing a tie and looks extra hot all dressed up. My fears subside when he squeezes my hand.

"Trust me."

We go up with Tuxedo until the elevator stops abruptly, bouncing as it comes to a halt. I reach for the wall to steady myself. The horizontal metal doors open, and we're on a rooftop. It's decked out with hundreds of string lights, white furniture, and a single bar. We step off the elevator.

"Have a good evening," says Tuxedo.

"Where are we?" I ask.

Daniel waves me over as he walks ahead of me. I follow. My heels thunder on the hardwood floor. From this view, I see the downtown skyline with tall buildings, office lights, and the faint outline of a mountain range. But the rooftop is empty. Just one bartender, Daniel, and me. Even Tuxedo is gone.

"Are you trying to tell me you're Batman? Like, the rich guy before he becomes a caped crusader."

"I hate to disappoint you, but I'm not independently wealthy like Bruce Wayne, and both of my parents are very much alive," says Daniel.

That's when I notice her. A Latina woman dressed in a white flowing gown sitting inside a glass enclosure. Inside is a white futon mattress. A small silver bucket. Nothing else.

"I got tickets to Melissa Mercado. The wait list is insane. Vee knows a guy who knows another guy."

Daniel gives a flourishing wave like I should know who Melissa Mercado is. I smile.

"Who?"

His smile turns into a frown. "Vee said she was *the* artist to see."

"I'm still not sure what's happening," I say.

There are two clear seats in front of the enclosure with our names on them. Daniel sits down in one. I hover over the other. The woman in the glass structure doesn't seem to notice us even though we're only three feet from her.

"Her exhibit is called *Solitary*. She sets up this structure in various spots around town and spends a week living in it. This week's performance is called *Hallow's Eve*."

"Oh. A performance artist," I say.

I move toward the bar and Daniel follows. I don't want Melissa Mercado to hear me.

"Daniel, thank you for organizing all this, but I don't enjoy performance art." I lower my voice to a whisper so that even the bartender doesn't hear us.

Daniel orders two ginger beers. We crack them open. I move to the edge of the rooftop. The city sparkles around us. From here, Melissa looks like a ghost floating in an invisible house.

"What's the value of performance art?" I ask. "No one but a handful of people can view it at a time in this secret location. Art is meant to be shared with lots of people."

"I get it," says Daniel. "In your view, art has to be popular to be of value."

He folds his arms over his chest.

"Rewind. I didn't say that."

"I thought it was cool."

"I just don't get the point of it. People always say that with all-white or all-blue paintings, anyone can do that, but for me, performance art seems to exist solely for shock value. Nothing more," I say. "Why dedicate time and energy into making something that only exists for a fleeting time period?"

"Is *Heartifacts* meant to last forever?"

"I hope I get more boxes to expand the exhibit and keep it going."

"For me, if one person is moved or thinks differently after a film I've made, then that's all that matters," says Daniel.

I can see what I'm saying is bothering Daniel, but I don't have the heart to tell him that without viewers, no one will pick up his film for a bigger distribution. I decide to switch the subject.

"Seems like this is a perfect opportunity to shoot," I say.

Daniel silently pulls out his phone from his blazer pocket. He directs me to stand against the city backdrop, focusing the camera lens on me. I stare into it. A few seconds later, Daniel hands me his phone. I hold it steady and point it at him as he walks toward the glass enclosure. I follow. He sits down on the clear chair. I film him from behind. Just the back of his head. I rest my hand on his shoulder while it records. I tap the red button.

"What do you think?" I ask.

He watches the footage.

"Great," he says. "Let's try it again for a second take. Just in case."

We repeat the same movements, but this time it feels more fluid. Rehearsed, in a good way. He replays it. I have to admit it looks better than I thought. I'm used to shooting in my studio with an overhead iPad mount, but it's actually fun moving the camera around. I hold my hands in the shape of a camera lens like I've seen Daniel do.

He gestures to the seat next to him. I sit down. Melissa Mercado is now lying flat on the ground, her dress clutched around her like a mummy's wrap. She stares straight up at the inky night sky. She's motionless. Daniel says nothing. We sit in awkward silence. I open my mouth to say something, but I stop myself. Instead, I watch this woman. Her stomach rises and falls with each breath. There's no artist statement. No music playing in the background. Just the hum of Los Angeles below us. Car honks. A helicopter whirring overhead. I fidget in my seat, wiggling one foot incessantly. This is eerie.

When I turn to Daniel, he's got his phone lens focused on me. I'm startled and realize he's had his phone on me this whole time. I hold up my hand over the eye of the lens.

"Can you please not record right now?"

"The look you're giving me is priceless."

I stick out my tongue, then fold my arms over my chest. "I'd rather not."

He slowly lowers his phone and presses stop.

"You looked perfect," says Daniel.

We stare into each other's eyes. For a moment, it's just us. It disappears when Daniel turns back to the artist.

"What I see is someone who is comfortable with herself," says Daniel. "Who doesn't place herself in the context of what she's doing to be someone."

I scoff. "Would you watch a movie where nothing happens? If someone stuck a camera here and recorded this nothingness, then screened it in a room with only you and me, would you watch it?"

"People watch puppy cams."

"In the background. While they do other things," I say.

Daniel turns to face me. Our knees touch. He taps my right knee. I lean forward.

"You hate this," he says.

I glance over at the woman on the floor. Surely, the glass isn't soundproof, so I whisper. Even if I don't like her performance piece, I don't want to insult her to her face (or the side of her face at least).

"This is my worst nightmare."

"Being alone?"

"Creating an exhibit that no one sees," I say.

"We're not no one. The exhibit is timed entry. Viewers have thirty minutes to observe. It's sold out until the end of the year," says Daniel.

Melissa stands, stretches, and then moves to the silver bucket. She lifts the edges of her white dress, and squats.

"Oh my god, Daniel, is she peeing?"

His brown eyes widen. "I believe she is. I mean, she doesn't leave the glass case for a week, so she must."

An unmistakable sound of pee happens. I leap up from my seat and rush toward the edge of the rooftop. Daniel follows me.

"In New York City, I saw people pee all the time. Drunk guys, toddlers in the park, and parade revelers. But I usually looked away," I say.

He pats my shoulder. "Want to go?"

"Yes, please."

"One sec," says Daniel.

He rushes back to our two clear seats and pulls off our badges.

"The artist requested all patrons take their name tags with them," says Daniel.

He hands me my laminated label and wraps his blazer around my shoulders again. We are close. I rest my head on his shoulders. The service elevator looks less scary now. As we spill out into the alley, I wobble in my too-tall heels. My feet are killing me. The narrow front squishes my toes.

"Thank you. I know you put a lot of effort into this scene. It's just not my thing," I say. "Now, I beg you, please get the car and pick me up here before I die in these heels."

"I'm not leaving you in this alley by yourself. I can carry you."

"I'm way too heavy."

"Nonsense."

He stretches his arms in front of me. I shake my head, but oh my god, the pain from these godforsaken shoes shoots through my ankles. So I nod and he sweeps me off my feet. I am pressed against his body.

"Wrap your arms around me," he commands.

I do. Suddenly I'm aware that his lips and mine are awfully close. Kissably close. I lean forward. My lips pucker. But he pulls back. I am left with my mouth hanging. Cool. I try not to radiate disappointment. He holds me tight as we exit the alley. We're on the sidewalk. His car is two blocks away, and he carries me the entire way without a single grunt. I must admit that my feet and toes are thankful not to be mashed on the cement anymore. When we reach his gold Toyota, he rests me gently on the ground.

"My feet and I thank you," I say.

Why the hell do I mention my feet? Not romantic, Chloe.

"You're very welcome."

He unlocks his car. We slip in. As he drives me home, I type in *Melissa Mercado* into my Instagram and see that she has posted several videos of what we just watched. The most popular one has 4,967 likes. Wow. Apparently, people like people-cams more than I thought. I still don't get it. Why would anyone want to watch this woman do nothing? Seems like a ginormous waste of time.

I switch over to my account and mindlessly scroll through

my posts. My most liked posts are my *Plan It Girl* vertical layout instructional videos. Then, it hits me. I should post Daniel's film to my community. That's how I'll get *Heartifacts* to go viral. Daniel said Melissa Mercado's show is sold out until the end of the year. This is how I'll make it happen.

"When we're done with the short film, can I post it on my Instagram?" I ask.

"I was hoping you would," says Daniel.

"I think it'll be good promotion for *Heartifacts*. Can we add a title card at the end with the show's website and social?"

"Sure. Of course."

I turn to see the mountains against the sky. There's a full moon, heavy and bright. I trace the outline of the moon in my car window. Daniel turns on music in his car. As we follow the signs to the 110, I make a promise on the moonlight. *Heartifacts* will be a huge success.

Stepping into a 99 Ranch supermarket is like walking into a candy store. I hold Ahma's hand as she steadies herself, using the cart as a makeshift walker. When I was a kid, I loved roaming the aisles and examining the packages written in Chinese, Vietnamese, Japanese, and Korean. I filled the cart with candies, cookies, and giant Asian pears while Ahma haggled for the price of a live lobster in the giant seafood tanks.

But today, my mission is singular. Follow the list of pineapple cake ingredients I have compiled so far and find the exact ones my ahma uses. I try the baking aisle first with its white boxes of Mochiko sweet rice flour and tapioca flour with a winged horse as its logo.

Ahma pauses at the rows. I watch to see if she reacts to anything she sees, but her expression is blank. I've never gotten used to seeing her stare into space. My ahma was always expressive—a single look could shut down grown men.

I pick up a bag of Sun Right fortified all-purpose flour. The yellow and red package is mostly written in Chinese and there's a picture of steamed baos. This must be the flour she uses for the pineapple cakes.

I bring it to her, holding it out, hopeful.

In Hokkien, she asks me, "What is this?"

I put it back. I try another brand. Another flour. Steamed cake flour. But she shakes her head to each. I carry an armful of flours, only to discover that Ahma has left the baking aisle. Crap.

I toss everything into the cart and dash off to find her. She's wearing a bright yellow sweatshirt that says *Strong Arm Gym* across the front and matching sweatpants. How hard could it be to find her?

I zigzag through the store. I credit my days zipping to the subway, always late for something, for giving me the ability to dodge Asian kids nagging their parents for candy, older grandmas, and 99 Ranch employees stocking cans without bumping into anyone.

It takes me ten minutes and an adrenaline rush before I find Ahma standing in front of the lobster tank. It smells fishy and salty. She pokes the thick glass with her pointer finger. A mass of lobsters with purple rubber bands clamping their claws shut are in various stages of climbing over each other.

"Ahma," I say.

She doesn't hear me. For a moment, I just watch her. Dad told me that his brother Eddie loved lobster. He'd crack it open and suck out the meat the moment it was cooked. According to my dad, his older brother got everything he wanted. Ahma would argue with the seafood mongers until she'd get a two-for-one deal for lobsters. I can still remember the clacking sound the lobsters would make in the steaming pot.

I approach her from behind. I see her face reflected in the

tank's glass with a frown embedded into her wrinkles. Her eyes are filled with tears.

"Ahma? It's time to go."

She waves me off and clicks her tongue at me. When I touch her shoulder, she smacks my hand.

I don't know what to do.

I text my mom, relaying the entire situation. She tells me my dad will come soon. Wait there, she urges.

So I stand behind Ahma as she talks to the lobsters. I can't understand anything she says. I suddenly realize how silly it was to think that I could fix this on my own. That I could stick bags of flour in her hands to recreate a recipe that's long been lost in her mind.

I stay close to her until my dad arrives. He hugs me tightly.

"It's okay, kiddo. I've got it from here."

He coaxes her out by whispering to her. He is the only one who can still reach her no matter what. Maybe because he looks like his brother.

On the car ride home, I am quiet as my dad talks to Ahma in Hokkien.

A text from my mom buzzes: You tried your best, Chloe. Ahma is not the same anymore.

I type through my tears: Maybe we should stop trying to figure out the recipe. Maybe it's better if we give up.

My mom doesn't respond. I toss my Recipe Planning notebook on the car floor and stomp on it, leaving an imprint of my shoe on its pink cover.

I copy the message I sent my mom and paste it into a message to Daniel.

Daniel: Don't give up. We can figure this out.

Me: It feels impossible.

Daniel: Impossible = I'm possible.

Me: That's corny.

Daniel: Promise me you won't give up. I need those
pineapple cakes in my life.

Despite my craptastic mood, I smile.

Me: Fine. I won't give up yet.

Daniel: Text me what you have so far.

So I pick up my Recipe Planning notebook with my foot-print on it, and I send him pics of my detailed notes. We text back and forth about ways we can figure it out. Brainstorming what we can check. Who we can ask.

Me: Thanks, Daniel.

Daniel: You can thank me with a tray of pineapple cakes.

Me: Done!

By the time we get home, I have hope again.

Teens, dudes with skateboards and tattoos, and older couples in designer clothes wait on a line for the Broad Museum, with more people wrapped around the exterior of the white honeycomb structure. I hold up our free tickets and wave at Daniel. He stops to chat with a street vendor selling fruit. When he reaches me, he holds a Ziploc bag full of fruit and two plastic forks.

"Hey," says Daniel. "I can never resist the fruit and Tajín bag."

He hands me a fork.

"What is in here?"

Daniel's eyes widen. "Only the best thing LA has to offer." He points to the various fruits. "You've got fresh coconut meat, watermelon, mango, some cucumber, all doused with Tajín, which is the perfect blend of chili peppers, lime, and salt."

"Back in New York, I've only ever had Tajín with mango." I dig into the bag and spear a watermelon cube dotted with red spice. It tastes deliciously sweet with a nice kick of heat at the end.

"This is amazing," I say. We silently devour more. I gesture toward the long line. "I had no idea it would be so busy here."

"When it first opened, it was impossible to book tickets. Vee and I went last year for the first time. We couldn't stop talking about the Kara Walker silhouettes."

"Jake loves her work. He took me to see her exhibit at MOMA. Oh, and I read there's some Takashi Murakami pieces here too."

Daniel nods. We slowly move as the line juts forward. I usually hate waiting for anything, but it's a nice warm day. The sun is shining. A gentle breeze cools us. Our hands touch briefly over the last piece of pineapple. Daniel nudges the fruit to my fork. I take it.

"Who's Jake?"

"My ex."

He nods again. I blather on about how we broke up, and how Jake dumped me via the US Postal Service. Daniel is strangely quiet so I keep talking. I cannot shut up. I'm a GIF on repeat. I mention how Jake is a super cool artist who knits massive murals. Some are about social justice issues. Others are portraits of his grandmother. He's done concert band logos for some up-and-coming musicians. Daniel cracks a small smile. Somehow, we're at the front of the museum now. The first floor is crowded.

"I like to start at the top and work my way down at museums. That way, I don't miss anything," I say.

"Lead the way," says Daniel.

We escape to the stairs and make our way to the third level. I am immediately in love with this museum. I stop at a giant furniture exhibit. A brown chair towers over me.

"Stay right there," says Daniel.

His camera is on me as I stand underneath the chair, resting against the leg. I look like a tiny person in a giant's house.

"Can I move now?"

Daniel nods, holding his phone steady. I slip under the wooden table. It looks like something out of a storybook, like Goldilocks and the giant furniture. Daniel joins me and points the camera at us. We are together, at least on screen.

We move out of the big furniture room when I see Takashi Murakami. His work is like Andy Warhol's pop art, but mixed with anime. It's an explosion of color. Murals of walls with bright yellow flowers with happy faces. I am in awe. I've only seen some of his work online, but in person, it's way more thrilling.

"Your face right now is pure joy," says Daniel. "Watching you study art is worthy of any painting in a museum."

He's across from me. A statue between us. A group of pre-teens near us hovers a selfie stick. I move out of their way before they bump into me.

"Let's go out for real," I say.

I suck in my breath. Maybe it's the Takashi Murakami art, or the fact that he said he loves my face, but I go for it. I reach for his hand and hold it in mine.

"A real date. Not just for the movie. Probably *not* performance art. Dinner and a movie."

His tan face is growing paler by the second. He gently lets go of my hand. Suddenly, all I can hear is my heart thudding loudly in my chest. I'm not shy about asking guys out, but rejection is never fun. I'd rather eat glass.

"Or maybe not," I say.

"You're great."

"Words every person loves to hear," I say. "There's a *but* somewhere."

"I'm not boyfriend material. I'm the nice guy who goes on one date with a really cool girl and she ends up hooking back up with her ex. Trust me."

"I'm over my ex," I say weakly.

"Jake, the amazing artist who gets commissions from really cool bands?"

Hearing Daniel repeat my words back to me sounds awkwardly painful when filtered through his voice. Can I help that I still admire my ex-boyfriend? He's really talented.

"Chloe, I'll tell you what will happen. We will go on one amazing all-night sort of date. We will have a great time. Laugh all night. We'll do something fun. Except for dancing. I'm a terrible dancer. At the end of our magical date, I'll drive you home. We'll share a few brilliant kisses. You'll hop out of my car. Tell me you had a fantastic night and can't wait to do it again. I'll drive home with a dopey grin on my face. I'll text Vee that our date was one of my best. Then, the next day, I won't hear from you. The day after that, the same. Soon, a week will pass. I'll run into you in the neighborhood. You'll feel guilty, but you'll tell me that you got back together with Jake. You realized that you missed him and I'm a really nice guy, but you're not over him."

When Daniel's done with his monologue, I am flabbergasted.

"How many times has this happened to you?" I ask.

Daniel counts on his hands. "At least five times. Six if you count Rachel Lyon, but Vee says she doesn't count 'cause she was rude."

"Wow. I'm not sure what to say."

"Chloe," he says, taking my hand in his. "I really like you. Like, a lot. You're a really cool girl. We have fun together. When you talk about art, I want to hear everything you have to say. But if we date while you're still into Jake, it's not going to end well. And I can't risk giving up my favorite neighborhood café to be your rebound guy."

I finally find a wide white bench and I plop down. I didn't think I was still hung up on Jake, but if Daniel can see it, then I must not be as over him as I thought. Sure, I still talk about Jake. Selena always says: *Forget the ex with someone next.* I always thought she was nutty for saying that. Was that what I was doing with Daniel? Finding someone new to bury my old relationship?

"Friends?" asks Daniel.

He reaches out his hand. I stretch out mine and we shake.

"Friends," I say.

"It's better this way," says Daniel. "Trust me. This way, we won't end up hating each other."

"Is that how the other dates ended?"

"Let's just say I have to avoid my favorite pizza joint because she works there. I can't handle the awkwardness of her free slices. Like I'm a street urchin who accepts pity pizza. Vee thinks I'm being ridiculous. Plus, he says free slices are awesome. *Use it or lose it,* he says. I'd rather lose it."

We get up and walk through the rest of the museum. I'm in a daze. I let Daniel do most of the talking. I'm over Jake, right? I boxed up his things. I unfollowed him on all social. Hell, his stuff is the first box in *Heartifacts.* Is there a time frame when you're over someone?

"For our last scene, the big breakup, I thought we could have a movie night. Stage it to look like we're at two different places. The theme of the night: we choose a film we think would make the other person sad. We really want to make it look authentic that we're heartbroken on camera."

"Of course," I say.

"Do you think it'll be too cliché if we ate pints of ice cream in the scene? Too much?"

"When Jake dumped me, I did the opposite. My dad had to remind me to eat."

"No food then. My umma and halmeoni are going to a church function on Halloween. They've given up trying to drag me there. How about you come over then? We'll have the entire house to ourselves."

"Great," I say.

Daniel talks at the rate of someone who had three energy drinks with a side of straight-up sugar. I nod along, but don't really hear anything he's saying. I want to play the role of a friend who doesn't care that she was flat-out rejected by her crush, but I don't think my performance is very convincing because Daniel finally stops talking.

"You okay?"

"You know, I ate a taco earlier and I'm feeling a little queasy from it."

"Okay, sure, how about I get you home, then?"

I hug him. "I'll catch a Lyft. Stay. Enjoy more of the museum."

I walk away before Daniel can say anything else.

arrive at Daniel's house with my favorite movie snacks: kettle corn popcorn, matcha Pocky, and several homemade mochi my mom insisted I bring over. Daniel answers the door with a towel around his waist, his black hair dripping with water. I can't help but stare. I have eyes. He's not sporting a six-pack like Jake, but there's something very cute about a guy in a towel.

"Oh hey. You're early," says Daniel.

I glance at my watch. "I'm preciously on time."

"You're early for LA."

I steal another look at his bare chest. My eyes wander down. A very Selena thought pops into my head: *Screw that towel.*

"Be right back."

He runs up the carpeted stairs with the towel still fixed around his waist. Why do I keep hoping that the towel falls off? I shake my head. We're just friends. Better as friends. But if I'm still hung up on Jake, why am I staring at this boy's butt? I turn away and focus on setting up my snacks next to his. I lay everything out so that it's the perfect array of snacks. I snap a pic and send it to Selena who sends me back an eggplant and peach emoji.

I roll my eyes and laugh at the same time.

He's already put out some cans of key lime LaCroix, a large red box with gold Korean letters on it, and extra-hot wasabi peas. When I see *extra hot* in the red writing, I think of Daniel's butt. The next second, he's in front of me. He holds up the red box with a small chocolate pie on it.

"These are my favorite," says Daniel.

"What are those?"

His brown eyes bug out. "You've never had a Choco Pie?"

Daniel opens the box and takes out one individually wrapped treat. He unwraps it and offers it to me. It looks like a puffy chocolate cookie. I take a bite. Whoa. The combo of yellow cake, marshmallow, and chocolate is deliciously sweet.

"Right?" asks Daniel.

"Where have these pies been my whole life? I thought you said my ahma pitied you because you didn't have sweets at home."

"We don't. These are contraband."

He holds his finger to his lips and wiggles his eyebrows. He's way too cute.

"Are you expecting more people? This package is huge."

I wave at the giant pack of Choco Pies and his cheeks turn bright red. What did I do? Oh my god, did I say something about a huge package? *Chloe. Get your mind out of the gutter.* But I can't help it. His butt is fine. I bet the rest of him is too.

"Why is everyone here obsessed with this weird sparkling water?" I hold up the cold green can. "They look like something out of an eighties VHS exercise tape that my mom still watches when she works out in the morning."

Daniel tugs the can out of my hands. Our hands briefly touch.

"Excuse me," says Daniel, covering the can as if it can hear us. "This water is a gift from the heavens. The rumor is that it's a Midwestern staple. Most TV writer assistants come from the Midwest, and since they're in charge of ordering for their shows, they stocked the writers' rooms with LaCroix. Now everyone drinks it."

"Everything in LA is superficial," I say.

Daniel raises his eyebrows. I'll say anything to get him to raise his eyebrows. It's so freaking adorable.

"I'll have you know I have a digital subscription to *The New York Times*."

"Fine. You're the exception to the rule. It feels like all everyone talks about at school is the film industry." I put on my best LA accent: drawn out and spacey. "*Oh, that actor. My dad produced his last movie and says he's a jerk. Does no one here read a book?*"

"Ouch," says Daniel. "What is this book thing you're talking about?"

I smack his arm. He smells so nice and fresh from the shower that I resist the urge to get closer. Instead, I plop on the couch.

"My bestie Selena and I always go to the Village Halloween parade. This year, she convinced me to wear a sexy costume with her. The only good thing about moving here is not being a sexy goldfish," I say.

Daniel coughs. "I'm imagining an elaborate orange sequin jumpsuit."

"You're not far off." I find the photo that Selena sent me of a tall blonde with orange plastic fins and a fish head.

"If you like parades, the one in WeHo is pretty awesome. Makeup artists go all out," says Daniel.

I shrug my shoulders. I have no idea where WeHo is, or what that means. "I don't really have friends here. And Halloween's not the same without Selena."

"I hope you consider me a friend," says Daniel.

That *friend* word again. I change the subject. "I picked my movie. It's on Netflix."

"Great. Mine is too. Who goes first?"

"Rock, paper, scissors," I say.

"Old school," says Daniel. His stupid dimples come out and I do everything in my power not to lean in toward his lips.

We play rock, paper, scissors and I win two games out of three, so my pick is first.

"Matcha Pocky? I haven't eaten these before."

"A delicacy," I say. "I order them in huge packs. My mom has tried to make homemade ones, but I prefer the preservative-filled version."

He nibbles on the end of a green matcha cream. I take one and tap mine against his Pocky stick.

"What do you think?"

"Best Pocky ever. Though I am Team Chocolate Pandas."

"Of course you are. Pandas are cute, like you," I say.

Daniel's cheeks turn red. Chloe, you've got to stop. He said *friends* like he means it.

"I mean. Everything is cute. This can of LaCroix is cute. *Cute* is my word right now. Cute everything, you know?"

He nods, looking away from me.

"What movie are we watching?"

"*Always Be My Maybe*. One of my favorite romantic comedies. I've seriously watched it, like, a billion times. Now, a billion and one times."

I see the panic in Daniel's eyes like when my fave gel pen runs out of ink.

"It's more com than rom. Trust me. It's hilarious."

I hit play on the movie. Daniel and I sit side by side. I devour several snacks to keep my mouth from saying anything else stupid. When dating Jake, I kept my cool together the first time we met, and I was a big fan of his work. Why can't I keep my mouth from saying silly things to a guy who is clearly not interested in me?

Halfway through the movie, Daniel laughs so hard when Keanu Reeves comes into the restaurant scene. Randall Park, the main romantic interest, bemoans Keanu arriving in slowed-down dialogue. I love how Daniel's face crinkles when he laughs. As we reach the end, I find myself conveniently closer to Daniel's body. We're mere inches from each other. I can easily touch his thigh. He must have some psychic abilities because he jumps up suddenly.

"Let me grab my phone."

"Cute," I say.

At this point, I figure if I'm going all in on claiming *cute* as my word, I'll use it for anything. Daniel sets up a black tripod and his phone.

"I put the lens solely on me, so you won't be in the scene since technically we broke up."

"Cute," I say.

"I have to ask though. Why did you pick a rom-com as something that would make me sad?"

My real answer is that I thought we'd end up hooking up because of the rom-com vibes, but clearly that ship has sailed.

"It came from our last convo that romance made you sad."

"Oh," says Daniel. His shoulders sag. "Do you think I'm a sad person?"

"No! I mean, I didn't think you'd enjoy rom-com movies, so it might make you sad. Like anything with a happy ending."

"I'm busting your chops," says Daniel. "You're totally right. This kind of movie makes me want to cry. It sets everyone up for failure. Whenever I've had an ounce of a feeling with a girl, she ghosts me. Like in this movie, Randall Park is mopey-loser attractive, but he's still a romantic leading man. I'm more best-friend, side-character material."

Daniel falls back into the couch. "Can you hit record? I think I'm in the moment."

I rush over to his phone and hit the red button. I stay away and watch Daniel through the screen on his phone. He doesn't cry but I feel his ache. Ever since Jake and I broke up, I tear up at the slightest suggestion of heartbreak. A song. A celeb couple announcing their breakup. I'm so lost in the moment that I don't hear Daniel ask me to hit stop. Suddenly, he's next to me. He presses the stop button. I want to touch the back of his head and bring his lips close to mine. I want to whisper that I am the girl who wants to date him. Instead, I look away.

"My turn," says Daniel.

"What did you pick?"

"*My Octopus Teacher.*"

"I haven't seen it."

"It's a great documentary. Gorgeously shot. And you love animals," says Daniel.

"I do adore animals. Sea creatures are so cool, especially the ones in the deepest parts of the ocean, like the ones who glow in the dark."

My phone buzzes, lighting up the room. I glance at it.

Selena: I need updates, girl! Like now.

I shove my phone back into my pocket. I had a different vision of the evening. Netflix and chill, but apparently I'm the only one with that in my head. We watch Daniel's movie. It's about a filmmaker who free dives into the ocean in South Africa and befriends an octopus. I didn't expect to feel all the feels about a random octopus, but I do. I also didn't know that octopi only live for one to two years, so at the end, she dies by turning white. The remains of her body are eaten by sharks.

I am sobbing. Daniel's arms are around me.

"Chloe, I'm sorry. I shouldn't have picked this documentary. It was a mistake."

He clicks off the TV. The room is now dark. I'm still crying, nestled tightly against Daniel's chest, even though the movie is turned off. I am soaking his white T-shirt with my tears.

He strokes the back of my hair and I touch his cheek. We are so close right now when I look up at him. He wipes a tear away.

"I love how much you love animals," he says.

I respond by kissing him. I curl my hand around the back of his neck. His lips are warm and soft, and our kisses are gentle, then urgent. I wrap my arms around his neck to pull him closer to me. He responds by stroking my back with his hands.

Then, suddenly, Daniel stands up.

"Chloe, I can't. I really like you," he says.

"I'm not sure what the problem is. When two people like each other—"

"I know how this is going to end. Trust me. Just wait."

He connects his phone to the Apple TV so his phone screen projects onto the TV screen. He scrolls through his photo albums. He picks one labeled *Rebounds*.

"You have an entire photo album of your ex-girlfriends? I'm going to need another Choco Pie."

I tear open the package as Daniel dims the lights even more. The first photo is a blurry dark photo of what looks like a concert venue with Daniel and a Latina girl smushed together, taking a selfie. I bite into the Choco Pie. As the chocolate melts in my mouth, Daniel moves to the TV screen and points to the dark photo.

"Case number one. I went to see the Wild Ones at the Wiltern with Kate, and the band played two encores. It was amazing. Kate and I had a blast. I even got backstage passes with the band. I go to kiss her and she says, 'I'm not over my ex,' and runs off. She completely disappears into the crowd, and I was there all by myself."

"At least you had the backstage passes?" I offer meekly.

He flicks to a new photo. It's a selfie with Daniel holding a froyo container that says *Yogurtland* on it. He's frowning. In the background, there's a white and Asian couple making out like a kissing photobomb. Daniel points to the blur of black hair.

"Case number two. Esther. Our second date. We went to a double feature of Werner Herzog. Her suggestion. We talked for hours about *Grizzly Man*. She suggested we go to Yogurtland. There's, like, eight million, but she wanted to go to the one in Eagle Rock. We go, and her ex Meredith is working. Wow, what a coincidence. They flirt in front of me and then Meredith says she misses her. I kid you not, her ex-girlfriend took her break and they started making out in front of me."

I stifle a laugh because Daniel is so serious. It comes out like a weird honk. I excuse it as hiccups. He moves on to the next photo. It's a view from a hiking trail. There's a white girl on a rock and Daniel poses in front.

"Case number three. I sent this pic to Vincent after he set me up with Grace and we went to Runyon Canyon for a hike. Everything was going great. She and I talked about our favorite hikes, and we petted all the happy dogs we met. Some dude was running with a Bluetooth speaker and suddenly Grace says, 'That's our song,' and the next thing I know she's bawling on a rock. Several people gave me dirty looks because they thought I was responsible for her crying, like I had broken up with her. One blond guy said, 'Way harsh, bro. At least wait until you get to the car.'"

Daniel says this and I can't hold in the laughter anymore. It's bad. When I get like this, I cannot stop laughing. Like, I try, then I hear the thing that made me laugh and I'm stuck. Tears stream down my face.

"Please stop."

"There's more, Chloe."

My sides ache. My cheeks burn. Daniel clicks to the next photo. This one is dark too, but instead of a concert venue, it looks like a big movie theater. Daniel presents one photo of him eating from a clear plastic container of popcorn. The next photo is of someone dressed in a black uniform with his arms around a pretty Black girl who is smiling. The photo is blurry, but her smile and the way she's holding hands with the uniform guy is very apparent.

"Case number four?" I ask.

"ArcLight movie theater. The Dome. You know how the usher comes out and greets the audience?"

I shake my head.

"I've never been to the ArcLight."

A movie theater disaster date requires kettle corn popcorn. I grab a fistful and munch on it.

"You've never—what? So you've never really seen a movie. Okay, we'll revisit that. Basically, at every ArcLight movie, the usher comes out and does this whole greeting and talks about the volume and staying to make sure that the movie sound quality is up to the theater's standards. Well, this extremely handsome Black usher comes out and when he says the bit about *please come see me if you have any issues during your movie-going experience,* my date pops up from her seat and shouts, 'I miss you.' They have this magical movie moment as she rushes down the aisles and people clear out of the way. He says, 'I miss you too,' and then they kiss as the entire sold-out audience starts clapping. I'm there with my expensive caramel popcorn as they go off hand in hand together."

"Ouch. That's pretty bad."

"I'm not done yet."

"It gets worse than the movie theater rom-com?"

Daniel scrolls to the last photo in his album. He's dressed to the nines in a tux with a pink rose corsage. The limo driver is in the back seat with him.

"Case number five. This is Anthony. Charlotte Kim was my long-time crush. Right before prom, Vee told me her boyfriend broke up with her, so I thought it was the perfect time to ask her out. Charlotte needed a date and I had wanted to go with her since we met freshman year in the film enthusiasts club."

"Why are you in the back seat with the limo driver?"

By now, my hands are coated in Choco Pie chocolate and popcorn pieces. I wipe them clean.

"Just as we arrive to Henson Soundstage in Hollywood, Charlotte gets a text from her ex. He wants to talk to her. She tells me she'll be a minute and she darts out of the limo. Chloe, guess how long she was gone?"

"Ten minutes?"

Daniel scrunches his face. "Two hours."

"Yikes."

"I was too damn embarrassed to get out of the limo. I still had her corsage in the plastic florist box. She had my ticket to prom in her tiny purse. I texted her, but she didn't respond. Anthony played my favorite songs on his stereo system. He told me a bunch of his breakup stories to cheer me up."

"Why did you wait there?"

Daniel hangs his head. "I kept hoping she'd come back. I had the biggest crush on her for the longest time. We hung out a lot before she had a boyfriend. I thought we had a connection. She always read everything I wrote. We even exchanged poems."

I pat the couch seat next to me. "Come sit."

He does but decides to sit a few inches away. The mood in the room has completely changed. I crack open a now warm key lime LaCroix and hand it to him. He takes a big swig.

"All of that sucks, but seriously, Charlotte Kim is a jerk for ditching you at the prom. That's not your fault. It doesn't mean girls don't like you."

"They don't like me enough to date me beyond two dates. Listen, Chloe, I really dig you. You're funny, sweet, and creative. You're someone I want to get to know more. You're hella cute too, but your boyfriend just dumped you. I've been there and done that. I know you think you're ready to date someone new, but you're not. How long have you been broken up?"

"I'm not counting days."

"Approximately?"

"Three weeks," I squeak out.

"You're not ready. You're in love with the idea of love. Classic post-breakup symptoms."

I reach for a key lime LaCroix. I take one sip.

"This tastes like a flavorless Sprite."

Daniel covers the can with his hands. "Don't take out your relationship problems on key lime."

"Okay, what are the other classic post-breakup symptoms? I assume you're an expert based on the evidence that you've presented."

"The line *I'm totally over him/her/them.* Everyone says it and doesn't really mean it."

I have said this exact line to him. Yikes.

"Stalking their social."

"Ah! I've got you beat there. I unfollowed Jake on every social platform."

"Do you still check it?"

I blush. My cheeks warm at the thought that I still do nightly checks on what Jake is doing.

"See," says Daniel.

He starts to clean up the snacks, and I grab the plates and follow him into his kitchen.

"Anything else?"

"Keeping their ex's stuff in hopes of getting back together." He raises his eyebrows. "I don't want to point out the obvious, but you have dedicated an entire exhibit to your ex."

I place the plates in the sink and spin around to face Daniel. "Jake's box was my inspiration for the idea."

A thought occurs to me. Daniel's slideshow is the perfect visual for the museum exhibit. With the short film of us as a couple and his slideshow, it would add a whole new visual element that I'm lacking.

"How would you feel about using your Rebounds slideshow in *Heartifacts*? I have this vision of it running on a loop on the wall when you first enter, like the endless cycle of getting dumped. No offense."

Daniel nods. He tilts his head. I continue.

"I would project our short film on the large wall so that viewers would see it as a backdrop as they walk through the breakup boxes and stories. By having your slideshow up front near the entrance, it welcomes the viewers with a sense of humor."

He grabs his phone and scrolls through the photos.

"How would anyone know what the heck is happening in my photos? Without captions, they'd be pretty random," says Daniel.

"You could use title cards for the captions."

"I don't know."

"No pressure. The exhibit can feel emotionally heavy, like the world's worst Valentine's Day, but your short personal story at the beginning, it'll break the tension. Not in a *look at this poor guy's life* kind of way. More like, *damn, we all feel this way*," I say.

Daniel nods. "It's a great idea, but I'd rather not."

"I understand."

I pick up a blue dish sponge and wash the dishes from our movie night. Daniel joins me and dries them.

"I enjoy that we are each other's creative partners. We can bounce ideas off of each other. Go to exhibits together. Hey,

Vee has been on me about hitting Highland Bowl for the teen free bowl night. Join me for a group hang. You'll see how much better it is that we're friends."

I try to forget how warm his breath felt against my lips. I force a smile.

"Cool," I say.

Even though I'm not.

Chapter
14

Under the glowing lights of this hipster bowling alley, I totally see how hot Vincent is with his chiseled cheekbones, muscular arms, and hair like a Korean boy band member. I look around for Daniel, but don't see him. Francesca is already there, scarfing down a slice of pizza. Several groups bowl with blue bumpers down each row.

"Hey," I say.

Francesca gives me a nod as she pulls on the stringy cheese on her pizza slice.

"I'm starving. Came here straight from dishing out froyo. Eat up. It's so good."

I shrivel my nose at the steaming pizza pie in front of me.

"I'd rather not."

My stomach is rumbling, but I don't like pizza here. It's greasy cardboard at best. Nothing compares to real NYC pizza, even though this smells good.

"New Yorker?" asks Vincent.

"Guilty as charged."

He grabs a slice and places it on a paper plate. "Daniel mentioned."

"Where is he?"

Vincent waves his hand back at the entrance while eating his pizza. "His shoot is running late. He's working on this doc to submit to the Santa Monica Teen Film Festival, and he booked an interview that's going long."

"Bummer."

I haven't eaten dinner and thought I'd grab something here, only to find out that they only serve *pizza*. Great.

"I know you," Vincent says to Francesca. "Angela Alvarez's ex. You two were always making out in the back stairwell."

Francesca wipes pizza grease from her mouth. "Until she dumped me for a UCLA freshman."

"That's busted."

"Thank you," says Francesca. "What's Daniel's documentary about?"

Vincent chuckles. He looks around the bowling alley before answering. "Do you want the real tea?"

Francesca mimes holding a teacup. Vincent laughs, then bowls and knocks down eight pins. "His take on Valentine's Day is that it's a mass-market holiday solely to make money. It's all numbers, business guys in suits, and stock shots. His documentary is as boring as a dining table. I don't have the heart to tell him though," says Vincent.

"Ouch. Aren't you his best friend?" asks Francesca.

"We've been best friends since sixth grade," says Vincent. "Someone left graffiti on my locker that said *Bi now, gay later,* and Daniel washed it off with me," says Vincent.

I fall even harder for Daniel.

"He's your ride-or-die," says Francesca.

"What's boring about it?" I ask. I roll my sparkly pink ball down the lane. I knock three pins down. Grr. I don't even like bowling, but it sucks to be bad at something.

"Honestly, it's way too serious." Vincent looks at his phone. "Speak of the devil, Daniel says he'll be here in an hour. He's been chasing this particular guest forever and he finally scored an interview with him. Plus, that boy can talk to a wall for ninety minutes," says Vincent.

We continue bowling. Vincent is kicking our butts. After about thirty minutes, I finally eat a slice of pizza. Turns out: not bad. I won't Instagram it, but it's not the cardboard covered in ketchup that I thought it would be. Vincent teases me about my pizza snobbery. I launch into my hate for LA bagels, which are basically carb hockey pucks. He waves his hand at me.

"Girl, I ate a burrito in New York City and that's a mockery of the word *burrito*."

I laugh so loud that I end up dropping my pink bowling ball in the lane. It slowly rolls down the alley.

"You got us there," I say.

Francesca nestles her bowling ball in the ball return. "I'm gonna grab more slices since Ms. New Yorker here ate the last ones."

I hold my hands up. "They were pretty good."

Francesca and Vincent exchange a smile. Francesca leaves. Vincent is up. He steadies himself before throwing a perfect strike. Damn. Vincent smiles and pats the bench. I sit down next to him.

"Daniel talks about you incessantly. It's annoying," says Vincent.

"He said we'd be better as friends."

"He showed you the slideshow."

"Yes!"

"I told him to delete that shit. Daniel goes for girls who are still hung up on their exes because he's afraid of having a real relationship."

"I have a huge crush on him."

"I know. It's obvi. I've tried to get through his thick skull that he's a total catch. Here's what we're going to do. When Daniel gets here, I'll corner him and gently nudge him to ask you out."

I pick up his root beer cup and peer into it. "Do you have a magical elixir in there? Your boy has already turned me down."

"Daniel wants me to date this guy on his documentary crew who he thinks is perfect for me. I'll agree to it if he asks you out and you all go out on a real date."

I pick up my plastic red Solo cup, clinking it against Vincent's. "Done."

We keep playing. Francesca returns with a large cheese pizza that smells like tomatoes and garlic. Daniel finally arrives, apologizing profusely for being late, but none of us care. I anxiously stare at Vincent waiting for the moment that he whisks Daniel off alone. He finally asks Daniel to go to the bathroom with him.

After they leave, I kick Francesca's foot gently. "He's nudging Daniel to ask me out."

"I know you're hung up on Daniel and he's a sweet honeybee, but are you really, truly over your ex? Like, for real."

I nod a little too much. I haven't even checked him out on Instagram today, which is a huge accomplishment. I told myself that if I was going to hang out with Daniel I needed to let that go. I'm super satisfied that one day without thinking about Jake means I'm cured.

"I'll tell you that I'm not over Angela. I straight-up type out texts to her every single day. I have stupid dreams where we get back together. It's not as simple as you think."

I sip my soda, letting Francesca's words wash over me. Maybe she's right.

"But I really like Daniel. He's a really good guy. Should I let him slip away just because I am fresh from a breakup?"

"If you really like the guy, then the best thing for him is to let him go for now. Be friends. Get over your ex."

"How do I do that?"

"Me? I go to the gym every day. Skate at the park. Pour myself into my art. I do all the shit I like and yeah, I think about her. Cry over stupid songs that we like. Let myself get all mushy when I see something she'd like and resist the urge to text her."

"So you don't text her at all? Like, she's gone from your phone?"

"I don't. When I can finally not feel that ache in my body when I think about her, then I know it's over. What did you do with your other breakups?"

"This is my first."

She nods. "That's why. You're a newbie at this. Getting your heart broken is like fixing yourself first before you attempt to make out with someone new. Trust me. I went that route for a while. It makes you miss your ex even more. Go on a journey with yourself first."

I finish my root beer and grab the empty pitcher.

"I'll get us more," I say, heading to the not-a-bar-during-teen-night bar.

The line is long now. I hold the pitcher and absentmindedly grab my phone. Like a reflex, I open Instagram and type in Jake's username. I click on his account, scrolling mindlessly as I wait for the line to move.

Wait. Why are there palm trees in the background of his most recent photo? I full stop and look at the location geotag. Venice, California. Then, the date: November 5. That's today. What the hell? Why is Jake in LA and he never freaking told me?

"Can you move?" asks a stranger.

There's a six-foot gap between me and the person in front of me. I'm still frozen, but shuffle forward as my whole life unravels. Jake, my ex, is in Los Angeles right this very minute and he didn't text or call me. He hasn't since he sent the box. Hasn't answered my messages. His caption does nothing to fill me in: *Enjoying some sunshine!* The time stamp is two hours ago. I scroll through his past photos and they're all in New York City. I am vibrating with anger. My heart thuds super loud, like a subway performer drumming. I finally get the pitcher filled, but when I return, I've splashed most of the root beer on me.

"Dude, you were supposed to get more root beer. Why is half the pitcher empty?" asks Francesca.

By now, Daniel and Vincent are back. I am sticky from the soda, but I don't wipe my shirt clean. Shakily, I pass my phone to Francesca with my Instagram account open. She looks at it, her eyebrows knit together.

"Is this Jake?"

I nod. Vincent's perfectly shaped black eyebrows shoot up. His plan is falling apart because Daniel's sunny smile disappears in the cloud of my misery.

"Look at the location," I say.

"Dude, he's in Venice. I'm guessing you don't know anything about this."

"Bingo."

"Yikes!" says Francesca. "I'm gonna get us a refill and I'll be taking your phone with me before you keep doom-scrolling."

She dashes off with my phone and the root beer pitcher before I can say anything. It's probably better that she runs away. I am guilty of being exactly what Daniel said I was. I look at Vincent. His glare cuts through me. We had a plan and I messed it up. But also I want to cry. How could Jake fly all the way here and not even tell me? What did I do that was so bad he'd ignore me like this?

Then, I remember his solo show exhibit. He was so nervous that he spent the night in a closet with his meditation app trying to find his zen. I got everything perfect. Or so I thought. I even secured an assistant to the art critic at *The New Yorker* to come check out his show. I had this grand idea that I'd put music next to his pieces with Bose headphones. It was a merging of the music that inspired Jake and his art. I thought it was a fun idea and something that allowed his viewers to have their own unique experiences with each mural. I tested the equipment repeatedly until 2 A.M. that night.

But the day of the opening, the Bluetooth speakers weren't pairing properly so the wrong music played in the wrong headsets. By the time I figured it out and resolved the issue, people started leaving. The *New Yorker* assistant, who Jake took on a personal one-on-one tour, left early. It was a disaster. Jake hid out for weeks. I let him be as I wallowed in my first exhibit failure. I apologized. I sent cakes. I brought him bags of bagels. I stayed away from his studio. When he emerged three weeks later, he acted like nothing had happened. Like the past three weeks didn't roll through my heart. We didn't talk about it.

Then my ahma fell in the street. A neighbor found her and called my parents. They made the quick decision to move out to Los Angeles and take care of Ahma. I was so upset about my ahma and leaving New York City that I basically cried myself to sleep on the plane ride. Jake and I had a hurried goodbye at JFK airport in the JetBlue terminal. My eyes were red. I didn't want him to see me like that, but I had no choice. It was at the airport or nothing.

Now, as I sit in a hipster bowling alley in Highland Park with Jake on the other side of town, I realize that I messed up. I made all the mistakes. I should've never pushed him into that solo show. He was doing fine being in group exhibits with other young Black artists. He was a rising star. My stupid mistakes broke his trajectory and our relationship.

"Hey," says Daniel.

I have no idea how long I've been sitting there with tears streaming down my face. Francesca pours me a new cup of root beer. I sip, salting it with my tears.

"You okay? Want me to walk you home?" asks Daniel.

I nod. I mouth *I'm sorry* to Vincent who crosses his arms and frowns at me. My nose is dribbling snot. Really attractive here. Daniel ushers me out. We walk side by side. I feel awful. Daniel and Francesca were right. I'm not over Jake. Not by a long shot. I convinced myself I was, but now I know that I miss him terribly. The fact that his mere presence can reduce me to a snotty mess means I am not over this breakup. I never was.

By the time we arrive at my ahma's house, Daniel offers me several tissues that I take. I honk out my nose and I stuff the tissues in my back pocket.

"I'm sorry," I murmur.

"Nothing to apologize for," says Daniel as he walks me to my door.

He's too nice and I'm too much of a mess. I step inside my house, turning back to look at him. This sweet boy who doesn't deserve to be my rebound guy.

"I wish I could get over Jake, like, right now," I say.

Daniel nods, a small smile on his lips. "I understand."

"I hate that I'm another one."

"We're friends, Chloe. Remember? Friends are there for each other. You're not another one because we never went out."

I pat his shoulder. "Yeah, I guess you're right."

"It's all good. I'm still editing our short film. I'd love your feedback on the final cut."

"Of course," I say.

I slip into my grandmother's house, waving goodbye to Daniel who shuffles away quietly into the night. I thunder up the stairs to my bedroom where I flop onto my bed and let out all the tears in a loud, messy cry. Sesame wakes up from her slumber, then sits on my chest, rubbing her soft face against me. She always knows how to comfort me.

The last time I cried this hard was when I saw my grandmother all bruised up from her fall. I can't stop sobbing.

Chapter
15

It's 10 p.m. I flip open my Happy Memory planner to the divider I constructed with frosted white vellum paper and bright pink letter stickers that read *Operation Get Back Together with Jake.* I rip out the carefully made divider and throw it in the trash.

I make a new divider. *Operation Get Over Jake* in iridescent foil stickers. When I place a fresh Big Ideas dot grid sheet, I fill out the date, November 7, and after that, I stare at it blankly. I have no idea how to get over Jake, and there's no bullet-point list to fix this. I snap closed the cover.

On my @PlanItGirl Instagram account, I post my new divider with the caption

How do you get over your ex? Ideas in comments please, and three broken-heart emojis.

Later that night, I read their responses and, against all advice, I DM Jake. I compose several versions until I reach this one.

Chloe: You're in LA? I'd love to see you at my ahma's coffee shop, if you're game.

I send him the shop's Instagram. Even though it's well past 1 a.m., I keep refreshing, hoping for a response. Nothing. I check his account religiously, but no updates. Just that selfie on the beach. I zoom in close on his face. The face that I stared at up close and snuggled against. It hurts in my chest, so I toss my phone into my dresser drawer and swear I won't look at it.

I fall asleep with my phone against my heart.

In the morning, I look at my reflection in the camera. My hair is all sorts of knotted. My swollen eyes look like a goldfish and my mascara is streaked on my face like I ran in a thunderstorm. Cool.

I check Instagram.

Jake: Hey C-Lo. I've got time around 11am between meetings. How about we meet then?

The time stamp is thirty minutes ago. My heart races.

Chloe: Yes! See you there.

I add a bunch of smiley face emojis like a fool. I hit send before I can erase them.

Of course, I have less than thirty minutes to get ready and transform my scraggly look into something attractive. At least somewhat like Jake remembered, but somehow even better. I'm no makeup artist, but I run around until I can get myself in a shape I can see Jake in without feeling horrified. I stare at myself in the mirror for a hot second.

You can do this, Chloe. It's Jake. You can talk to Jake.

As I walk to the café, I remember the first time I talked

to Jake. I stalked him for weeks on social. Followed his yarn bombs around the city, tracking them on a bulletin board. Selena thought I was going all forensics on him, but the truth was I became obsessed with his art. I had to figure out who the mystery knitter was. Most of the city was tracking him too. He was a headline on *The Cut*: "Why No One Can Find the Yarn Bomber." Theories ran wild on Artstagram. Some people even claimed to be the one behind the masterful knit creations with messages in the murals stretched along subway walls.

When I finally figured out who he was through investigating the elements in the backgrounds of his anonymous Instagram posts, I messaged him to meet me at his favorite lunch spot, Blossom, in Harlem.

I asked him to join the young artists exhibit I was co-curating for the Teens Take the Met night. I told my supervisor I could secure the Yarn Bomber. She told me if I could get him to showcase at The Met she'd help me arrange my first solo show. I knew having my name in the mix would secure my future as a bona fide curator.

I didn't expect Jake to be my age. Or insanely hot. He flirted with me that day, telling me he was impressed. He called me *Sherlock* through the whole not-a-date lunch. In the end, I got him to agree to talk to my supervisor. I wowed him by telling him that Sally Greenly agreed to do the show and she specifically asked for him. It was all true. He was in demand. He thought The Met was too mainstream for his needs, but I convinced him that he had a real voice. The bigwigs in the art world needed his point of view. He needed to show that knitting wasn't solely for women. I gave him a whole rundown. He laughed and said that on sheer tenacity alone he'd do it. If I tracked him down, it must've meant something special to me.

I told him to trust me. He did. Soon, we were texting all the time. He introduced me to his crew, then to his grandmother June who runs Knitters for Justice to teach incarcerated men to knit. I didn't expect to fall for him. I just loved his art.

But now, as I stand in front of the café, I can see Jake chatting it up with my dad, and my heart leaps into my throat. Jake and Dad laugh.

Jake looks different. Maybe it's the sunlight beaming against his bronze cheeks. His muscular arms in a white T-shirt. The snugness of his slim gray sweatpants. Dad spots me before Jake does. Dad waves at me. He's always liked Jake. They could chat for hours, and did when Jake came over for dinner.

"Hey, C-Lo."

Jake wraps me in a hug. He smells musky today. Familiar. I resist kissing him, though it's hard.

Dad passes along some matcha lattes with hearts in them. Oh, Dad. He's a hopeless romantic. He winks at me as I usher Jake to a corner booth. I want to be alone with him as long as possible.

Our knees touch as we face each other. I squeeze his thigh with my hand before I freeze. Oops. His breezy smile lets me know it's okay, but I move my hand to my own leg and keep my hands to myself.

"Sorry I didn't ping you. Last-minute trip. My manager

arranged it," says Jake. He sips his matcha. "I've trekked the city for matcha this good, but your dad's is my favorite."

"Manager?" I ask.

"Mary Johnson. She's interning at an artist agency. She's a badass. Getting my name out there. Her boss has a list of buyers who want to commission exclusive pieces from me, and part of the proceeds go to Knitters for Justice."

"That's amazing."

Jake's grin is irresistible. I can't help myself. I place my hand on top of his and squeeze it.

"Mary's supervisor booked me a meeting with an assistant curator at The Broad."

"Oh, I went there with a friend. You'll adore it. They have a permanent Kara Walker exhibit that is so powerful," I say.

"There's a possibility that my piece would be in the same space as hers."

"Wow, Jake!"

"I know. It's surreal."

"I'm so happy for you."

I know people say that all the time, but I genuinely mean it. Jake has worked so hard to be taken seriously, ever since he was outed as the Yarn Bomber and photographed everywhere. Every major New York magazine and online outlet wanted an interview. Trolls said he only got attention because he's hot. Jake was pissed.

Jake squeezes my hand back. "How's your ahma? And Sesame? Last time I saw her, she was screeching in her carrier in JFK."

"Sesame meowed the entire flight. Ahma has her good days," I say.

"I bet she is happier that you're here."

I nod. Is Jake happier that I'm here?

Jake pulls a small black Moleskine notebook out of his back pocket. I instinctively reach into my purse, grab a blue pen, and hand it to Jake. He grins.

"Just like old times. Your trusty Pilot pen," says Jake.

"It writes better than anything else."

He flips through the pages of his notebook.

"This is my idea," says Jake.

He turns it to me. There's an intricate sketch spread across both pages, completely in black ink, name after name squeezed together so it almost looks like a giant sea of squiggles. I'm used to seeing his tiny replicas. I run my finger along the pages. Jake uses my pen as a pointer. He walks me through the sketch as I nod, biting my lower lip.

"This is ambitious," I say. "But amazing if you can pull it off."

"I didn't tell you the best part. Knitters from Knitters for Justice are contributing hats that I'll sew into the mural with each name listed here. Grandma's got a team of sewers to help me."

Jake shows off photos on his phone of the work in progress. I smile when I see pictures of his grandmother.

"How is Grandma June?"

"Feisty. She got Woolly Mammoth to donate even more skeins than they originally promised."

"Of course she did. Your grandmother could move an actual mountain if she set her mind to it," I say.

"She gave me a ripe scolding for breaking up with you."

We lock eyes. He puts his phone down. My matcha has gotten cold and less green. I stir it several times so that the oat milk swirls into a richer grassy green. He's said it. The thing I've been dreading. Up until now, it felt like our old selves. Plotting, planning, dreaming. Now, it's back to reality.

"C-Lo, I don't know how to do long-distance. With the manager booking me for meetings and showcases, I'm not around a whole lot. Plus, the time difference," says Jake.

He trails off. My face must reveal how mad I am because he stops talking. He stares out the window. I follow his gaze. A tiny pug puppy is outside, being pet by several children, and he wriggles from one kid to the next.

"You must be mad if you didn't even notice a pug puppy."

"Oh, I noticed him."

Jake reaches for my hand, but I pull it back. He doesn't want to do long-distance. He's too busy. The time difference?! What fresh BS is this? I blink my tears back. I stare at the puppy who is now belly-up. Damn. I can't even enjoy a pug belly or its curly tail wagging. The breakup box pops back into my mind.

"You could've called me. I got a box. And haven't heard from you since. Selena said it was cold-blooded."

"I know. I got an earful from her," says Jake.

"Why did you do it?"

"I chickened out, C-Lo. I tried to email you. Text. Even a

DM. All of it seemed harsh. I knew if we talked that I couldn't do it. Your voice would've hurt too much to hear." He lowers his voice, gathers my hand in his. "I've got to focus on me. My career. Ever since we met, you got me thinking and dreaming bigger. How I can take my message national. Blow it up. With you here and me there, I can't do both. You know how long it takes me to finish a piece. Mary has a wait list for my work. She did that in one month. We've got big plans, me and Mary. You know how I told you I've always wanted to get my grandma into a better apartment. One that's not freezing in the winter. An entire ground-floor apartment so she doesn't have to haul up and down stairs. It used to feel like an impossible dream. How could I ever buy property in Brooklyn? With this manager, I can see that future. The program can grow even bigger too. Grandma can hire real staff so she's not shuffling all her knitting gear back and forth and managing all the volunteers."

Jake brings my hand to his lips. I don't resist. In fact, I cup his cheeks. Stubble is there, prickling my hand. I stroke his beautiful face.

"I know how much this means to you, Jake. But we can do it. Long-distance. I don't need you to be my twenty-four-seven boyfriend. It's exciting you can do this for your grandmother and yourself. Let me be there with you. I don't need much," I say. "I just need you in my life."

I say it so softly that maybe he didn't hear. He rests my hand back on the table.

"I hate to go, but I need to jet to this meeting."

I instantly regret my desperate plea to get back together. I don't understand why my resolve dissolves within seconds of being close to him. Touching him. I feel like a failure again.

Jake hops out of the booth. He leans down to kiss the side of my cheek, not my lips, not looking me in the eyes.

"Later, C-Lo. Take care of yourself," he says.

I nod. The bell on the door rings as Jake slips out and into an Uber. The car zips away. I look down at the notebook in my hands. Jake's notebook. All of his sketches. He was so desperate to get away that he left it. I know I shouldn't, but I flip through the pages. More sketches. Some scratched out or bare wisps of an idea.

That's when I see a Black girl's face. A sketch. She's gorgeous. High cheekbones. Beautifully full lips. Her black hair cut short. Beneath the sketch, *Mary Johnson, October 10*. I snap the notebook shut.

Jake sketched me a year ago in Washington Square Park. He dated it at the bottom with a heart next to my name. I wanted to rip it out of his notebook to keep. I had never seen myself like he did. But he wouldn't let me take it, telling me I'd always be in his notebook. Tearing it out could mean losing it.

I dare myself to flip open the notebook to look at the sketch again. Even though it hurts, I check.

There's a heart by her name.

My tears drop into my matcha like raindrops.

My mom convinces me to try again with Ahma at 99 Ranch—together as a family, that way I'm not alone. I don't want a repeat of last time. Dad's idea is that we load up the cart with everything we think is right, then we work backward by showing each item to Ahma, then taking out anything that is wrong.

That's how I find myself back in the baking aisle, filling our cart with brown sugar, cane sugar, powdered milk, and powdered sugar.

Ahma clings to my dad's arm, stroking his cheek. He bends down to whisper to her. She points and he picks it up and puts it in the cart. In her clear moments, her mind is sharp. We try our best to work within those moments without overloading her.

It's a narrow window.

I stand in front of the dizzying row of different flours and starches. My mom carries flour sacks like babies.

"I used to hold you like this, Chloe," says my mom as she tosses a bag of Flying Horse rice flour to her shoulder. "I'd pat you on your back and you would let out the biggest burps."

"Cool. Thanks, Mom." I pat her arm and take the flour out of her hands before she demonstrates how she used to change my diapers.

It occurs to me that my mom and I have spent a ton of time testing out different flours, but my dad is the one who spent his childhood with his mom baking these treats.

"Dad, we need your opinion."

His face lights up like I told him he'd won *The Great British Bake Off*. He slowly brings Ahma to us. She shuffles in her khaki pants covered with red and white flowers, and grips him tightly. She looks tiny next to him.

He bows to me. "At your service, madam."

"Aren't you sweet?" My mom leans over to kiss my dad's cheeks. He gently taps her butt.

I cough loudly. They stop. For now.

"Can we get back to business?"

"Certainly." Dad waggles his eyebrows, making my mom laugh. I roll my eyes.

"Look at all these flours. Does one seem familiar? Something you might have seen in Ahma's kitchen growing up."

I gesture to the long row. Dad bites his lip. He touches a few, pokes at them, and squints at the packages. Most have Korean, Japanese, Vietnamese, or Chinese characters on them. Mom and I are by his side, investigating like detectives on a forensics TV show. By now, everything looks the same to me. All the characters blend into one language.

Then, Ahma points at one: Sun Right cake flour. It has a bright yellow sun on it with a smiley face.

"This!" Ahma says in English.

"Cake flour!" I shout so loud that a few shoppers stop to stare at me.

"We've been using all-purpose flour this whole time," says my mom.

Dad grabs a few sacks of it, and we hold them up like winning lottery tickets. We hoot and holler, acting like fools. Even Ahma breaks into a huge smile.

"I'm glad we didn't give up," I whisper to my mom.

"Me too, sweetheart." She caresses my cheek.

"Bring it in, family," says Dad.

We form a circle around Ahma and hug her. She lets out a laugh. Something we haven't heard since we arrived in

Los Angeles. Then, Ahma grabs my face and gives me loud smacking kisses, sucking in my cheeks like she's devouring me whole. Just like when I was a kid.

While we wait to pay, I text Daniel the news. He sends me five hand claps and three heart emojis. I tell my brain not to think too much about the three hearts he typed out, but my heart is like, *hell yes*. I smile even wider now.

If I could bottle this moment to keep forever, I would.

M y Lyft driver dropped me off here, but I think I'm
in the wrong spot. There's no line. I clutch a flyer
that has half the face of Lady Gaga and the other
half of Beyoncé, squinting at the tiny writing at the bottom,
verifying that today's date, November 8, matches the one on
the flyer. It does.

It's dark and I'm under a freeway overpass with zipping
cars overhead. My New York City spidey sense tingles. I'm a
girl in a skin-tight low-back dress with no one around.

Me: Where am I?
Daniel: Call me.

Over the phone, he safely navigates me to where I'm supposed to be. Francesca and Vincent are laughing very hard
about something, and Daniel looks ready to split.

"Hey," says Vincent. His arm is around Francesca. "Your
friend here is the absolute best."

I smile. He sounds high as hell. Francesca's eyes are heavy-
lidded like she just woke up, so I nudge her.

"Did you all have some fun before I got here?"

Francesca and Vincent burst into a fit of giggles as a response. I poke Daniel in the ribs. He grimaces. He's clearly
sober.

The line is full of different people. Teens like us. Older gay couples. White boys with sparkly glitter eyeliner. Latina girls in goth wear or barely-there tops. I never went dancing this time of year because it's like an iceberg in New York City, but here, you can wear a cutout halter crop top and not shiver in the slightest. Selena would be mad jealous. She's always moaning that I hibernate in the dead of NYC winter. Excuse me if I don't like my thighs turning into icicles and my face crystallizing. I text her a quick shot of me and Daniel and the flyer in my hand. She immediately sends back a yellow-faced emoji with its tongue sticking out.

"Long time no see. How's the editing going?"

"Good. I can show it to you soon."

"You look like you'd rather get your teeth pulled," I say.

I touch his arm gently. He pulls back like my fingers are electric shocks.

"I'm a crappy dancer." He raises his voice. "I only agreed to this because my best friend here told me he needed to get out!"

At this, Vincent releases himself from Francesca and smooches Daniel's cheek.

"You're the best!"

He raises Daniel's arms, which are slack, and jiggles his arms so Daniel's dancing with him. Soon, the people behind us start a rhythm with claps and foot stomps. Vincent twirls and spins around Daniel. His moves are elegant. It's clear he's a dancer. Daniel crosses his arms like the ultimate grinch. The entire line is watching as Vincent executes a flawless routine that shows off his leg muscles, even in those black droopy crotch pants. When Vincent is done, he takes a bow, and the entire line is hooting and hollering.

"Damn, Vin," says Francesca, "you can bust it."

"And this is why I don't want to go out dancing with you, Vee. I'm basically a block of tofu, awkwardly standing there while every person around is salivating to be near you," says Daniel.

Vincent puts his arm around Daniel's shoulders.

"You are too chicken to try. You just stand there, but I bet there's some sick moves in there if you got out of your super-serious head," says Vincent, tapping the side of Daniel's head.

Daniel playfully pushes Vincent away. "I'm here. Isn't that enough?"

The line starts slowly trudging forward and Vincent and Francesca are two birds chirping away. I weave my hand through Daniel's arm. He doesn't immediately move away from me, which I take as a good sign.

"Stick with me. We can be basic dancers together. My BFF Selena is, like, a dance-floor goddess so I totally understand."

Daniel finally smiles that ridiculous dimpled smile. For a second, I feel like we're on a real date.

"We can hide out in the corner then."

The room is the bottom floor of a Mexican restaurant. There's a small stage with a DJ cramped at one side. At first, there's ten people scattered around, then the room fills up as people from outside squeeze in. A disco ball rotates from the ceiling, illuminating the walls with rainbows. Daniel and I head to the bar that serves mocktails with glow sticks as stirrers. Vincent, as predicted, already has a crowd around him.

It's glorious to watch him move, graceful, chaotic, and loud at the same time. He takes off his black leather moto jacket to reveal a skin-tight black bodysuit with a scoop neck. The crowd whoops. Even I can't help but stare at his banging body. Next to me, Daniel sips his ginger beer straight out of the brown bottle.

"And now you can see why I never go out dancing with Vincent. I could be naked and no one would notice," says Daniel.

"Oh, I'm sure someone would notice," I say.

Daniel laughs. "Thanks. I made a promise when Connor dumped him that I'd even go out dancing with him if he'd leave his room."

"Promises are promises," I say. "Come. We can moodily dance together to fulfill your promise to Vincent not to be a complete wallflower."

I take Daniel's hand and lead him to a small spot near the stage. I rest a hand on his shoulder and sway to the music. The mashup of "Single Ladies" and "Alejandro" is so fun, even Daniel moves his body a little. Still holding his hand, I turn and spin. It's been too long since I had fun.

Suddenly, two drag queens in matching red sequin gowns come out with gold microphones in hand. They lip sync to "Telephone." The white queen performs as Lady Gaga. The Black queen as Beyoncé. The crowd rushes the stage. Daniel and I are in the front row. Daniel places his hands on my shoulders. I gently lean back. Now, my body is on his. He doesn't pull back. Instead, he holds me as we dance together. At the end of the song, the drag queens snap down into two splits on opposite sides of the stage. The crowd roars in delight and I can't help but wildly holler as they take their bows and bound off stage. The club returns to itself. Bouncing light and full of energy.

Now, Daniel and I are close together. I wrap my arms around his neck. His hands on my waist. The song is now "I'll Never Love Again" and "Listen." I rest my head on his collarbone. I didn't plan on dancing with Daniel like this, but it feels so nice and I don't want it to end. We are locked like this until the end of the song.

I glance up at his face and his cheeks are red.

"I should go find Vincent," he says. "Thanks for the dance."

He's gone before I can say anything in response. I scan the crowd for where he might have gone, but now it's just a sea of faces with a swirl of colored lights. It's impossible to tell who's who. I sip my Lady Beehive mocktail, a delicious blend of honey and sparkling water. I scan the room.

Until I see Jake. That can't be right. What is Jake doing here? Then, I see the girl from the notebook with her arm around his waist. Even from a distance I can tell she's more gorgeous than the sketch, if that's somehow humanly possible. I look down at my drink, suddenly wishing it were spiked. Maybe Jake won't notice me. I slink off the dance floor, weaving in and out of people. I barely move.

"Hey, C-Lo."

His voice is unmistakable. I don't turn around immediately. I have to act calm, cool, collected. Like I'm unfazed he's here with a stunningly beautiful girl and we broke up a month ago. By the time I turn around to face him, she's there. I'm glad I've had a hot second to see what she looked like because she's way prettier than the sketch.

"Funny running into you here. Mary told me about this mashup night."

Jake gestures to her and her name sounds so familiar to me, like I've heard him say it before. Then it dawns on me. Even when I saw the sketch I didn't put it together. Mary is the one helping his career. When he said she worked at an artists agency, I expected her to be an older, dowdy woman who knew all of old-money New York City. I didn't expect to meet someone close to our age.

"Hi. I'm Chloe Chang."

We shake hands. I'm pressed against the wall, wishing I could sink through it and disappear. No such luck.

"Nice meeting you, Chloe. Jake, I'll grab us some waters. It's hot in here," says Mary.

Jake nods and his hot girlfriend effortlessly makes her way to the bar. Now, it's just us. The song fades to "Irreplaceable" mashed with "Monster." Someone pushes behind Jake with an *excuse me,* and Jake is now in my arms. I hold on to him for a second. We used to dance for hours with Selena and our crew. Sometimes until sunrise. Now, he awkwardly takes a step back.

He gestures toward Mary. "I should've told you."

I reach out to hit his chest. He blocks me, then holds my hand.

"You left and everything happened so fast with Mary. I

wanted to tell you, but your ahma was still in the hospital. I didn't know when to tell you."

I yank my hand away. My vision is blurry, so I stumble along some steps. This whole time I thought Jake was mad at me for his solo show, but he was busy hooking up with Mary. A hand catches my arm before I fall down. It's Jake.

"I'm sorry, C-Lo."

He wraps me in his strong arms, and I fall into his embrace. I hate myself for not running away from him, but the truth is I like being comforted by him. He pets my head like he used to do when I got off FaceTime calls with Ahma and she didn't remember me. I should walk away, but I don't.

Jake whispers, "I still care about you, even if you think I'm a horrible jerk."

Mary returns with two drinks. I don't notice her until I finally look up. In the distance, I see Daniel who has a peculiar look on his face, like he's swallowed an entire lemon. I step away from Jake.

"Later, Jake," I say.

I don't say goodbye to his new girlfriend/manager. He can explain me to her. I head to the nearest bathroom and use a rough paper towel to clean up my messed-up black mascara. I stare at my reflection, at this girl who somehow can't get over her ex.

"Hey, girl," says Francesca. "I've been looking for you everywhere."

One glance at my face and the crumbled towel and she gets it.

"You okay?"

I shake my head no. She's by my side. Her arm around my waist.

"We will leave and get some fries. Tell me everything."

I nod as Francesca leads me out of the club, arm in arm. The cool night air feels good against my hot tears that keep coming down. I follow her to Brite Spot Diner, and we squeeze into a booth together. Francesca orders. As we wait for the food, I spill my entire story to her.

She shakes her head at certain parts, her eyes bulge in others. It's the first time we've ever sat down to talk. After I'm done, we devour the fries in front of us. She licks her fingers.

"There's nothing that French fries can't fix," says Francesca.

I sip on my chocolate-peanut-butter milkshake. "Damn right."

"Do you want my unfiltered opinion?"

I nod. "Please."

Francesca wraps her hands around her tea mug. "Jake was too chicken to tell you the truth. That's why he was shady and broke up with you through the mail. He flew here and didn't even tell you. Why do you even like this guy? I mean, I get he's hot, but hotness can only get you so far. I've known you for a minute now, and I can tell you're whip-smart and you've got creative skills to pay the bills. If this guy bounces because things got hard, then you don't need him."

She lifts her tea mug to my milkshake glass and waits. I hold mine up, click against her glass, though I am not entirely convinced I don't need him.

"He's talented. Sensitive. He cares about making art."

"How does he treat you? Your grandma was in trouble. Did he call you? Text? Find out what's happening on your end?"

Her questions are like pointed jabs. I focus on the remains of my milkshake, getting every inch out with my straw. It's easier than answering. She scrolls on her phone.

"Vin wants to meet up with us here. Is that cool?"

"Totally."

"Girl, before Daniel gets here, what's going on with you two? Daniel was wrecked when you and Jake were working out your thing."

"Did he say something?"

"He didn't have to. He saw you and Jake all snuggled against each other and his face was shattered like glass."

"I don't know what's going on with us. I tried to kiss him, and he freaked out. He said he's a rebound guy. Showed me that photo slideshow."

"Right."

"We're friends."

"Sure," says Francesca. She types out a message, then slips her phone into her tiny black purse. "That boy is into you. Do yourself a favor. Don't double-dip."

When Vincent and Daniel show up, Vincent slides in next to Francesca, squishing against her body. Daniel takes a seat next to me. He's on the edge of the booth with one butt cheek on. I try not to get hurt that my mere presence makes him uncomfortable, but then, I'd probably feel weird if he were hugging some gorgeous girl.

"Get this," says Vincent.

He hands over his phone to Francesca and scrolls through. Francesca's eyes are huge. Vincent flips the phone to me. I peek. Vincent is shirtless and, wow, his body is beyond. I can't help but stare. Next to him is another hot Asian guy. Also shirtless.

"Cool," says Daniel. "I can't wait to show up to our next Asian guy meeting and have to explain how you two have set us all back. I'm the Pillsbury Doughboy and everyone wants Henry Golding."

Francesca and I exchange a look. Our eyebrows are basically touching the sky. Vincent tucks away his phone.

"The club asked if I wanted to join the band set and I said yes. Chris would be my partner for routines."

"That's awesome. Does that come with club passes?" asks Francesca.

"Definitely," says Vincent, stealing a fry.

"Count me out," says Daniel. He suddenly gets up from the booth. "I'm gonna head." He leaves before any of us can say anything.

Vincent's smile fades. He climbs out of the booth. I touch his arm. "I'll talk to him." Vincent nods and I leave.

Daniel is outside waiting for a car. He scrolls through his phone. The blue light illuminates his face. People walk behind us. A girl in tall gold heels sways back and forth as her friends hold her up. I move closer to Daniel to be out of her path.

"You okay?"

He shrugs.

"Not all of us want Henry Golding. I mean, he's fine, but I'm not interested in muscles only."

"Interesting. Your eyes told a different story when you saw Vincent's photos."

"Any human with a pulse would respond to those photos. Did you see me and Jake together tonight?"

Daniel stares at the ground, suddenly interested in his shoes.

"It's not what it looked like. I was crying into his shoulder."

He looks up, concern in his hazel-brown eyes. Suddenly, I feel incredibly vulnerable sharing this with him, but I feel like I must.

"I'm not really over him. I thought I was, but I'm not. I got to meet his new girlfriend who is also his new manager. She's stunningly gorgeous. We've only been broken up for a month and he found someone new. He found her before he even sent me the shoebox."

Daniel is by my side. I rest my head on his shoulders.

"That sucks."

"Royally sucks. You were right. I thought I was immune to breakup symptoms, but apparently, I didn't get my shots."

"I know," he says.

"Can we go back inside with our friends?"

He taps on his phone, canceling his ride.

"Let's go."

Daniel offers his hand to me. I take it. We walk back in hand in hand. Vincent and Francesca are collapsed together in a fit of giggles. I can't understand anything they're saying. By the time they've recovered, they relay the story, and it takes ten minutes before Daniel and I can comprehend what happened. All I got is that somehow the waitress thought they were dating, and they thought it was so funny that they went to kiss but banged noses instead. We order more fries, waffles, and a mountainous ice cream sundae.

The rest of the night, Daniel and I sit close, legs touching, strictly as friends, of course.

Chapter 17

Two days later, I get a DM from Jake.

> Jake: I know we left things in a weird place. Can I see you? Mary already flew back. I'm leaving tomorrow morning. I'd like to see Heartifacts.

I screenshot it and send it to Selena and Francesca so they can weigh in.

> Selena: Give him a chance. Jake isn't a horrible jerk. He did jerky things to you, but he's not terrible.
> Francesca: Delete it and move on, girl!

Neither of them are helping. I take a shift at the café to get my mind off things and, of course, Daniel arrives.

"Strictly as a customer," says Daniel after I take his order.

Great. I can't think about Jake with Daniel being all cute and chatty. I ask Dad to cover me for five minutes and hastily type out this message back.

> Chloe: Sure. Come by at 8pm. Ruby Street is the gallery space. See you there.

Even though Daniel can't see the DM, I feel guilty I'm still seeing Jake, even after I spent the night holding hands with Daniel and wishing I were over my ex.

"I have a cut of the movie, if you want to see it. I could bring it to Ruby Street tonight so we could screen it on the wall and get the full effect."

"Tonight?"

"Unless you have plans?"

"Tonight's not great. I told my mom I'd get groceries at 99 Ranch with her."

"Tomorrow then?"

"Tomorrow is perfect!"

"Fantastic," says Daniel. "I'm excited for you to see it."

Technically, Daniel and I aren't dating. It shouldn't matter if I meet up with Jake. But if Daniel knows, he'll think I'm part of his Rebounds club. I shouldn't lie to Daniel, but I need a minute alone with Jake to figure this out. If I'm truly going to get over him and move on to a new guy, then it's time to see if we still have feelings for each other.

I don't tell Francesca what I'm about to do. I Marco Polo with Selena to get her opinions on my outfits. She tells me I should wear something that says, *this is what you're missing*. I choose a white top with an open back and my favorite blush-pink floor-length skirt with silver sequin stars on it. As I walk by, Sesame bats at the bottom hem and gets her claws stuck in the skirt.

I pick her up and nuzzle her head. "Are you on Francesca's side too?" Sesame meows in response.

When I'm at Ruby Street, I put on a playlist with some of our songs. Songs Jake played in his studio while he worked. Songs we listened to together on the subway, sharing his AirPods. Maybe he'll remember. Francesca strongly advised against this last-ditch effort to woo Jake. Straight up creepy was her message, but I don't care. I have to know if I still have something with Jake.

I light some candles. One with a rose quartz crystal embedded in it. Before living in Los Angeles, if you had told me a pink rock could change my love life, I would've knocked it into a subway grate. But here I am, wishing on a gemstone for luck.

Before he arrives, I stand over our box and read what I've written:

Why we broke up: I'm still figuring this out. Maybe it was because I let him down. Maybe because I moved. Maybe because there's three thousand miles between us and we are too young for a serious relationship. When I figure it out, I'll update this card, but until then, this is all I know: I miss him. I miss NYC. I miss how it felt to see my face in his sketchbook.

"The light in here is amazing," says Jake.

"Hey."

I lean in as he kisses my cheek. His lips are warm against my face. His muscular arms look amazing in a fitted dark blue T-shirt.

"And you're right. Los Angeles galleries have way more space. This one is special."

"It used to be a church, then the owner, Lourdes, renovated it to be a coworking and event space, but she kept the stained-glass windows," I say.

The moonlight streams in through one of the windows of disciples gathered around Jesus, who has a heart in his hands. It casts a red hue on the floor.

"Mind if I take a look around?"

"Be my guest."

I anxiously wait as Jake takes his time, walking through the exhibit and examining each box with intense scrutiny. I try to occupy myself with rearranging boxes, but it's pretty useless. All I want to know is what Jake thinks. When he's finally done, he sits down at a table and gestures for me to join him. I placed fresh peonies on the table. His grandmother's favorite. I thought it would remind him of the time we searched all over the city for pink peonies for her seventieth birthday, only to find out that everyone else in Jake's family had snatched them up before we could.

"Pink peonies," Jake says. A smile forms on his lips.

"They were easier to find this time around."

His eyes soften as he looks at my face. The way he studies me makes my heart skip, like he's memorizing me.

"I read your note by my box."

I glance at the flowers and focus on their soft, wispy petals.

"I'm sorry I left you wondering what happened. I should've been clearer with you. You deserve that," says Jake.

He holds his hands out. I place my hands in his.

"I care about you, C-Lo, but it's time for us to end. Move on. You're here and I'm there. Even if we stayed together long distance, things would fall apart eventually. You've had a plan for your life since I met you. I'm only just starting to discover my path. We need to go our separate ways."

One of my hands sinks to my side. The truth feels like punishment. Suddenly, I want to leave, so I remove my other hand from his and get up and walk out. Jake calls my name, and I don't respond. I keep walking like he's not even there. When I arrive home I stumble up the stairs to my bedroom. I was foolish to think I'd somehow remind him how much I care with some stupid flowers and songs. Maybe Francesca is right. He's a selfish jerk who only thinks about himself. I need to move on.

My phone buzzes.

Jake.

I answer.

"You can hang up and tell Selena what a jerk I am and I get it. Just give me a minute. What you've done, Chloe, is amazing. It's so heartfelt, honest, real, and vulnerable. I love it. I've always known you'd achieve anything you set your mind on. Hell, you found me, and I didn't want to be found. It's not easy to see our breakup through your eyes, but the moment I saw our box and read your words, I finally understood. I didn't give you a chance to weigh in. I acted impulsively. Selfishly. And I'm sorry. I'm getting on a plane early tomorrow morning and I swear I'll leave you alone. You won't hear from me. I'll disappear for a bit. But if you ever want to talk, I'm here. I'm coming back in March for my debut at The Broad. An opening night invite is yours. I understand if you don't want to come, but I'd love for you to be there."

I am silent. I sit on the edge of my bed, staring at my

phone. Jake says my name over and over again. I press my phone to my ear.

"I'm here."

"Thanks for listening."

"Bye, Jake."

I hang up. I toss my phone across my room.

When Daniel arrives for the screening the next day at Ruby Street, I make it my mission to delete Jake from my brain. Daniel sets up his phone and a projector so that his movie can be shown on the white wall.

"Get anything good at 99 Ranch?" he asks.

"Oh yeah."

"I still devour those lychee-coconut gel cups. It was the one sweet thing my mom let me eat," says Daniel.

I nod, acting like I did indeed go to 99 Ranch with my mom and wasn't trying to woo my ex-boyfriend. I am a terrible actor, so I don't even try to say anything else.

"I don't have the exact right song that I want to open with," says Daniel. "I asked my musician friend Jung to put something together, but he made it too romantic."

He runs his fingers through his black hair.

"And if you don't like it, be honest."

I grab his hands. He looks down at the ground, at his black Converse shoes. I squeeze his sweaty palms.

"It's me."

Daniel bites his lip. I want to kiss away his nervousness. He hits play. I watch us—the fake romantic us—on these dates. It almost looks real. I didn't realize how many times he had the camera trained on me because he captured moments I had forgotten or didn't see. I never realized my face is so serious when I'm looking at a new piece. Watching us kiss for the first time, I feel a dull ache in my heart for not only losing out on Jake, but losing out on Daniel too.

Suddenly, I realize Selena's been right all along: I need to ditch my ex and delete him from my life. I'll take the advice from my @PlanItGirl followers and finish my step-by-step plan for Operation Get Over Jake. I'll follow each step, and poof, heartache gone. Then, I'll convince Daniel that I'm 100 percent over Jake Miller and we belong together.

"What do you think?" asks Daniel.

"Can you replay it?"

I zoned out there. He hits play again and this time I walk around the gallery space, taking it in from different angles. I imagine myself as someone coming to *Heartifacts* for the first time. The images are splayed against the backdrop of the wall, so it looks like a movie theater screen. What's cool is that at any angle, you have a perfect view.

I stop in front of the projection. An image of me is directly on top of me like an identical twin.

"Wait," says Daniel. "Hand me your phone."

I oblige. He snaps photo after photo as I stand in the light. When he's done, he shows me the photos. It's weird to say this, but I love it. It's a hall-of-mirrors effect.

"I might use these pics in my doc, if that's cool with you."

"Sure. When can I see a cut?"

Daniel scratches the back of his head. "It's such a mess.

Even Vee hasn't seen it yet. The structure isn't right yet. I'm missing some key interviews."

I touch his arm. "I'm sure it's not as bad as you think. Every artist I've ever worked with says that exact thing."

"Even Jake Miller?"

I can't escape Jake.

"Jake would swear he'd made a rat's nest of a piece, and I'd see it, and it was gorgeous. Artists, I've found, are too hard on themselves," I say.

Daniel finally smiles. "I'm really happy with how this short turned out."

"I like how you can see it from all angles in the gallery wherever you are."

"Me too," says Daniel.

"Can I take you out for a celebratory doughnut at Mochinut?" I ask. "Strictly as friends, of course."

"Who am I to turn down a celebratory doughnut?"

As we walk out, I turn back to the exhibit space with its twelve boxes. With Daniel's film and more boxes, I can turn *Heartifacts* into something bigger, better, and Instagram-worthy. I want everyone to be talking about this exhibit. The success of *Heartifacts* means I can finally get over my past failures.

We walk along York Boulevard and dodge food truck lines. The thumping drumbeat of a concert rumbles out of the Hi Hat.

I make a vow to myself: I'll prove to Daniel that I'm 100 percent officially over Jake. He won't be my rebound guy. He'll just be my guy.

use my cherry-red glitter pen and choose three stickers—Plan For It, Make It Happen, You Got This—and place them in a triangle on the bottom right of my page like my mini-cheerleading squad. On my Big Ideas dot grid sheet, I formulate my five-step plan to delete Jake from my mind.

I scroll through the comments my @PlanItGirl followers left on how to get over your ex. I synthesize their advice into five easy steps.

> Step 1: Unfriend and unfollow all of Jake's social accounts. Don't be tempted to take a peek! Peeks turn into rabbit holes of doom-scrolling and jealous rages.
> Step 2: Spend time alone enjoying activities you love.
> Step 3: Exercise. At least twenty minutes a day. Body movement helps get you out of your head.
> Step 4: Read Breakup Bootcamp by Amy Chan. (She has a real-life retreat where people go to get over their exes!)
> Step 5: Rewrite your breakup story and reframe how it helped you change in healthy ways. Future you will thank you!

I reread each step like a mantra. Ew. Los Angeles has me saying words like *mantra*. Never tell Selena. She'll stop sending my NYC bagel care packages.

Now that I've laid it out in my Happy Memory planner, I've totally got this, just like my black-and-gold foil sticker says.

Four months from now when Jake comes back in March for his Broad Museum debut with his beautiful girlfriend, he'll see I don't need him. He'll regret dumping me. And I won't care anymore because I'll be with Daniel. It's perfect! I don't even care that Jake's here.

I start with step one. Cold turkey on Jake's social.

I open my planner and make a big red checkmark next to step one. Easy peasy.

Now that I've figured out how to get over Jake, I take out my Goal Planning journal and write down: *make* Heartifacts *a huge success.*

Reach out to art social media influencers
Organize a special influencers night
Get more boxes and expand what I have
Invite VIP guests (ask Francesca for contacts)
Set up a photo booth
Ask Mom to make kawaii-inspired *mochi*
Reach out to local media to cover the event

It's 1 A.M. I should go to sleep since it's a school night, but my mind is buzzing with ideas. All the time I wasted thinking about Jake can now be devoted to growing *Heartifacts* into a mega-popular installation art showcase. Bonus: I'm already on step two because planning an art show is one of my favorite activities ever. It's all coming together. I almost smugly text Selena with this update, but don't. She'll know soon enough.

I asked Jake for his advice on getting *Heartifacts* to go viral. I texted him, so technically, I didn't violate step one of my Get Over Jake plan. That's how I end up on a FaceTime call with Jake, the breaker of my heart. He's wearing a black tank, which means he's working in his studio. I grab a notebook and ignore his muscular arms.

> Jake: Hey.
> Me: Hey, yourself.
> Jake: You want to pack the space?

I nod, trying not to get sucked in by his dark brown eyes. They are not mesmerizing. *They do not sparkle, Chloe.*

> Jake: Here's what I would do. Strip away the detailed placards and mission statements.
> Me: What?! No. How will anyone know what each piece is?
> Jake: People don't want to read tiny pieces of writing. Serve fancy passed hors d'oeuvres from a caterer.
> Me: But my parents cater.
> Jake: Your parents are great, but people are paying for a scene, atmosphere. Trust me.

My heart sinks. My parents will be crushed when I tell them.

Me: How am I going to afford a fancy caterer?
Jake: Sponsors. If people know influencers are coming,
    they'll shell out.
Me: What else?
Jake: Invite influencers to contribute breakup boxes
    too. Ditch the why-we-broke-up essays and
    Photography Prohibited sign. Make it all about the
    objects and visuals. It's gotta pop in photos. Like
    the Museum of Ice Cream.
Me: Basically change everything.
Jake: I don't make the rules. I play by them.
Me: This doesn't sound like you at all, Mr. Yarn
    Bomber.
Jake: Mary's helped me see that if I do one of these
    schmoozer nights, then it funds my next project. Oh
    yeah. Wear something corporate.

I scrunch my face. Jake laughs.

Jake: I know. It's a drag, but it'll make you look older,
    and people take you more seriously when you're in
    a suit.
Me: I don't own anything that's not a shade of
    pastel.
Jake: Rent something. Oh shoot. I gotta go. Later,
    C-Lo.

He hangs up and I stare at the blank screen. I look over my notes. If I want to make *Heartifacts* successful, Jake's right. It's time to step it up from amateur hour. Plus, this one night can help establish me as a real art curator in Los Angeles.

The next seventy-two hours are a whirlwind.

Dad calls in a favor with a sushi-chef friend who agrees to provide fancy rolls in exchange for social posts.

I buy a black business-suit thing. It's uncomfortably tight, but I do look older.

Jake's manager sends me a curated social media influencer list as a *favor to Jake's friend.* I eye-roll at her email so hard I hope she can feel it.

The influencer boxes arrive. I peek inside. It's basically a bunch of beauty products.

Jake said to ditch the mission statements and art placards, but it felt like sacrilege. I worked late into the night to write the perfect text.

I rent a 360-degree photo booth for the night that takes 3D images and comes with oversized props like feather boas and neon glasses. My budget is bursting. I'll make back the money, I tell myself.

The guest list swells as influencers invite other influencers.

I blink. Then, it's here.

When I arrive at Ruby Street, Lourdes is surprised by how different the space looks. I assure her that I'll leave everything in perfect condition (even if it takes all night to clean). Lourdes gives me her blessing for a successful night before handing me the keys.

I answer questions via text while running to check on the box setups. The photo booth is stuck in 405 freeway traffic. I am pure sweat. Daniel arrives with Vincent one hour before to help. They are dressed in similarly matched polka-dot bow ties, navy blue blazers, and sleek black jeans.

"Why are you two twinning?" asks Francesca.

"Because Daniel is my soul partner," says Vincent.

"The real truth is I don't have any decent clothes, as deemed by Vincent."

"People are going to be photographing. Young filmmakers have to look dapper and professional. RuPaul says if you want to make money, you gotta dress like money," says Vincent.

"Right on, Vin," says Francesca.

She and Vincent slap high fives.

"Help me with the projector," I say to Daniel.

"Gladly. Treat it well. I saved up for months to buy it."

Ever since my tech fail at Jake's show, I've decided it's best to leave machines to someone else. Daniel looks around the room and grimaces.

"You made a face."

"This place looks really different," says Daniel.

"The photo-booth rental company said their truck is stuck by the Getty Center on the 405. Whatever that means."

Daniel sucks in air. "I hate to tell you this, but your photo booth's probably not arriving on time. Traffic on the 405 is like the La Brea Tar Pits. You get stuck there for hours."

"Please don't say that."

I wipe my hands against my black slacks.

"You okay? You look like you've had too much caffeine."

"Do I really look like a mess?"

He connects the cables to the projector and his phone. I glance down at his screen and see that he's labeled the video as *Me and Chloe*. I don't know if it's my nerves, but my palms are now extra sweaty.

"You look great. But jumpy, I guess."

"How do you feel before you screen a film of yours?"

"Like throwing up."

"Roughly the same here."

Daniel places his hands on my shoulders, pulling me face to face.

"Look at me."

I steady myself in his brown eyes. My heart thuds so loud I'm sure everyone can hear.

"Close your eyes. Root your feet into the ground. Imagine deep roots forming below your feet. Imagine your arms are the branches of that tree and stretch them to the sky. Take a deep breath in through your nose. Slowly let your breath out through your mouth. Now open your eyes. How do you feel now?"

"Wow. What was that?"

My palms are no longer sweaty puddles of perspiration.

"You can thank the weekly meditation class Vincent takes me to. He says it helps with his dance performances. He calls it *centering*," says Daniel.

"Thank you."

"Of course."

After that, I feel more prepared to tackle the last twenty minutes. It's a choreographed dance. I move through the room, checking on every single box and making sure that nothing is out of place. I place a stack of confidentiality forms next to the anonymous boxes with a prominent sign: SIGN FORM BEFORE VIEWING. NO PHOTOGRAPHY ALLOWED FOR BOXES IN SECTION B. The photo booth arrives in the nick of time. It's 8:05 P.M. There are throngs of people outside.

I step out from behind the black rope to see the line is growing. It snakes down the sidewalk and spills around the corner. Whoa. I take a deep breath, fix my suit jacket, and head back inside.

I'm all smiles and *hello*s, greeting the crowd as they come inside. For all my stress, the 360-degree photo booth is a huge hit and already has a line. I've never had a crowd this big before. A girl with the most amazing green sequin jumpsuit grabs my arm. She shimmers as she moves closer to me.

"Chloe the curator?"

I nod. It has a nice ring to it.

"Girl, I'm gagging. I can't wait for my ex to see me here with his garbage!"

She squeezes my shoulder, then flitters away with a gaggle of friends trailing behind her. I take a moment to look around the room. People are posing, snapping selfies, and scarfing down sushi like it's going out of style.

I see my parents in the corner of the room, sharing one tiny plate of sushi. I try to wipe Dad's frown from my mind from when I asked him if his friend could cater instead. I make my way over to them, but every few seconds, people keep waving me down to congratulate me. I pose for pics.

By the time I reach my parents, they have their coats on.

"Proud of you, sweetheart," says Dad, kissing my cheek.

"Enjoy the party!" says Mom.

"Thanks, Dad. Thanks, Mom."

They disappear behind a wall of people. I decide to duck behind a pillar to check my phone. I see a text from Jake.

Jake: Damn! Heartifacts is popping.

I flip over to Instagram and search #Heartifacts. Hundreds of posts with thousands of likes. I notice the photos they're taking are blocking off the art, but under the #Heartifacts tag, there are six thousand posts. Wow.

I take a moment to relish in the popularity. After my failure at Jake's solo show, it feels a million times more amazing to finally break through and have my first super-successful show. I dip back into the crowd. I answer questions and smile for more photos. I feel like I'm full of espresso, sugar packets, and Los Angeles sunshine.

I pose with different influencers. Names I've already forgotten, though we look like BFFs on Instagram.

Out of the corner of my eye, I see Daniel's film is projected on top of people's bodies. No one can see the actual movie.

A beach ball floats above the crowd, tapped back up into the air by random hands. I have no idea where a beach ball came from. I make eye contact with Francesca who raises her eyebrows at me.

I shrug. The crowd loves it. Who am I to stop the fun? I jump up when the rainbow-colored ball hovers over me and smack it hard. Then, I hear a rip like scissors slicing through fabric. Suddenly, my uncomfortable suit is very comfortable.

I grab the side of my pants, gripping them tightly, and hustle over to the pillar.

Francesca must've seen because she meets me there. Her eyes are wide as plates.

"Damn. Okay, wait here. I have denim overalls in my bag."

"No. Not overalls."

She raises her left eyebrow. "It's overalls or ripped pants."

"Fine! I'll meet you in the bathroom to do the switch."

"Oh, girl, the bathroom line is longer than Pink's Hot Dogs."

"You are speaking gibberish."

Francesca waves her hand at the pillar. "This pillar is your best bet, babe."

She rushes off. I peek from behind the pillar at the crowd that continues to grow. I scan to find Daniel and Vincent. Vincent is flirting with a very hot Indian boy while Daniel stifles a yawn. Yikes. My eyes turn to Daniel's movie. Our film.

I see what happens next in slow motion as I hold my pants.

A group with a selfie stick is right by Daniel's projector. The one he saved up to buy.

One person with a buzz cut raises the stick. The group squeezes together. They bump against the table with Daniel's projector.

I stifle a scream as his projector crashes to the hardwood floor with a loud thud. The projector is flipped on its side. I feel sick inside. Francesca finally returns and uses her body to block mine as I change into the paint-splattered overalls.

I whisper as I hook the denim suspenders, "Daniel's projector is dead."

"Oof. Vin says Daniel treats it like an endangered species because it's hella old."

When I get to the projector, Daniel is sweeping glass shards off the floor. People continue to crunch the remains under their shoes.

"I'm so sorry, Daniel. I'll pay for a new one."

Vincent helps him clean it up. Daniel holds his projector against his chest like an injured sea turtle.

"This specific projector can't be ordered anymore." Daniel waves his hand toward the crowds. "People here just want a selfie. They're not looking at anything. What about the heartbroken people who gave you their objects and trusted you with them?" asks Daniel.

Inside, I know he's right. I traded trust for a hashtag.

"I wanted more people to see *Heartifacts*," I say.

"You succeeded." There's an edge to his voice.

"I think it's best if we go, Chloe," says Vincent. "Come on, D."

I watch as Vincent wraps his arm around Daniel's shoulders. They walk out together. I don't try to stop them.

The beach ball is near me again. This time, I jump up and whack it hard. The crowd cheers as it floats over a sea of faces.

I did it. I duck behind the pillar again for a minute. This is not at all what I thought it would be, but it's a huge success. I check Instagram: ten thousand posts. The line is nonstop. This is what I wanted. It's happening. Finally. So why does it feel like my heart walked out with Daniel?

So why does it feel like something has gone horribly wrong?

The next day, after my twenty-minute morning jog (step three!), I check my Instagram. Thirty-eight DMs. I click through each one. Some are cool. People share *Heartifacts* in their Insta stories. Some random spammers. A good chunk are from people who want to send in their breakup objects and tell their stories.

Then there are long messages from people who are in the exhibit.

> Dear Chloe,
> I am really disappointed. I saw photos from *Heartifacts* last night and somebody posted a photo in front of our box with the caption *Vegan losers!*
>
> El is mad at me. They had no idea they were in it.
>
> We were already in a crappy place and now El says they don't trust me.
>
> When I sent you the box, you said that it would be anonymous, but I'm seeing random strangers make fun of the *Vegan AF* socks I got El, and I feel like crap.
>
> Please take my belongings out of the exhibit and ship them back to me.
>
> James

There are more messages like this one from the other people featured. I read through them all. Before I respond, I look up the photos tagged with #Heartifacts and what I see makes me feel ill.

The art is in the background. It's all selfies and photo booth strips. As I scroll, I realize the gallery space is packed, but no one cares about the objects. Daniel's movie is nonexistent. I found the no-photography forms on the floor stamped with footprints. I should've known better. No one reads anymore.

I text Selena and Francesca. I screwed up.

Selena: I saw the takedowns. Want to talk?
Francesca: You gotta make it right.

I plop my phone on my bed. Whenever my brain feels like it's on fire, I grab a paper planner. With my fine-tip markers and stickers, the world seems less insane. I sit down at my desk to write.

What should I do now? Francesca said to make it right, but what does that mean? Things got out of hand. Not only did some of the objects get destroyed, but no one even cared about what they saw.

A knock. The door opens. Ahma shuffles in. She holds her gold watch out to me. The watch face is blinking the wrong time. I press the small side buttons and adjust it until the time is correct.

Ahma sits on my bed. She gently pets Sesame who purrs at her chin scratches. My phone lights up with notifications. I toss it in my dresser drawer. My grandmother puts her watch back on, strapping it on slowly. It hits the ground with a thud. I pick it up and help her fasten it.

Ahma caresses my cheek. "So smart," she says.

I smile. I feel anything but smart. She pads out of the room. I go back to my trusty planner and jot this on the dot-lined paper: *I cared too much about making Heartifacts super successful. I let influencers influence my decisions. I didn't think about my original creators.*

I draw a pink rectangle at the top of the paper.

How do I make it right?

Underneath the rectangle, I add three thick lines.

1. Apologize
2. Offer to give boxes back
3. Contact influencers to delete certain posts.

I make lists under each number of who I need to contact. It's a start. At least, I hope it is.

At dinner, I take small bites of broccoli while Dad talks about his success at Ruby Street. He's got regulars now and more people are visiting Sweet Yen because of the cross-promotion. His words. I smile and nod when he looks my way.

The last time I made a mistake like this—when people left Jake's exhibit without even going through it—I spent three weeks indoors under the covers. I blamed a terrible head cold, but the truth was I wanted to sink through my bedsheets.

I thought I had made all the right plans. Maybe I should

stick to my planner world, make more videos, and forget about art.

The doorbell rings. Dad answers it while I continue to spiral.

"Daniel's here!" says Dad in a singsong voice. He looks directly at me, then winks. Real subtle, Dad.

I pop up. "What are you doing here?"

I thought he was still mad at me. Behind Daniel are two people I don't recognize, but Ahma does. One is a white woman dressed all in black who grasps hands with my ahma, bending down to chat with her. The other is a tall brown-haired half-Asian man with a basket of sunshine-yellow lemons. They smell so fresh, I can practically taste the sour lemons on my tongue. Ahma greets them in her light blue swan-covered dress. She stands and bows, saying *thank you* several times.

"I'm Clark. Daniel posted on Nextdoor about your grandma's pineapple cake recipe and how you all were trying to figure out the right ingredients. I brought these." He holds out the lemons. "I always saved a few for her every time they ripened. In return, she dropped off a tin of pineapple cakes."

The other neighbor guiltily holds up a small, clear bag with square silver tins.

"I'm Sutton. Your grandmother asked me to send these to Emily when you all lived in New York. I forgot. They've been sitting in my cupboard for months. I'm so sorry."

My mom reaches out for them. "The pineapple cake tins! We've been looking for them everywhere."

"Come on in, everybody. Let's make pineapple cakes!" says my dad.

Within minutes, our kitchen becomes a makeshift bakery. Dad passes out aprons. Mom grabs all the measuring cups she can find. Sutton measures the ingredients. Even Ahma helps out by cracking the eggs. Clark opens a bag of sugar. Daniel drains the canned pineapple.

When everyone is busy, I purposely sneak closer to Daniel. He's diligently stirring the crushed pineapple in a warm pot. He's got my pink Hello Kitty apron on.

"Please don't get anything on that apron. It's vintage Kitty."

"On my honor," he says.

I want to tell him that he looks adorable in it, but I bite my tongue.

"Thank you," I whisper close to his ear. He smells sweet, like fresh cane sugar. "I can't believe you did all of this."

He grins, killing me softly with his dimples. "Selfishly, I did it for the fresh pineapple cakes."

I could kiss him.

All of us work together to flatten the soft, pale yellow dough. Daniel adds the jam-like pineapple. Ahma shows us how she pinches the dough around the pineapple, then rolls it into a ball. We place each rolled ball into a square tin.

"I've got it from here," says my mom.

She scoots us out of the kitchen as Dad urges everyone to sit and eat something he whipped up quickly. I sit next to Daniel. He chats with Clark and Sutton. Suddenly, the problems with my exhibit don't feel so heavy.

Eventually, Mom comes out of the kitchen with a tray of freshly baked pineapple cakes. The air is filled with sweet citrus. I've never seen her so happy. Her smile is going to fall off her face.

"I think we did it. We made them."

Everyone claps. We surround Mom in a hug. We don't notice that Ahma is right by the hot tray. She screams.

One pineapple cake hits the ground with a sickening thud. The butter crust crumbles into sand. The yellow insides are splayed out.

Ahma yelps, clutching her right hand to her chest. Everyone moves quickly. Dad grabs an ice pack. I bring her to a couch. Mom wraps the ice pack around her hand. Clark examines her hand while Sutton sits close to Ahma. A red welt raises hot and hard.

"We should take her to urgent care," says Dad.

"You guys go. We'll clean up," says Daniel. Clark and Sutton nod.

The tray is on the dining table as we rush off.

It's late by the time we come home from the urgent care center. Ahma whimpers because her hand hurts. My parents bring her to bed while I get a new ice pack. By the time Ahma is asleep, it's 12 A.M.

I could sleep right through Thanksgiving break.

I hear my phone buzz in my drawer.

There's buzzing in my dreams.

In the morning, after checking on Ahma and getting her some tea, I decide to write back only to the people in the exhibit who are upset with me.

Dear James:

I am sorry *Heartifacts* disappointed you. I began *Heartifacts* as a girl who had gotten dumped. I wanted to connect our stories together because even if we love different people, we all go through the same heartbreak.

I understand why you would want your most special objects returned to you. It's clear I didn't handle them with care, and I allowed people to treat them carelessly.

But I do hope you allow me to keep them for a little longer. I am putting *Heartifacts* on hiatus to take time to figure out what's next. I will share my next steps with you and everyone involved.

Again, I apologize for what has happened.

Chloe

I send the same email to everyone in the exhibit who is pissed at me. I have piles of emails, messages, and texts, but I don't respond to them. The only people who need to hear from me are the ones I hurt by my need to be super successful. Everyone else can wait.

At school, Francesca hangs with her friends. She tries to sit with me at lunch, but I tell her I need some time alone.

"I'm here when you're ready," she says.

The last time this happened with Jake, Selena came to our apartment with a huge quart of ube ice cream and two spoons. But I ushered her out. She kept showing up until I talked to her.

When I get back to our house, Daniel is sitting in the living room with Ahma. He pours a cup of tea for her. A pink box of egg tarts is on the table. One tart in front of my grandma. Another on a small green plate for Daniel. I pause in the doorway as Daniel delicately holds the pastry for my grandmother to nibble since her right hand is still bandaged with white gauze. She wears dentures so it's hard for her to chew, even soft things like custardy tarts. Daniel waits until she's done before he sets it back down.

"Hi," I say.

"I wanted to come by and check on your ahma," says Daniel.

"She appreciates your company."

I lean down to kiss her cheeks.

"You go," she says, shooing us away with her left hand. "Talk, talk."

"We'll be close by," I say.

I lead Daniel over to our couch. He sits close to me.

I whisper, "We don't like to leave her alone too long."

He nods. "We do the same with my halmeoni. She hates it though."

I study my grandma from behind. She hunches over her tea. The last time Daniel and I talked he was mad about what happened with the exhibit. I can't say I blame him.

"What's the final damage for your projector? I'd like to pay for it."

"It's in the photo shop on York. He said he'd call me when the parts arrive."

"I'm really sorry. I screwed up big time with you and my

contributors. I didn't listen when you said I wasn't ready for a new relationship. Or when you turned me down. I pushed for what I wanted. I've decided to close *Heartifacts* to regroup."

"I appreciate the apology. You made mistakes, Chloe. It's okay. We all do. But can I ask you something?"

I nod.

"Why did you start this exhibit?"

I open my mouth to respond, but quickly shut it. I fall back into the couch cushions, wishing I had an answer for him. I usually ask artists why they started a piece, but when I'm asked, I am blank. He gets up and pulls out his phone from his black messenger bag.

"I want to show you something. From your original exhibit. When only ten people were checking it out. Tell me what you think."

It's footage from the moment he walks in with Vincent. Vincent clutches his arm.

In the video, Vincent says, "I don't think I can do this, Daniel."

"You can. I'm here with you."

I'm in the background, fussing with a flower arrangement. The camera pans over the whole scene. People are standing by each box, reading the placards, and looking over the objects. Then, the focus is back on Vincent, who finally finds his box.

"This is it," says Vincent.

Out of his pocket, he pulls a photo booth strip that matches the one in front of him. For a few minutes, I am

transported back there when Vincent first saw Connor's trib-
ute to him and their relationship.

"Do you see this?" asks Vincent. He points to the placard.
To the place where it says, *Why we broke up.*

Vincent holds his own face as if to keep the tears inside.
Daniel moves closer.

"You okay?"

Vincent shakes his head. Daniel places the camera down.
We see a ceiling view now, but we hear these words:

"I care about you, man. It doesn't matter what Connor
wrote. You are a good person."

What unfolds next is my guest star cameo. I reach over to
pause it.

"You should put this in your documentary."

"No. It's terribly shot. Some of it has the ceiling. I'm showing it to you so you can see what *Heartifacts* was before it
became a huge success. It was something special," says Daniel.

He picks up his phone and slides it back into his pocket.
"There's no way I can use this in my documentary. My tone is
serious. This is way too sentimental."

"Yes, I know. The commercialization of Valentine's Day
and romantic relationships. But this scene is about relationships. Vincent's relationship with Connor. Your friendship
with Vincent. It's about love—friend and boyfriend. It's perfect," I say.

"This is lit terribly. No one will take me seriously if I put
this scene in. No, this video was just for me to document the
moment for Vincent. He asked me to record him so he could
replay the video if he ever felt like calling Connor. Plus," says

Daniel, using his index finger as an exclamation point. "I'm playing it for your eyes only."

I move closer to Ahma as she stiffly gets up from the table. My hand goes to her curved back. Crust crumbs hang on the edges of her lips. I wipe them away.

"I sleep now, Emily," says Ahma.

When she mixes me up with my mom, I know it's time for her to get back into bed. Her medication makes her drowsy, which can lead to falls.

"I'll be right back."

I gently lead her to her bedroom. I pull back the covers and tuck her in. I sing a few lines of a lullaby she sang to me when I stayed at her place overnight. These are the only words of Hokkien I remember by heart. She closes her eyes. I watch her sleep. Her hair is getting grayer by the day. As I leave, I shut the door quietly to not wake her.

When I'm back in the kitchen, the table has been cleared and Daniel is washing the dishes from his teatime with my ahma.

"She called me your dad's name," says Daniel.

"Her memory fades more in the late afternoon. By nighttime, she's gone somewhere else."

"That must be hard," says Daniel.

He finishes and puts the dishes in the rack, wiping his hands on a kitchen towel.

"She always talked about you. Her smart granddaughter who is going to be a big deal someday."

I burst out laughing. "This is the only time I'm grateful her memory is fading."

"Hey. Don't talk about my friend like that. You are going to be a big deal someday. Yen doesn't mince words. So why does *Heartifacts* matter to you?"

I sit down at the kitchen table, grab a tart out of the box, and nibble on it. I shrug.

"In the video you shot, it seemed so simple. Curate people's found objects. Things that mattered to them in the moment. Like, by itself the object is meaningless. A blue ink pen is nothing to someone else, but to you it might mean everything. We might love differently, and the circumstances are different for breakups, but we all know what it's like to stare at an object that once meant something to you."

I don't notice until now that Daniel has his phone trained on me. Normally, I would freak out that he's filming me, but being around him, I realize he's always recording something.

"When Jake sent me back my things, I wanted to throw them out in the dumpster of my parents' coffee shop. Francesca saw me and asked if I was okay. I knew her from around school, but nothing else. We were basically strangers. But once we both realized we got dumped, it was funny to share our objects with each other. It felt like we spoke the same language. I bought her stuff because I had the idea that if we could bond over our mutual breakups, then more people would be affected too. We could find each other this way. Instead of hiding out at home or doom-scrolling through our ex's feeds, we could come together and say, *I see you. I'm in the same place too.*"

Daniel's phone is still fixed on me as I say, "I should write this down."

I rush up the stairs to my bedroom to sketch out a new plan for *Heartifacts*. A reimagined version of the original without the influencers. A pared-down exhibit that focuses on what matters most: bringing people together to get over their heartbreak together. Not in isolation, but with friends and others to witness our pain, and even joy.

Daniel knocks on my door. "I gotta go. But I sent you a Dropbox link with the videos I just recorded and the original one from the exhibit, in case you want them."

I hug him tightly. "Thank you. Now go. I have some work to do."

It comes back to me. That one question—*Why does* Heartifacts *matter to you?*—cracks open the inspiration I desperately need. I grab my arsenal of supplies: Post-its, notebooks, planners, multicolored pens, and stickers. I lay everything out and get to work. Usually when I plan, everything has its place, but now, my room becomes a whirlwind of ideas. I put ideas down on Post-its and place them along my bedroom wall. I give myself two and a half months to revamp *Heartifacts*.

Instead of my detailed spreadsheet of media and influencer contacts, I pull together everyone who has expressed interest in being part of the exhibit. I find the relationship expert who wrote *Breakup Bootcamp* and ask to interview her. I read countless articles on how to get over a breakup.

I listen to my curated *Heartifacts* playlist and write down song lyrics that speak to me. Finally, I rewatch the two videos Daniel has sent me. I take notes. What I like. What needs improvement. I rewatch them over and over, especially what

I've said about the meaning of *Heartifacts*. I write it down verbatim so that all my words are exactly as I said them.

I stare at my mini-monologue in my notebook. This is my new mission statement. This is what I want people to first see when they walk through the door, before they look at the boxes.

I send this video to the twenty participants who trusted me with their objects, so they can hear my new intention. I give them the option of backing out or staying with me. I ask them to let me know by December 10.

When I'm done reaching out to them, I text Daniel.

Me: Thank you for reminding me of what's missing the most from Heartifacts—my heart. I had spent my time chasing success. I thought a sold-out show would prove I'm worthy of being a curator, but the power of your videos has shown me I need to dig deeper.
Daniel: You're welcome. I'm happy to hear it, friend.

I want to type this: *You are amazing, talented, caring, and I wish you were my boyfriend.*

I send this instead: I'd love to see your documentary, no matter what shape it is in. As a fellow creative to another. Can you screen it for me?

Daniel: Maybe.
Me: I've got key lime LaCroix and Choco Pies.
Daniel: Sold.

My bedroom is a mess of papers, notebooks, and Post-its. I haven't showered in three days. Mom and Dad are worried about my sweatpants game, but I tell them I have my period. The only part of my room that's pristine is my desk, outfitted with my iPad mount and soft box lights. I haven't filmed this week's episode because my Ballet Slippers gel manicure is chipped and also because I didn't plan it out.

The truth is: as much as I put myself in my YouTube videos or on social media, I like to hide out sometimes. I have a certain look to my followers. I am calm, cool, composed. But right now, I feel anything but that.

I haven't heard from anyone who exhibited in *Heartifacts*. I can't blame them. I would be ticked off if I gave my personal belongings to someone and saw them get mocked on Instagram.

I pull out my phone and open my @PlanItGirl Instagram and hit live.

In a few minutes, there are 321 followers active.

I haven't done a live in a while. I want to be real with you. My
plans to get over Jake worked, and now there's this new
guy. I can't get him out of my head, but he just wants
to stay friends. Also, I decided to put my *Heartifacts*

exhibit on hiatus after a disastrous influencer night. I'm
sure you've seen what happened. Usually, I'm your gal
to come up with big plans, but I'm stalled. My Big Idea
sheets are blank. I am taking a momentary break from
my #PlanWithMe videos and hope to come back in
December when I've got a plan for how to fix my messes.

I see messages and emojis flying up from the bottom of
my screen, but I click off. I've never taken a break from my
planner channel, even when I had the flu. But I'm not exactly
in the headspace to plan anything. I am a blank page and
there's no amount of motivational stickers that can soothe
me right now.

Selena must have seen the live because she texts me immediately.

Selena: I'm worried about you. How many bagels should I
send? Call me. I'm serious. Don't do that deep dive down
into silent mode.

Francesca and Vincent text me to check in. I cover with
overly enthusiastic emojis and promises to get together soon.
Selena always said my *Let's get together soon* was a precursor to
my disappearance. As always, my BFF is right.

Daniel is coming over to screen his documentary. He keeps
calling me *friend* over text and I tell myself it's totally normal
to dress up for a friend's visit. I take a long, hot shower. Brush
my hair. I put on my favorite pick-me-up outfit: a pastel
multicolor midi skirt with a gold glitter waistline and an

oversized green T-shirt that says, *Done is better than good.* Pink lip gloss and a gold hair tie complete my look.

I put out Daniel's favorite snacks, including cold key lime LaCroix and a Choco Pie, and wait for him in my living room. I purposely asked him to come over when my parents were at the café and Ahma was resting. I want to give his movie my undivided attention.

Classic Daniel arrives fifteen minutes after he says he will.

"I'm so sorry. I got caught up in editing the end. It's still not where I want it," says Daniel.

He looks so cute in his black hoodie, clutching his laptop like it's his own heart in his hands. I usher him in and we settle into the couch, side by side. He sets up his laptop with a small portable Bluetooth speaker.

"Keep in mind this is a rough cut. Definitely not ready for the festival submission yet. It's way too long. It needs to be a tight twelve minutes total."

I place my hand on his knee. He stops chattering.

"I'm not a film critic. I'm a friend who wants to see what you've done. I know you've worked really hard on this, and it's only one part of the creative process."

I reach over to hit play on the screen. Daniel bites his nails as the title sequence begins.

Voiceover: In 1913, Greeting Cards, Inc., churned out mass-produced Valentine's Day cards in Kansas City, Missouri, and it launched the start of an annual holiday. And since then, corporations with vested

*interests have overtaken this once obscure holiday and
turned it into a chocolate-covered money-making
machine. In 2018, Valentine's Day sales hit $73 million
with card companies, confection brands, and florists
raking in the most profits.*

Whoa. This is intense. I don't look over at Daniel, but I
can feel him fidgeting, bouncing his right knee up and down.
The doc opens with a scene inside a corporate office. Daniel speaks off-camera as the person—a white man in a blue
business suit—answers his questions. He's a spokesperson for
Greeting Cards, Inc. He talks about how his company started
by selling greeting cards and found Valentine's Day was always a big spike in sales.

I stifle a yawn. The interview is slow, meandering, and way
too long. I don't have the heart to tell Daniel because his eyes
are glued on the screen. The next scene is a stock video inside
a pharmacy as people fight over cheap boxes of chocolates.

*Daniel's voiceover: Chocolate sales in the month of
February account for $18 million of overall holiday
profits. More than any other time of the year, people
want their relationships to be reduced to gifts in the
form of fancy dinners, flowers, and mass-produced boxed
chocolates. I investigate further into why material objects
and an annual date mean people drive themselves crazy
to demonstrate their affections to each other. If true love
exists, why must it be reduced to red rose bouquets?*

Dread fills me when I see that twenty minutes have passed, and I have liked zero parts of Daniel's doc. Vincent was right. It feels like watching a research paper. What do I tell him? Should I be honest or sugarcoat it?

He hasn't even opened his LaCroix can.

Twenty minutes later, I pick out some details I can share that I liked: the music, visuals, and his interview questions. As the credits roll, I mentally run through lines I'll say. He snaps his laptop shut and finally turns to me.

I blurt out: "I enjoy the music you chose for the opening. Your skyline shots of Los Angeles were straight-up gorgeous. And your interview style is effortless." I say it all so fast it sounds like a run-on sentence.

Daniel sighs loudly. "You hate it."

"I didn't say that."

"The opening music? Shots of the sky? You might as well compliment my font choice," says Daniel.

I pause. He packs up his laptop into his bag.

"What did you really think? One creative to another."

I debate whether I should tell him what I thought honestly. Then, I think about how he gave me feedback on *Heartifacts*. It won't help him submit to the Santa Monica Teen Film Festival if I'm nice.

"You're talking about the commercialization of romance, but you don't interview anyone who's actually been in love. The focus is on corporations and the history of Valentine's Day, but what about the footage you took of Vincent when he came to *Heartifacts*? Even though I sound like a total jerk in that video, it had the real heart of what you're saying."

Daniel puts his bag down and sits again. He nods slowly, then grabs a notebook out of his bag and jots notes. I take this as a cue to continue.

"Who is your intended audience? Everyone has either been in love, had their heart broken, or had an unrequited crush at some point. Some people hate Valentine's Day, and others go all out for it. Some schools have flowers that get delivered as part of a fundraiser."

He scribbles fast. I've said enough so I stop myself there. Daniel looks up. There's a streak of blue pen ink across his chin.

"You have pen on your chin."

"Shoot. I do?"

He rubs, but it only makes the streak worse. I wet a napkin and gently wipe his chin clean. We are close again. He smells so nice. I'm super glad I showered before he came over. For a moment, I think we're going to kiss, but then Daniel moves away.

"Thanks for cleaning me up. And the notes. I'll keep them in mind when I head into my next cut," says Daniel.

I stay away from him because it's clear he doesn't want me too close.

"The short film we made together. I saw how you could capture real emotion in those short scenes, especially how you edited it all together. Have you ever thought about using the short film as a template for your documentary?"

Daniel grunts and exhales loudly. "Documentaries are serious. I'm not shooting a rom-com."

"Oh," I say softly.

"I appreciate your notes, but I don't think you get what

I'm trying to do here. I'm exposing the reality of this mass-marketed commercialization of Valentine's Day," says Daniel.

"You could merge both styles together and add some humanity to the final cut."

He tucks his notebook into his bag and gets up to leave.

"Got it. I'll consider it. See you later, Chloe."

He leaves without waiting for me to walk him out. As the front door shuts, I remember this exact feeling. Jake would act in a similar way when I gave him feedback on a piece he was still working on. He'd get all snippy and tight. But a few days later, he'd look at his work in a new way. Maybe he'd change it. Sometimes he wouldn't, but he'd say afterward, "You gave me some fresh eyes on this," and he'd get back to polishing it.

I hope Daniel feels the same way. I really hope I haven't ruined our friendship.

Later, Francesca comes over for dinner with Vincent. Vincent and my ahma slow dance in the living room. She's dressed in Mickey Mouse sandals with white socks, a quilted floral jacket, a paisley top, and loose denim pants. Her favorite jade earrings sway as she moves with Vincent.

"Your ahma has moves," calls out Vincent.

They are barely moving. Ahma presses her cheek against Vincent's. Her bright smile is huge. I haven't seen her this happy in a long time.

My grandmother sees me and says in Hokkien, "Why is he not your boyfriend? Such a handsome, nice boy." She smacks his cheeks gently.

I immediately turn red. Ahma is always trying to set me up with boys.

"Ahma," says Vincent in Hokkien, "I'm not interested in a relationship. Did that. I want my dating life to be like Costco. Sample all the goods before buying."

"Ay!" Ahma starts laughing so loudly that Francesca, Vincent, and I can't help but join in. She responds in Hokkien, "You are very handsome and the best dancer."

To me, Vincent says, "I will be coming over here every day."

They continue their soft slow dance, my grandmother holding Vincent close. Francesca helps me set the table. My parents have a meeting with Lourdes about expanding their hours at the coworking space. It's just the four of us.

"I ordered way too much food from Joy," I say.

"Never. Those bao sandwiches are basically mini bites," says Francesca.

It turns out I didn't order enough because Vincent and Francesca can eat anyone under the table with their voracious appetites. I might as well have brought two horses over to eat. During dinner, Ahma talks with Vincent nonstop since she discovered he could speak Hokkien. They are speaking so fast I have trouble keeping up. My language skills are lackluster. Vincent cracks her up and it makes my heart happy to see her so happy.

"Vincent can charm a ghost out of a haunted house," says Francesca.

He grins widely at Francesca and continues chatting with Ahma at a rapid pace.

"So," I say.

Francesca holds up her hand. "Don't tell me you have an agenda for a casual friends dinner."

I snap my mouth shut. Francesca slaps her knee in response.

"Oh my god. You totally do! Spit it out. What's on your mind?"

"I want to revamp *Heartifacts* with local artists involved and I want your help." I say it so fast it sounds like one word.

Francesca tilts her head like a puppy trying to understand what their human is saying. She taps her wooden chopsticks against her bowl and points them at me.

"Girl, can I be real with you?"

I nod. Uh-oh. This is not the conversation I thought we would be having.

"You're intense."

"What?" I'm so loud, even Vincent and Ahma pause their rapid-fire conversation to look at me, as if I shouted a curse word.

"Vin, she's intense."

"Definitely."

"Oh my god. What. Just 'cause I'm organized?" I respond.

"Like, right now, your eyes are all buggy and you have that intense straight back like you're standing in front of a group of seven hundred people."

I purposely hunch over, which makes Francesca laugh even harder.

"Girl, you make relaxing look hard. Listen, I admire your sheer tenacity. You will organize the crap out of anything. But artists don't want to be rushed. Like, even when you're not

hovering, it feels like you're hovering," says Francesca. "I'm not sure if my artist friends want to get involved."

Ouch. Jake once called me intense. I thought it was a good thing. He was impressed I tracked him down after no one could figure out who the Yarn Bomber was. That's how I won him over.

Apparently, it's not good to be intense.

"The collective is a pretty laidback group full of talented artists, but none of us want to be treated like a commodity. Does that make sense?"

"Yeah," I say, glancing down at the table. The food is fast disappearing. "I got dessert," I add.

I lay out three containers of forbidden rice pudding, dotted with purple taro balls. As we dig in and savor the coconut rice sweetness, I let Francesca's words wash over me. Jake's solo show was a result of his artist friends all dropping out of the larger gallery showing I had organized. He said I pressured them to *hurry up*. I never said that! Okay, that's a little intense. I look over at Francesca and Vincent and they radiate confidence effortlessly. Dang. I've been in La La Land long enough to think things like *radiate confidence*.

"I have an idea, Francesca. Come with me. Take me to your artist friends. Let's start some conversations. I can present some ideas I have and see if they want to participate. No hard deadlines. No pressure."

Vincent pauses what he's saying to my ahma and points his chopsticks at Francesca. "That's what I did with Daniel."

"Yeah, that guy is the definition of intense," says Francesca. "I took him to some movie screenings and told him if he

asked one question, I'd watch any documentary he wanted," says Vincent. "Oh my god. I endured some rough stuff, but damn if that boy can speak up now. He'd get all in his head and talk himself out of asking a question to a director."

"Exactly. Help me be better at working with artists. I'm rough around the edges, but I'm committed," I say.

"Toss in some fresh homemade mochi and you've got yourself a deal," says Francesca.

"Deal."

We shake hands and it's done.

Afterward, Francesca leaves to finish a piece she's working on, but Vincent stays to help me clean up. Ahma's dance energy has withered in the last thirty minutes, so she calls Vincent by my dad's name. I help her to her bedroom and set her up with *Single Ladies Senior,* the volume turned all the way up.

Vincent is washing dishes when I return. He passes me plates and I dry them.

"Thanks for helping. And for hanging out with my ahma. I've never seen her so happy," I say.

"She's a feisty firecracker. Reminds me of my nai nai. She's in Taiwan. My parents dropped me there from ages three to ten so I could learn Hokkien. I visit her every year."

"I used to visit Ahma every year too until we moved here. Her dementia was worsening every few months until she was in the street in her pajamas."

Vincent stops washing dishes and gives me a hug. I rest on his shoulder, the weight of reality hitting me.

"You miss New York."

"Every single day. It's weird here. The vibe is so different than the city," I say.

"You just said *vibe* so I think you can cross that off your LA bingo card."

I start laughing and return the dishes to their original spots in the kitchen. "What else is on that LA bingo card?"

"Get a parking ticket."

"I don't drive," I say.

Vincent's brown eyes go wide. "Okay. I lost my mind for a second. You have to learn. You get one of those cars with the big STUDENT DRIVER sign on the top."

"Not interested. People drive here like it's a racetrack."

"Spot a celebrity. That's the free spot in the middle of the LA bingo card."

"Done! I saw the back of Randall Park's head on Melrose."

Vincent laughs and grabs his brown leather satchel.

"I should go. Thanks for dinner. I'm definitely coming back to hang with your ahma."

He starts to leave but pauses.

"I don't think I should be telling you this, but Daniel told me about your feedback on his documentary. He was crushed."

"Oh," I say.

"For what it's worth, I agree with you. It feels so divorced from human connection. Daniel's a great guy, but he takes himself too seriously. Like, if he could skip straight into adulthood, he would."

"I feel bad. Maybe I shouldn't have told him the truth."

"He can handle it. I know him. He'll go into a rabbit hole

for a few days and then he'll emerge with an even better idea of how to fix it. Just give him time," says Vincent.

He walks out the door with a wave. I check on Ahma one last time by cracking open her bedroom door. The hallway light spills into her room as a sliver. She is resting peacefully. I sigh with relief. I quietly shut her door.

"Co-hee," says Ahma.

I stop immediately. She hasn't called me by my first name in a while. I open the door again.

"What's up, Ahma?"

In Hokkien, she says, "Your friends are right. You take yourself too seriously. Laugh at yourself. Have some fun."

My listening skills are better than my speaking. I enter her room and respond in broken Hokkien that I'll try, and she should get some rest. I lightly kiss her forehead. Despite her seventy-two years, her skin is so smooth. She loudly smooches back at me. When I shut her bedroom door again, I make a vow to be less intense. Whatever the hell that means.

show Francesca the three ideas I have, on three Post-its on my giant corkboard. She sits on the edge of my bed and Sesame hops into her lap. Francesca reads them over for what feels like hours. She tilts her head back and forth. A few times she says, "Huh," out loud as she pets Sesame.

Finally, she points at a neon pink Post-it where I've written, *What Love Is and What Love Isn't*.

"Tell me more about this," says Francesca.

"I thought this could be an open-ended question we pose to the artists and our viewers. What they define as love and how they define what love isn't. The artists could interpret that however they want in whatever medium they choose. For our viewers, it would mean writing their responses on Post-its and posting them under *What Love Is* or *What Love Isn't*. Low-tech interactive," I say.

Francesca snaps her fingers, tapping the pink note with her index finger like an exclamation point. "That's it. You came alive when you said it. Clearly, it's the right idea. Leaving it open to interpretation by the artists and the viewers is great. It'll give you a nice range of what it might look like. It's uncontrolled."

"Exactly. Would your artist friends be interested in that?"

"Why don't you ask them yourself? I've arranged a club meeting," says Francesca.

"When?"

"Right now. Come with me."

She walks out of my room at a fast pace. I trail right behind her.

"But I haven't had time to prepare!"

Francesca doesn't respond to my many questions and instead grabs her skateboard parked right by our shoe rack. Soon I'm jogging behind her as she skateboards toward Highland Park High. I am out of breath, but still listing the many reasons why it's a bad idea for me to come to a meeting with nothing prepared. Francesca has gone full silent mode and I'm sweating as we enter the Arte Para La Gente meeting space/art studio.

I quickly count twenty people. Some are still in the middle of sketching, painting, or knitting. The chatter in the room dies down as Francesca stands up on a chair.

"Hey! My friend Chloe here wants a minute of your time," says Francesca.

Oh my god. One minute?! She gestures for me to get on the chair after she steps down. Does she want me to climb Mount Kilimanjaro after this too? The room is silent now. I tentatively climb on top of the chair.

Twenty faces stare at me. I have nothing prepared. My mind is blank like all my words disappeared. My mouth is dry. It's now or never, Chloe.

"Some of you might remember me from *Heartifacts*. I decided to close it for a bit and revamp my idea," I say.

A pink-haired girl with a nose ring says, "Slow down. You're speaking too fast."

I nod. I start again.

"I started *Heartifacts* at Ruby Street. I shut it down because it lost its way. I want you to help me get back to the heart of it. I had an idea to involve this community of artists and our viewers so that the exhibit is more of a low-tech interactive experience. I'm asking artists to interpret two questions. What love is and what love isn't. Interpret those two phrases however you want. Whatever medium speaks to you. Heartbreak and falling in love are universal, but we think we're the only ones who feel this way when we get dumped or meet someone new. It's brand new for each person. I want to connect us all together. A community collective answer to these two big questions."

I stop talking. No one says anything. Twenty pairs of eyes blink back at me. My hands are sleek with sweat. My heart is in my throat, but I'm still alive. I did not die from sheer unpreparedness. I step down from the blue chair. I finally make eye contact with Francesca who smiles and nods at me.

A hand goes up.

"Yes?"

"Is there a deadline?"

"I'd like to give everyone time to fully develop their piece, especially since the two-week holiday break is coming up," I say.

"Chloe and I can set up one-on-one meetings right after the break to check in. Help you brainstorm. Chat. Or if you want us to buzz off, you don't have to," says Francesca.

A few people nod their heads. Francesca scribbles a few things on a blank sheet of paper.

"Sign up if you're interested. This isn't a hard commitment. But I do think we have something important to offer to our neighborhood and the art world at large. Most people only see romance as being between two white characters. We can represent the love and joy in our relationships through our art. We don't always have painful backstories. We don't always have to be the background best friend. We can be the main characters in this love narrative," says Francesca.

One person claps. Then another. Soon, the room erupts in hoots and hollers, including me. Damn, Francesca is such a good public speaker. By the time the sheet makes it around the whole room, it's completely full of signatures.

Yes!

Even though I don't plan to, I stay for the entire meeting, talking with different artists. One is a Muslim sculptor who uses gum wrappers and garbage to make little figurines. She takes me through her current lineup of political figureheads from around the world. I can't believe what she can do with paper. Another shows me baskets he's woven out of black-and-white photographs so that tiny Latine faces peer out. I see a white artist with huge pink headphones on, face fixed on their painting, like no one else is in the room. I don't approach but watch in awe at how the blank canvas has morphed by the time I leave.

It's actually fun because I get to hear their ideas. It reminds me of when I started my first-ever gallery show in eighth grade to raise funds for an art program in my middle school. My principal thought I was a silly kid with a big idea until I presented my zero-budget plan for raising money for a thriving after-school arts program. I relish hearing what artists have to say and this idea sparks all sorts of cool interpretations.

After everyone leaves, I hug Francesca.

"Thank you. I couldn't have done that without you."

"Psssh. Of course you could. You are a badass. I gave you a platform to say what you needed to say. Plus, I think Arte Para La Gente can bang it out of the park with this one. Lourdes and I have forever talked about a way to get my group to do a show there and this idea is popping."

I take the sign-up sheet from her.

"But you should've seen the look on your face when you got on that chair. Like you had seen a serial killer running around with a chainsaw."

I start laughing so loud it comes out in one big honk. Francesca folds over with giggles too. When we finally calm down, I put an arm around her.

"I'd like you to be my co-curator. I can learn a lot from you. Plus, you are the one who knows this community inside out."

"For real?"

"Please."

She holds up her hand for a high five. "I'm down. Co-curator credit is badass. I've got ideas, girl."

"I will have some planned meetings though," I say.

"Of course you will. We've got this. Just you wait and see. We'll blow the roof off of Ruby Street," says Francesca.

We leave school with our arms linked, chatting about a million different thoughts. Our sentences swim over each other. The only other time I co-curated was with a Met intern who thought I'd never pull off what I proposed to our supervisor. She was plain old shocked when I came in with Jake Miller. Her eyebrows practically touched the ceiling of The Met. But with Francesca, it's totally different. Her ideas make me excited, and she has a ton of good feedback on mine. There's no competition. We are one brain in sync.

When we get back to Ahma's house, I try to write it all down and make plans for what's next as Francesca reaches out to her contacts.

Mom drops off warm cups of tea and mochi, which delights Francesca and Mom both because Francesca *ooh*s and *ahh*s over her cooking and Mom eats it up. It's late when we finish chatting. I rub my eyes. It's been nonstop since we started talking, but I feel the rush of adrenaline from inspiration. Francesca skateboards home while I continue writing in my journal.

I text Daniel: Can we talk?

He responds immediately: Want to go for a walk?

That's how I find myself on York Boulevard waiting on the line with dozens of others in front of Mochinut as the waft of sugared dough and chocolate frosting comes out each time the front door opens and closes. Daniel actually arrives on time.

"Did pigs start flying?"

"Ha. I was around the corner when you texted. What's up?"

I spill out the details Francesca and I hammered out together. Daniel nods, asks questions, and taps his finger on his lips, which means he's mulling it all over. As we move in the line, I take out my notebook and share some sketches of how I'll revamp the space we're in. He chimes in with his own ideas. I write them down as quickly as I can. What I like about brainstorming with Daniel is that he gets the same fever I get, like you can't talk fast enough to get the words out. One thought leads to the next. Chasing a balloon before it floats up into the clouds to be forgotten.

I don't realize I've said this out loud until Daniel says, "Exactly. Chasing balloons. Sometimes they pop up at one A.M. and I try to write them down before I forget."

I blush at the realization that my inner thoughts are now outer, but it feels really good to know someone else gets it. We order our doughnuts and hover at the counter, still chatting a mile a minute. The white glaze from his cookies and cream doughnut rubs against his chin.

"You have some," I say, pointing, then hand him a napkin.

"Here?"

He dabs at the wrong place. I reach over, take the napkin, and remove the glaze gently.

"Thanks," he says. "Did you know there are some people who don't have constant running thoughts in their head? There's a psychology study that reports twenty-five percent of people don't have an inner monologue."

"No!"

"It must be nice," says Daniel.

"I can't imagine what it's like to be walking around without a constant inner narrator," I say.

He bumps elbows with me. "I'd miss it."

We finish our doughnuts, and Daniel walks with me outside. We wander the neighborhood that, somehow, doesn't feel so foreign to me. My first week in LA, I'd always get lost, walking in circles. But now, I'm starting to recognize where I am, and that feels good. We stop at a playground that used to be a gas station. Daniel sits on a bench as kids scream, running up the slide.

"How's the editing going?"

Daniel makes a *phhhh* sound. He shrugs his shoulders, then throws his head back toward the sky. Oh no. Not a good sign.

"It's a horrendous mess. I've spent days with index cards on my floor. I dream in colored index cards. Nothing makes sense anymore. Maybe I shouldn't enter the festival this year."

Every artist I've worked with has had what I call a *crisis of faith*. A moment where they doubt their work, want to chuck it in the garbage, or start all over. They deem the current work in progress as *awful,* and can't see their way out of it. I saw Jake do it after every single piece he finished.

But with Daniel, it's different. He spirals further down the rabbit hole. He talks about being a total failure, having nothing important to say, and no one caring. I sit and listen. Nod when appropriate. If I've learned anything, it's that artists just want to be heard, even if they sound completely irrational.

I wait until he's done to speak. By now, the moon peeks out. The playground is empty. I reach for Daniel's hand. Not in a couple kind of way. In a *I'm a friend who cares* way. We sit in silence. I wait for his breath to calm down and the redness in his cheeks to stop blooming like red roses.

"Why does this story matter to you?"

When I say this exact same sentence to artists, some are

struck silent. Some rage at me. Others answer as a monologue. Daniel starts to speak but clams up. He sighs.

"Because I've never been in a relationship. I want to prove
that love doesn't mean ultimate happiness. I don't know. I see
my friends in serious relationships and I can't get beyond a
second date. I am just a rebound guy. I thought if I analyzed
the data, I'd get some answers. When you watched it, I saw
how it wasn't connecting. How it felt like a diatribe. A man-
ifesto. I want to be more than that. Maybe I'm not anything
more than that."

I hug Daniel tightly. I cup his face in my hands.

"You are more than a rebound guy. You are the guy who
helps my ahma. You care about this community. You bring
people together. You are the kind of friend most people wish
they had. Sure, your documentary needs some revisions, but
you are clearly talented and have a vision. Don't throw out
what you've done because you got lost along the way."

I bring my forehead to his. Our breaths intermingle. His
brown eyes linger on the soft foam of the playground. I brush
his right cheek with my fingers. For a few minutes, we don't
say anything. It feels totally natural to do this, but also terri-
fying because I know I played him for a rebound guy without
meaning to. I am part of his problem.

I retreat from physically touching him. He stands. We
walk side by side.

"You're good at this," says Daniel.

"I like it. I like combining my creative eye with my planning side and a dash of pep talk in there."

"Like an artist coach."

"Something like that. If I could make that my job, I would."

"So I shouldn't delete all my footage and start over?"

"No. I won't let you."

I wrap my arm through his. "Show me where you're at. If that's okay with you. I know last time, my feedback felt . . ."

"You were right. After every critique, I have a day where I reject all the notes, then a few days later, it all seems to make sense. Like the clouds part and I can see the sky again," says Daniel.

We end up back at his place. His grandmother makes us dinner, and we take it to his room. I mull over the Post-It Notes and index cards thumbtacked to his giant corkboard.

I pause over an index card simply labeled *New footage?*

"Did you shoot more?"

Daniel nods his head. I read through his storyboard— index card by index card.

"Herzog is adamantly against storyboards. He says a story-board is the instrument of cowards," says Daniel. He combs his fingers through his thick black hair. "But I can't see the whole twelve minutes without each scene in front of me."

"Every artist works differently. You do you. Let your film idol do his thing," I say.

I suggest some changes. We move cards around. He shows me some new footage. I stand over his laptop and see a new voice emerging. A more personal approach. I encourage him to keep going. Add his own voice into the mix.

The narrative comes forward: a Korean teenage boy who doesn't see himself as the lead of his own romantic life. He watches the world through a lens. Images. Other people's In-stagram feeds. His best friend. He adds in his own rebound slideshow, per my suggestion.

It's late now. The tea has gotten cold. We nibble at the japchae on our plates, half-eaten. I know I should go home soon, but I don't want to. This reminds me of late nights in Jake's studio, but better because we're not stopping to make out, and hours go by.

We're focused.

Slowly, the changes come forth. A new version emerges. I'm starting to see Daniel through the shots. The interviews and data are still part of the project, but now, we have a central character. Someone to root for. Daniel Kwak. Even though I'm cringeworthy in it, I let Daniel add the Vincent video from the original version of *Heartifacts*. It fits in the narrative, and it feels so real and human.

Heartbreak as a universal feeling.

Oh my god. I need to use this.

"Daniel, can I use that original video in *Heartifacts*?"

"I thought you hated it?"

"We can play it on a loop. As long as Vincent is okay with that. His reaction is so real I'm positive other people will feel the same way. Like he's expressing what we all feel inside when we see objects from our past connected to someone we once loved. Someone we couldn't live without, until one day we did," I say.

"You should write that as your new mission statement," says Daniel. "It sums up everything that's great about *Heart-ifacts*."

I write down what I just said on a yellow Post-it Note and tuck it into my pocket. I glance at my phone.

"Wow. I should go."

"Thanks for chasing balloons with me. I feel tethered again. I can see the sky," says Daniel.

I hug him. "Good night, Daniel."

don't use the word *deadline* when I email Arte Para La Gente, which is like asking me not to plan my entire week. Francesca suggests we instead schedule check-in times with each person a month after my presentation. Our first compromise. Francesca reminds me artists don't like to be hounded and everyone needs a holiday break.

Our first stop is Monica, the Muslim artist who makes sculptures out of gum wrappers and garbage. Francesca takes the lead. I shadow her. I see these exquisite tiny human forms out of candy wrappers and discarded coffee-cup filters.

"Wow," I say.

I bend down to examine the intricacies of each curve in these paper dolls. One silver doll is leaning closer to the brown doll who is somehow looking at the silver one with literal heart eyes.

"How did you get the red in the eyes like that?" I ask.

Monica says, "Twizzlers."

Francesca laughs. "Is that why you had a giant pile of candy last week?" Francesca turns to me. "This girl looked like she had gone trick-or-treating, but she's so silent about what she's making I had no clue."

"I ate so much I never want to see candy again," says Monica. She touches her belly.

I know the dolls are made of Tootsie Roll wrappers, the

inner linings of Juicy Fruit gum, and Twizzlers, but they somehow look real. I snap a photo of it.

"I won't post this anywhere. It's just for organizing the layout of the gallery," I say.

"Cool," says Monica.

The sculpture even smells sweet, like it was dipped in honey and coated in sugar. It's almost sickening.

"What's that smell?"

Monica points to the paper in her sculptures. "I soaked the paper in a sugar rosewater solution for a few hours to create a saccharine floral scent."

I snap my fingers. "Yes! This piece is perfect for the *What Love Isn't* section."

Monica nods her head. "Yup. I wanted to show a scene that seems super romantic, but it's not real. We don't get actual hearts in our eyes when we're in love. Love isn't super sweet all the time. It can be hard."

"Do you need more time, Monica?" asks Francesca.

Monica's blue hijab moves in waves as she nods. "I want to add more to the scene, like, setting it in an actual place instead of free floating."

"You know," says Francesca. "Just my two cents, but I like it without a place. It could be anywhere. Any couple. It's nondescript. No gender. No human faces. Just the embodiment of a feeling. What do you think?"

"I like how you're talking," says Monica.

Francesca and Monica slap a high five. "You know how Mr. Cardona is always asking us to edit our own work, not stuff it with more?"

Monica nods.

"This is it. Don't stuff it."

"I hear you," says Monica.

We walk ten minutes to our next stop: a random studio on York Boulevard. Francesca nods hello to the white woman working the counter and heads straight to the back where we find Julian with a series of black-and-white photographs hanging from a long wire, air drying. He and Francesca exchange a fist bump.

"Hey," says Julian. His curly black mop flops over his amber eyes.

The room smells like chemicals. It gives me a headache.

Francesca cracks open a window and a gust of fresh air floods in. Thank goodness. I inhale a few breaths before I check out the photos hanging up. There are dozens of faces. Some solo people. Some couples. Each shot is incredibly detailed. A denim jacket's every crease. An older couple's faces crisp like crinkled paper. Francesca isn't looking at the hanging photos, but instead stands in front of a black desk with strips of paper littering it.

"This is bananas," says Francesca. "You take an X-ACTO knife to these edges?"

Julian says, "Yeah. I've gone through six blades so far."

"Dang. It shows."

I join her to look. The strips of photo paper are intricately woven together so the originals blend together. I've never seen anything like it before. Most photography students I know in New York City would die before cutting up their carefully made prints, but here, Julian has delicately sliced up each one. Glossy white photo paper strips line the floor of his tiny studio space, like confetti after a New Year's Eve party. I peer at the picture and somehow he's made multiple faces come together as one. A wrinkled eye from one person melds into an eye of a younger person with heavy dark eyeshadow. The crinkled hands of an elderly Latine person intermingle with a child's hand, woven with such placement that it's beyond my comprehension.

"How did you do this?" I ask.

Julian pulls out a sketchpad with wafer-thin sheets of graph paper. He flips through the sheets to show me how he's planned out every part of this woven photograph in pencil with tiny numbers inside each blue graph box. My mind is completely blown. I can barely read what he's written, but it's like a blueprint for a house.

"Julian has microscopic eyes. I don't know how he sees everything so small, but he does," says Francesca.

Francesca continues to look through his sketchpad, nodding and *um-humming* at certain parts. She touches it and compares the sheets to the in-progress piece in front of us. I can't make out anything that's written.

"You need more time. This bottom half is even more complex than the top half," says Francesca.

"I have this thing in my head I can't seem to get the paper to do," says Julian.

"I hear you. I used to get so mad I couldn't make what was in here," says Francesca, tapping the side of her head, "happen on my canvas. But here's what I do. Take a walk. Wander around. Let it float to the back of your mind. Then, when you're crossing the street, it hits you. Maybe you see someone in blue and it reminds you of a blue piece that's perfect in the spot you thought was reserved for green."

"Chasing balloons," I say.

Both Francesca and Julian look at me with their heads cocked. I explain the term Daniel and I came up with about being creative. They nod their heads and Julian stands over his piece.

"I'm gonna need at least another week. Maybe two."

"Sure," I say.

Francesca gives me a thumbs-up. I take a picture of his work and put it in an album labeled *What Love Is*.

"Take your time. If it's not coming together the way you want, step away. Get some fresh eyes on it. I'm happy to meet up in a week at Sweet Yen. We can talk it out. Look at new sketches. Whatever works best for you," I say.

Julian finally smiles at me. His mood, up until this point, has been as silent as Sesame jumping on my desk. He raises one thick black eyebrow at me, then nods.

"I'd like that. Thanks, Chloe."

Our next artist works entirely outdoors. I recognize the white painter with the giant pink headphones with kitty ears on top. I notice their petite frame, broad shoulders, and short, wispy, dark brown hair. Their baggy jean overalls are covered in splotches of paint in different colors like a rainbow of skin and denim. I look down at my white-and-pink sequin Keds and wish I had put on different shoes. They splash paint on the canvas. Francesca taps them on the shoulder, and they jump slightly, yanking off their headphones.

"I didn't hear you," says Sam.

Sam hugs Francesca, who is now covered in a blend of paint colors. I wave hello. I gingerly step toward the canvas, attempting to dodge the puddles of blue, green, red, purple, and yellow on the ankle-high grass. Sunflowers tower on long limbs. Tomato plants heavy with fruit. A messy pile of orange pumpkins. Francesca pulls on Sam's headphones. They hit play, and she listens to the music, studying the canvas for several minutes. I can vaguely hear the sound of drums, but not the singer. Francesca closes her eyes and sways her head to an invisible rhythm I imagine. They are watching her, standing so close they are touching Francesca's back. When she finally opens her eyes, tears stream down.

"It's beautiful!"

Francesca passes me the headphones. I step closer to the painting. To me, it looks like a jumble of colors and lines. Some splotches so thick the stretched canvas is weighted down, dipping like a pothole. None of it makes sense, then I listen to the words of the love song. It's not a song I've heard before. The singer describes the joy of falling in love through a series of shouts and screams. The sounds are up and down. "*It's oh so quiet . . . until you fall in love.*" The brass horns match the singer's wail. Then down again. As I gaze at the painting, I see it. How the shapes match what I'm hearing. It's the energy of falling in love. Chaotic, joyful, overwhelming, like you caught a rainbow in your mouth and the light pours out of you through every pore. I tilt my head and see how the lines squiggle in the sections that feel loud in the song. The painting visualizes what I'm hearing in the headphones.

I had wanted to do this very thing with Jake's first solo show. Then, the Wi-Fi and Bluetooth went haywire.

"I can't do it again."

"Do what again?" asks Francesca.

"Nothing," I mutter.

"Tell us. Please," says Sam.

"I messed up my ex's exhibit with the same concept. I picked the perfect songs to go with his murals. I had headsets installed on the wall. I tested out all the equipment. Listened to it dozens of times. Then, it all crapped out on the actual day, and everyone left." My voice cracks.

I keep my eyes on the canvas. I can't look them in the eyes. Maybe they'll finally see I have no idea what I'm doing. I am not an art curator. I'm not even that clever.

Francesca taps my shoulders and gently guides my chin up. We are at eye level.

"It was a mistake."

"We broke up because of it. Now he's dating Mary, who's perfect in every way I'm not," I say.

"He's not the right guy for you. And you're not perfect. Can you say it with me? I am not perfect," says Francesca.

She nods at Sam who says it like a mantra. Los Angeles is getting to me because I open my mouth and say it.

"I am not perfect."

We chant this in a trio until I start laughing.

"Okay. I get it. But seriously, what if the tech doesn't work and the beauty of this painting is entirely missed since someone couldn't hear the words?"

Sam shrugs. "Who cares? Sure. It would be great if they

could hear the song that inspired this piece. But the song is one part of it. Maybe someone can't hear or can't see. I want people to touch it. You know how at museums you get scolded for standing too close?"

We nod.

"I want my viewers to get intimate with it. Get close. Touch it. Feel it. It's part of the process. You get what you want to get out of it."

"What if it gets messed up?" I ask.

"I'll make it part of the piece."

"Like touch-ups?" asks Francesca.

They nod. Inspired by their speech, I approach the piece and put my entire palm on a section that's raised and bumpy. I close my eyes and run my fingers over the canvas. Some parts are still wet. Others are hardened and dry. It's weird, but I get a different feeling like I am getting to know the painting. Like we're hanging out, chatting about whatever.

Like how I feel when I'm with Daniel. A lump lodges in my throat and I swallow it down, opening my eyes. I am in love with Daniel. And not because Jake left Los Angeles. We talk for hours, and we still have more to say. He chases balloons like I do.

"It's wonderful," I say.

"Thanks," they say. "I want to add more layers. My own found objects from my last relationship before I came out as nonbinary. Parts of my old self too."

Francesca hugs Sam and they share a quiet moment. Francesca nudges me close and soon we are in a big hug together.

After we leave Sam's backyard, Francesca comes over to my

house so we can discuss the possible placement for each piece. Mom has dinner on the table. Ahma is watching TV with Daniel on the couch. Her eyes are glassy, which means she's not fully here. She calls Daniel by her brother's name. My uncle has been dead for five years, but it's no use explaining that to her now. Daniel goes along with it, patting her knee and nodding along to whatever question she is asking her brother.

The revelation I had when I was staring at Sam's painting comes back to me, and suddenly I can't look at Daniel. I feel flushed even knowing he's here. Francesca talks a mile a minute and I'm in and out of conversation. When we're finally done eating, Francesca follows me to my room and closes the door immediately.

"What's going on with you? It's like you're daydreaming, but you're still answering me."

"I'm thinking about next steps."

"Something happened when you were touching Sam's painting. You went somewhere. I got a vibe," says Francesca.

I roll my eyes at the word *vibe*. Next she's gonna mention something about my chakra energy.

"Does it have to do with the guy downstairs?"

"No!"

Francesca's green eyes go wide. "The lady doth protest too much."

"Anyway. What do you think about the order? I had some ideas after our visit today. I know we have three more artists to check on, but hear me out."

Francesca riffles through the shoeboxes stacked in the corner of my room.

"Are these the new ones?"

I nod. "I haven't sorted through them."

Francesca peeks through the boxes, one by one. I lay out index cards on my corkboard with the artists' names and their artwork on them. I fiddle with where to place them. Maybe it doesn't make sense to put Julian next to Sam. Their painting is huge, so it'll need ample space. I put blank index cards for the remaining artists and shuffle things around on a board that looks like a mini version of the Ruby Street studio.

"What do you think of this order? It's not quite right."

I turn to Francesca. That's when I see her taking the lid off a box. The one with my stuff from Daniel. Items I've collected on our fake dates. A menu from Mochinut. The Broad museum map. The napkin Daniel doodled on from the Craft Contemporary café.

"That one's not for the exhibit," I say, reaching for it.

I attempt to pry it out of Francesca's hands, but she has a firm grip on it.

"Chloe, what is this? I thought your breakup box was already in the studio space. Plus, these items are different than what you displayed."

"How do you know it's mine?"

Francesca holds up my name tag from the Melissa Mercado performance art exhibit. She picks up each object I carefully placed in that box. I thought I had left it under my bed, but here it is, on display.

"This is a relationship box!" exclaims Francesca.

I snatch the box out of her hands and slam the lid closed.

"I have no idea what you're talking about. This is just some random stuff," I say.

"You're biting your bottom lip so you're lying."

"Oh my god, when did you become a detective?"

She approaches me with her eyes squinting. She points at the box.

"You are in love with Daniel! Everything in there is from your not-date dates."

"Shh! He's downstairs."

I collapse onto my bed with the box in my hands. It jangles, and I realize I can't deny it any longer.

"He already rejected me once. I'm verging into Creep Town. We should only be friends, like Daniel wants," I say.

"Girl, I hate to point out the obvious, but that boy's been at your house almost every single time I'm here, and it's not to hang out with your ahma. She's cool, but he's got the look whenever you come into the room."

"What look?"

Now she rolls her eyes at me. "Don't play dumb. You two are both gaga for each other. He's got it in his head that he's the king of rebounds and that you're still hung up on your ex."

Francesca sits on the bed next to me, holding my hand. "And you are pining for the guy who is literally downstairs. And yes, he was scared and said no. He said you'd be better as friends. That boy is scared shitless. You both are."

She opens the box lid and rifles through the items.

"You want to control everything. Plan it all out. Love isn't planned. It's messy. It's full of mistakes and stupid things you say. It's also dopey as hell. Makes you smile at some silly joke you two share. You collect objects and get a dumb grin when you look at them. Isn't that the whole point of *Heartifacts*?"

I bounce off my bed and stare at the long butcher paper where I'm still working on my mission statement. I grab my Muji black gel pen and write down Francesca's words. She stands behind me and reads along. She continues.

"If you want a perfect relationship, good luck with that. You have to be willing to be cracked open if you really want one. It's like a roller coaster you keep riding until you hate the ride, then you get off and find a new coaster. You made mistakes in your last relationship. Hello, that's life! You think we walk around with emoji hearts in our eyes, saying the perfect thing to the perfect person. I call bullshit. Perfect has got nothing on being so madly in love that you become a goober who collects random crap in a box," says Francesca.

"I'm a goober now?"

"Pretty much."

She wraps her arms around my neck. "Go tell him. Tell yourself the truth. Maybe he's not ready. Maybe you're not. But you'll never know if you collect stuff instead of actually doing something about it."

I lean back against her chest. She's right. Even though it terrifies me to think about getting rejected again, it's true that I am crazy about Daniel. I've tried to get him out of my head, but he's there. Francesca pats my back.

"Go," she says.

I head downstairs. Daniel is munching on some stale sesame candy that my ahma hands him. She keeps them everywhere.

"Eddie, you always choke when you eat too fast," says Ahma in Hokkien.

I quickly translate for Daniel, who exaggerates his chewing so it's slowed down. Ahma grips his cheeks and gives him a loud smacking kiss. She gets up and slowly shuffles to her room. I watch her go.

"Hey, I was wondering if you could meet me next week at the new version of *Heartifacts*," I say.

"In exchange for pineapple cakes?"

"Deal," I say.

He reaches out his hand to shake on it, but instead I kiss his cheek, surprising the hell out of us both. I bound back up the stairs with the stupidest grin on my face.

t's making me anxious to see the exhibit in scattered pieces, but I haven't been able to figure out the right flow of the room yet. I take Selena on a mini-tour of the Ruby Street studio via FaceTime, and she feigns passing out on the other end. Canvases are everywhere. Selena sees Post-its where I want pieces to go.

"What happened to my best friend? Did an alien abduct you?" she asks.

"Francesca has convinced me to keep the chaos, and we'll figure out the flow soon," I respond.

"You are so LA now. Next you're gonna tell me you actually like kombucha."

"I found this one brand that makes this awesome cherry flavor."

"STOP IT. I am booking you a ticket home. Fly your ass here and I will stuff you full of cheese pizza," she said. "By the way, the book you sent me . . ."

I grab my copy of *Breakup Bootcamp* and hold it to my camera.

"Isn't it everything?" I gush.

"It's something. Listen, I heart you, but a book isn't going to help you get over Jake. You had it bad for that guy. Like, hearts in your eyes twenty-four seven," says Selena. "You've got to get him out of your system. Flush him out like a rat in an NYC apartment bathroom."

"Ew!"

"Take the MLK weekend to enjoy the city on your own. Go to the beach or something equally annoying," says Selena. "I'm digging your new direction for *Heartifacts*. It's a little all over the place, but you'll figure it out. You always do."

"I'm still waiting for three more pieces to arrive," I say.

"Ooh, I've got to go. I'm way late for my belly-dancing class. Mwah!"

After we hang up, I stand in the center of this chaotic mess. I spin around. My eyes land on the painting by Sam, and I let them rest there. I plan to install a headset so people can listen to the song paired with it, but for the first time, I see it. I see the joy, the mess, the stars in the piece. Even though it's across the room from me and I've stared at it dozens of times, it's the first time I finally feel like I'm seeing it.

"Hey," says Daniel. "I've been calling your name."

"Oh, hey," I say.

"Wow. Looks entirely different. Messy?"

He's got large black headphones wrapped around his neck that aren't plugged in anywhere.

"Are you aware you're wearing headphones, but they're just dangling in the air?"

He looks down at the end of the cord. "Shoot. I'm knee deep in editing and I forgot they were on my neck."

I laugh. "Come over here and check out this painting. The headphones are perfect."

I wave Daniel over to it. I take the loose end and plug it into my laptop. Daniel puts the headphones on. I hit play. I don't say anything. I'm curious how he'll experience it. I love when someone sees a painting for the first time after I've seen it over and over again. I get to experience it through their fresh eyes.

As he listens to the music, I watch him. His black eyebrows bounce up and down with the music—the highs and lows. He bites his lower lip. I put my hand on the ridges of the painting. His eyes go wide and then he tentatively touches it too. He's surprised by how it feels. Our hands accidentally touch in the middle where Sam has put a red heart. Not a cutesy one, but anatomically correct. It's in the center and all the lines in the painting come from it. I don't immediately move my hand away. Neither does Daniel. For several minutes, we listen and study it together. When the song ends, Daniel tugs off his headphones.

"It's almost like the colors moved with me," he says.

"Exactly! I'm glad you got it. I'm debating whether to keep the headphones with it so viewers can listen to the song while they study it. What do you think?"

"Headphones definitely. It gives the piece an entirely new perspective. It's like the artist somehow pictured what I saw in my head and put it on a canvas," says Daniel.

I am smiling so hard I feel like my cheeks will burst. He gets it.

"Come see the rest."

I take Daniel on a tour of the new boxes, pieces, and mission statement written on brown butcher-block paper. He doesn't say much, which totally freaks me out. Maybe he hates it. It's so different than the last version. Less perfect. More of the fraying edges out. But part of me doesn't care what he thinks. It feels more alive than the last iteration.

It's more honest than I've ever been.

"What do you think?" I ask.

My heart is in my throat. Who am I kidding? Of course I care what he thinks. I care what everyone thinks about this exhibit. He's quiet longer than I'd like.

"It's real," he says slowly. "It feels like I get to see you. The real you. Not the planner girl. Not a part you played in my short film. And it's awesome. You've put yourself in here. Flaws and all."

I am full of fireworks now. Like they could actually shoot out of my mouth. Daniel touches the butcher-block paper.

"Did you write this?"

"Francesca and I did. She co-curated with me and she said this one night and it felt like the whole story of this exhibit," I say.

Daniel reads it aloud. "*You have to be willing to be cracked open if you really want to fall in love.*" He pauses. "It's inspiring."

He stares at my words on the butcher paper.

"I need to write something down," he says.

He goes to his black messenger bag and grabs his notebook, scribbling fast. I let him chase his balloons.

While he writes, I get the box. Daniel's box. I've kept it hidden behind the big abstract painting, in case he didn't show up. After Francesca discovered it the other night, I wanted to throw it out in hopes that tossing it would make my feelings disappear. But I knew it wouldn't work. My feelings for Daniel can't be contained in a box.

I sit and wait while he writes. *Are you sure you want to do this?* I say to myself on repeat. I consider putting the box back, especially as Daniel snaps his notebook shut.

"Thanks. There's a sequence I've been struggling with and reading your *Heartifacts* mission statement inspired me. I could see it. The flow. So I had to write it down."

"Snag the balloon."

"Yes."

"What's that?"

I suddenly remember I'm holding the box.

I stretch out the box to him like an offering. He takes it. I cover my hand over the lid so he can't open it just yet.

"Before you look inside, I want to say something."

I had planned what I'd say when I got to this moment, but looking into Daniel's handsome face, all the words whoosh out of my brain. The balloon has floated away. So I say what I can from my heart in all its messy awkwardness.

"You say you're not a relationship guy, and you have an album on your phone called *Rebounds*. You told me I wasn't over Jake so we couldn't date. But I kept this box of things from us. Our non-dates were the best dates I've ever been on. That's why I kept these things. The truth is I'm in love with you, Daniel. I am over Jake. Like, a million times over Jake. Another truth: I lied to you about going grocery shopping with my mom. I was with Jake. I showed him *Heartifacts*. I tried to see if there was still a spark there, but I was wrong."

Daniel backs away from me. I am losing him.

"I'm giving you this box filled with the things that remind me of you. I want to add more memories in here with you."

I am finally done speaking and I'm terrified because Daniel doesn't say anything for a few long minutes. He opens the box and looks through, picking up each item and examining it like he's a detective in a murder mystery. It's driving me crazy that he hasn't said anything yet.

This was a bad idea, Chloe.

"You're serious."

"Very."

"Chloe—"

I hold my hand up as if I can stop the words coming out of his mouth. The look on his face is enough to crush me.

"I care about you, but dating is a whole other level. If we mess up and break up, I'd lose this incredible person. This fellow creative who gets me. I don't want to mess up what's a very good thing."

I nod as he hands the box back to me. I'm definitely tossing this box out as soon as I can. It feels heavier now. I clutch it to my chest. I'm not sure how to respond. How to move forward when I feel like my heart is walking outside of my body.

"I need some time, Chloe. I know Vee will be so mad at me for not taking this chance with you. He thinks I'm an idiot for not going out with you. But I've been down this road before with other girls, and Chloe, you're not just some girl to me. You are *the* girl."

His words make me want to kiss him. Instead, I grab the box and rush out the door. Daniel calls my name. I keep moving. I don't turn back to see him because if I do, I will cry. I feel stupid for asking Daniel out and getting a big *no*. Again. I shouldn't have listened to Francesca, the hopeless romantic.

I somehow end up at home. I shut the door. Peek out the window to see if Daniel's followed me. No. Thank goodness.

Ahma is on the couch, writing on small slips of paper, practicing words she asked me to write out for her.

"Emily, I am writing a letter to Eddie. Come. Get me a stamp," says Ahma in Hokkien.

Even though I'm holding tears back, I get a stamp and an envelope. I play pretend with her, but I don't have the heart to wake her from her dream of writing to my dead uncle. I address the envelope to Selena, who will understand when it arrives. I bring the stamped, addressed envelope to Ahma, who stuffs in sheets of paper with *Hello* on them. She hands it back to me. I lick the envelope and seal it.

"I'll mail it later," I say in Hokkien.

Ahma grabs my hands and rains kisses on them. I reach forward and hug her tightly. Her body feels so frail in my arms, like she's disappearing in her clothes. I want to tell her what happened, how I told a boy I am falling in love with him and he returned my things, but she won't hear me or even have words to comfort me.

Instead, I make her dinner from yesterday's leftovers, pairing her favorites together, hoping she eats more than two bites. Slivers of orange sweet potatoes nestled in white rice with a black tea egg on top. She comes to the table when I rest the bowl down. I kiss the top of her permed gray hair—a cloud puff—and hand her the silver chopsticks my uncle gave her with her name engraved on them.

I sit with her as she eats. She tells me the same story she told me yesterday. How she met my grandfather on their wedding day. How handsome he was. So much older than her. With two kids already. She was nervous, but the moment he held her hand, she relaxed. He was a good man. I listen and nod. She pats my hand, still calling me by my mom's name or my auntie's name. I respond to her questions of if I ate already and what my workday was like, even though it's all made up.

I don't have the heart to tell her the truth because the truth, I'm learning, will break your heart.

Before I film my next vertical layout episode, I check out the comments and twenty-eight DMs on my @PlanItGirl account. I read through them and tear up. I have the best followers ever.

@pugprincess: Take your time, girl. We'll be here! We're not going anywhere. Plan Fam 4ever.

@makingplans: I loved seeing the real you.

@wishiwashi: When my ex broke up with me, I left two months blank in my Happy Memory Keeping journal. Straight up nothing. You'll get back to it when you're ready.

@stickersister: Hugs!

@LAMomma: The beach is my place to go when my head and heart are restless. Ocean waves are nature's white noise.

Selena's right. I need a break from analyzing Daniel and my failures with *Heartifacts*. On a Big Ideas dot grid sheet, I make a list of places I want to explore in LA over my three-day weekend:

LACMA
Griffith Park
Santa Monica boardwalk

I open my Happy Memory planner and pop out the pages for January 11 through 17. I lay them out in front of me, pulling out my Plan For It stickers and my Ooly fruit-scented glitter pens. Flipping through the rainbow of stickers, I smile. I pick out one that says *Weekend Adventurer* and place it on the bottom right of the page. On January 17, I draw a palm tree with my lime-green pen and a bright sun in banana yellow. In strawberry pink, I write *Beach Day*. I snap a pic to shoot over to Selena.

Me: Never thought I'd write Beach Day in the middle of
    January!
Selena: Shut up. My entire face is frostbitten right now.

I fill in the rest of my schedule and fall into my sticker rabbit hole of searching for the exact right one to complement the others. It feels so good to be back at my desk with my supplies. When I'm done with my vertical layout, I position it on my desk, flip on my ring light, and take several shots.

Thank you for the DMs that completely lifted me up.
I am so lucky to have the BEST followers. My Squad
Mentor @LAMomma suggested some beach time,
so I planned an adventure in the City of Angels.
What do you think? Stay tuned for my first time
Frankenplanning! #Planwithme

Over the next three days, I visit each one. LACMA with Francesca. A hike in Griffith Park with Vincent. I decide to go to the Santa Monica boardwalk solo. I take the LA Metro from Highland Park to Santa Monica. I have to transfer from the gold to the purple to the Expo line, but as a New Yorker, I'm used to changing trains. I'm mainly surprised by how clean the Metro is and how it is mostly empty. In NYC, an empty subway car means either no air-conditioning or a bad smell.

When I step out of the station in downtown Santa Monica, the breeze is sprinkled with salt. I inhale it. It's January, and I'm walking to the beach alongside people in wetsuits with surfboards tucked under their tan arms. How freaking bizarre. Normally, I curl under a blanket with Netflix streaming, but here, it's flip-flops, açai bowl cafés, and convertible cars. At the pier, I see a giant Ferris wheel slowly spinning in the foggy distance. I grab a cup of hot cocoa from a café and walk the length of the rickety wooden pier. All around me are mountains and ocean waves beating down on the sand. Children run up and down. I pick a brown bench to sit and sip my cocoa.

I never went anywhere alone in New York City, even though it's the perfect city to wander. No one cares if you're solo or not, but it felt weird to go to the High Line without Selena or Jake.

I shoot a video for Selena. She has to see this.

"It's January. Seventy degrees. Look at these surfers. Wild, isn't it?"

She's going to send me back a cursing message.

I pull out a notebook and sketch the Ferris wheel. I'm not an artist, but it reminds me of a box in *Heartifacts*. I've always hated Ferris wheels. Why would anyone want to dangle high in the air in slow motion? It's always in movies as this romantic gesture. A couple rides it together, declares something important to each other, and then they have an amazing kiss at the top of the wheel before it breaks down and they are stuck up at the top. The girl clutches the boy.

I sketch the Ferris wheel and the individual cars in it, thinking about the circle shape of the wheel while brainstorming. One part of *Heartifacts* doesn't make sense to me—how to make it intimate, personal, and heartfelt (pun intended). I draw the inner circle of the Ferris wheel, and pause.

That's it! A lottery wheel. I can put silly fortunes on it and people can spin it when they enter. Then visitors can walk through the main exhibit. At the end, there will be a blank wall, a stack of heart-shaped Post-it Notes, and different color markers. On the left side of the wall will be the question *What is love to you?* And on the right, *What isn't love to you?* People can write their answers on the Post-its and stick them up for others to see.

I write down *sponsors*. I'll reach out to the companies that make my favorite supplies and ask them to supply the goods. In exchange, I'll do a video showcasing how we're going to use each product for *Heartifacts*. With the sponsorship, I can open the exhibit to be free general admission to everyone, just like The Broad Museum.

Once the ideas open, I'm jotting down more and more. It's the best feeling.

I snap a selfie and send a text to Daniel: Chasing my balloons in Santa Monica.

We haven't seen each other since my confession, but he's busy editing *V-Day* for his screening in three days, so I'm trying not to be worried about it. My phone buzzes.

Vincent: Can we meet up?
Me: Sure. When?
Vincent: Today.
Me: I'm over in Santa Monica.

He sends me three wide-eye emojis.

Vincent: Hit me up when you're back in our area, like in three years.
Me: Hahaha. I took the Metro.
Vincent: You are killing me. Want me to pick you up?
Me: I'm good. See you later. Let's meet at Sweet Yen at 4:30pm.

He sends me back a thumbs-up.

On the Metro ride back, I finally map out the entire layout for *Heartifacts*. I make an extensive to-do list and action steps for what we need to get done in a month's time. Gulp. It's a lot. I text Francesca photos of my lists and the layout. She sends back: 100!

I still haven't heard back from Daniel. I know I shouldn't take it personally; he gets hyper-focused, especially with the deadline fast approaching.

When I walk into Sweet Yen Café, Vincent is already

there, sipping tea with Ahma. In front of them, two pineapple cakes on mismatched plates. Ahma hasn't touched hers. Then, I notice her outfit. A red velvet vest over a floral top and bright yellow track pants. She has on pink socks that say *My favorite salad is wine* on the side with a large wine glass. I can't help myself.

"Nice outfit, Ahma," I say in Hokkien.

She gives me a thumbs-up and points to Vincent.

Vincent says, "We went thrift-store shopping at Stash on York. She looks good in bright colors."

"Amazing," I say.

I sit down and pour myself a cup of oolong tea. It steams up. I grip the white cup with both hands and let it warm me up. I reach for a pineapple tart. Vincent smacks my hand.

"Get your own."

"Fine."

I go to the counter and Mom passes me one on a plate. The second to last one. I take a bite.

"Mom, this version tastes just like Ahma's."

"I know. We cracked the code," she says. She nods her head toward Vincent and Ahma who are sharing a laugh.

"Vincent's such a nice boy. Just like Daniel."

"You're right, Mom. They're the best."

I bring my tart back to the table. They are still laughing. I nibble and mind my business until the laughter dies down. Vincent pats Ahma's hand and speaks in Hokkien so fast I have trouble keeping up. Something about me and a boy. Ahma nods and gestures to me.

"She agrees with me," says Vincent.

"That's great. What are you both in agreement about?"

"That you and I need to plan a big romantic gesture at Daniel's screening next week."

I choke on my tart and cough out buttery crumbs. "Excuse me? You mean, the guy who has rejected me twice? I desperately tried to get him to fall for me during a Netflix night, and we both ended up crying. I've embarrassed myself enough with my creepster vibes."

Vincent makes a *tsk* sound and waves away my words. "We all act like fools after a breakup. I know you're freaked out Daniel will think you're obsessed, but Daniel talks about you constantly. Spoiler alert: I've seen the final cut of *V-Day*, and it's clear as a crystal ball that Daniel is in love with you."

I put down my tart and tea and listen. Vincent leans forward, touching my hand.

"In my humble opinion, he wastes his time with girls who don't deserve him, so good riddance. But I like you. We need to get through that thick skull of his."

"What are you suggesting? I already confessed my feelings for him twice. I kissed him. I've done my work to convince him that I'm completely, one hundred percent over Jake, and he still says he needs time," I say. "I'm done."

Vincent grabs my hands. "I told Daniel I'd moderate a Q&A after the screening. He resisted, but I insisted. At the Q&A, I'll call on you as the first question."

Vincent adds a flourish with his hands.

"And what question will I be asking?"

"I don't know. You're the creative one. Come up with something."

He looks over at Ahma and says something under his breath to her.

"Hey!" I say, "I heard that."

Vincent squints his eyes at me. "I was hoping you would."

"I'm not a chicken."

"Weren't you the one who figured out who the Yarn Bomber was?"

"I regret sharing the details of my life with you. Besides, I spent weeks tracking him down. You're giving me three days. And like I said, he's already said no. What one singular question am I going to ask him that will change his mind?"

Vincent shrugs his shoulders and sighs loudly. "You like him?"

"I more than like him. He makes me happy. He gets what I do. When we go to a museum together, I see the art differently. His feedback is invaluable. He treats my ahma like his own. He's basically the best person I know."

Vincent stands up, kisses Ahma on the cheek, and drops some cash on the table.

"Then you'll figure it out. Love has a mysterious way of inspiring the wildest of gestures. When Connor and I first started dating, he left me love notes in my car. He hid them in the dashboard. The trunk. Glove compartment. One time, he snuck one into the window so when I rolled it down, it popped into my lap. When you're in love, you figure out how to express it," says Vincent.

He leaves. Great. Not only do I have a massive to-do list, now I have to plan the biggest romantic gesture ever by next week.

It dawns on me that my *Plan It Girl* followers might have some ideas for me. I hop on to my account and post a question.

What's the last romantic gesture that made you swoon?
   Could be a movie, book, TV show, or your real life.
   Share away!

After I post, I realize Daniel might see it, but he's on a social media shutdown until after the screening. Phew!

I walk home with Ahma. Fix dinner for her. Shoot out some emails regarding sponsorship. When I finally get a chance to look at my poll question, I see hundreds of responses. I scroll through them.

@writeitdown Write a love song and play it over the school
   speaker system.
@colormepretty Send flowers with an inside joke as the note.
@planwithme Cook their favorite meal.
@iambookish For my promposal, my girlfriend got her cheer
   squad to ask me to be her date with an impromptu cheer.
@wishiwashi Flash mob that spells out, "I love you."

I don't know what it is about my readers sharing their favorite moments, but it makes me light up from the inside. This is what I should include in *Heartifacts*—the joy of falling in love. I've been so focused on the misery of heartbreak that I forgot why we crush in the first place.

That's what I have to show Daniel. He's focused on the pain. The disappointment. He thinks I am just another girl who will break his heart. I need to show him I could be the one who makes him really happy.

I grab a bunch of Post-it Notes. I replay the video of Daniel and me kissing in Craft Contemporary. Our first kiss, which reminds me of our second kiss: Halloween movie night. Closing my eyes, I remember every detail. Every heart-stopping moment. Then, I write down what I want to say, adding numbers to the top of each note. When I'm done, I stare at my words.

Vincent wanted a big gesture for Daniel, and he'll get one.

V incent has been texting nonstop since I asked for his help. He gave me a list of three people who will each take one Post-it Note. I slip the notes into my silver purse. I put on my best outfit—a sparkly jumpsuit I bedazzled myself with giant silver sequins. The shiny disks shimmer and rustle as I head downstairs. Ahma is watching TV.

"Aye. So pretty. Sit," she says in Hokkien.

I do. She takes my hand and clasps it between her tiny, wrinkled hands.

"Chloe, you like Daniel."

My jaw drops open. She pinches my cheek.

"He likes you. Every time you walk into the room, his eyes go to you. Your dad was the same way with your mom. Now, go. Enjoy party."

"Thanks, Ahma," I say. "Want to be my date tonight?"

She shakes her head. "Too much for me."

I kiss her soft cheek as she waves me away. It's been a while since she really saw me, and it feels amazing.

I take a car over to the screening room in Burbank. Daniel said he wanted something small, so when I arrive I'm surprised to see Daniel wearing a black suit, looking hot on a mini red carpet. He stands against a white backdrop, the words *V-Day* printed across it, with Vincent by his side.

Vincent greets a line of people behind a red velvet rope. He perks up when we make eye contact.

"Chloe, you're here!"

A flash goes off. Vincent gives me a quick dab on the cheek and moves me toward Daniel. Super obvious.

"Hey," says Daniel.

"I thought you wanted something small."

"This is all Vee's doing. Including the suit," says Daniel, waving at the carpet and backdrop behind him.

"He did a great job. The suit," I say as my eyes linger down, "is perfect."

"You look great too. Thanks for coming. Is it okay to admit I'm nervous and sweating through the armpits of this very expensive button-down shirt Vee loaned me?"

There's the Daniel I know.

"Umma, Halmeoni, this is my friend Chloe Chang," says Daniel, waving over two older Korean women.

His mother looks like him. Her black eyebrows arch as she looks me up and down. His grandmother has short white hair and Daniel's smile. I bow slightly and cobble together the little bit of Korean I know.

"*Annyeonghaseyo,*" I say as a hello.

I'm rewarded with a smile from his mom. His grandmother pinches my cheek. They turn their attention back to Daniel.

Before I can say anything else, a few of his friends arrive and he's surrounded by a group of people who want a photo with him. More and more people arrive so I shuffle off to

the side. I watch as he greets everyone with a warm smile or
a high five. He's in his element. I'm so lost in staring at him
that I don't notice Francesca has arrived until she's standing
next to me.

"Hey, girl. Where's my note?"

Oh! The notes. I riffle through my purse and carefully ex-
tract the notes. I've assigned her number two, which means I
have to go first and kick it all off. The notes are stuck together
and when I try to hand them to Francesca, the entire pile hits
the ground and someone steps on them.

A black footprint from the bottom of a shoe is all over
my note.

"This is a bad sign, isn't it?"

Francesca helps me collect the notes.

"It's a sign from the universe that I shouldn't go through
with this," I say.

"I thought you didn't believe in signs from the universe
or any of that hippie crap," says Francesca with a grin on
her face.

"Los Angeles is seeping into my soul."

She grips my shoulders and looks me in the eyes. "Listen,
whatever happens, you'll be fine. You don't need a guy to fulfill your life. Look at you. You curate art exhibits. You have a
wildly successful YouTube channel. If he rejects you, which
I seriously doubt he will, then it's his huge, big, gigantic,
stupid loss."

I hug her tightly. "Thank you," I whisper.

As the crowd slowly moves into the screening space, I look
at the text Vincent sent to help me find the three other people

who will read notes. He assured me these people know exactly what to do. He's filled them in.

1. Tasty D. He's the white dude in neon pink camo pants. His real name is Darren, but we all call him Tasty D.
2. Jujube. I forgot her real name, but this is what we call her since forever. She'll be wearing giant hoop earrings with the word hope on them. She's known Daniel since preschool days.
3. Mrs. Haefelein. Daniel has no idea she'll be at the screening so I saved her for last. She should be wearing a floral pantsuit. Make sure her note is the best one.

I work my way through the crowd. Tasty D is easy to spot in those pants. He gives me a head nod and tucks away his note in his pants pocket. Jujube is a super-tall Asian American girl. When I hand her the Post-it, she gives me a hug.

"Daniel talks about you all the time. Nice to meet you," says Jujube.

She reads her note and smiles. "Vee and I have been conspiring for years to get Dan Dan hooked up with a cool girl. My previous attempts turned into total Milk Duds, but Vee vouches for you."

"Thanks."

Now I'm even more nervous that my plan won't work. Every seat in the theater is full, which means an entire room of people will watch me fail miserably at being a romantic. Cool. Two women have floral pantsuits on. What are the freaking odds? I approach one.

"Are you Mrs. Haefelein?"

"Excuse me?"

The look on her face tells me I have the wrong pantsuit.

"Sorry, I thought you were someone else."

"Chloe? I'm joking. Vincent told me about the notes. I am happy to take one."

I hand Mrs. Haefelein the note.

"Young love is inspiring. I'm Daniel's freshman English teacher. He used to take every English assignment and turn it into a video. All of his essays were short films. His cinematic take on Romeo and Juliet as actual star-crossed lovers is a video I still use in my classes today. He created a constellation storyline to illustrate how their relationship sent ripples through the cosmos and changed the course of literature. I knew someday I'd be watching one of his movies on a big screen."

"It's pretty amazing, isn't it?"

The lights in the theater dim.

"Good luck tonight, Chloe," says Mrs. Haefelein.

I rush over to my seat and sit three aisles behind Francesca. Vincent suggested we spread out throughout the room, so it has a bigger effect. She looks at me and I give her a thumbs-up.

I see Daniel in the front row, biting his fingernails. Vincent takes his hand. The lights dim.

INT. HEARTIFACTS EXHIBIT—NIGHT

Vincent sees his Connor breakup box and approaches it.
Daniel places a hand on Vincent's shoulder.

CHLOE

(off-screen)

Hi! I'm Chloe, the curator of this exhibit. I'd appreciate
you not filming. There's a sign at the entrance about
video and photography being strictly prohibited.

*Vincent cries. He pulls out a black-and-white photo booth
strip. He places it on the table next to the other half of
the photo strip in the exhibit display.*

VINCENT

I told you it was here, Daniel.

FADE OUT.

INT. DANCE STUDIO STAGE—DAY

*Vincent, dressed in a black body suit, sits on a metal
stool.*

DANIEL

The first time you knew Connor saved those objects was
at the *Heartifacts* exhibit?

Vincent bites his lower lip.

VINCENT

Yes. It gave me [*pauses*] closure. We went from talking
every single day to nothing. But when I saw what he
saved, I realized we meant something to each other, even
if the relationship was done.

The opening title sequence begins. As it moves forward,
I see Daniel took my note and dialed back on the intense

interviews with corporate CEOs and the stark history of Valentine's Day and made it more personal. He manages to weave in the historical elements with the companies that make chocolate and greeting cards, and the florists with human stories about love and loss. Some sections are new to me, which means he had to shoot and put together a lot of footage in the past few weeks.

INT. DANIEL'S BEDROOM—NIGHT

Daniel sits in a director's chair. Movie posters on the walls.

DANIEL

I don't normally work in front of the camera, but a good friend told me I needed to add more heart to this story. With that, here's mine.

Slideshow of Daniel's baby photos: Daniel in a red onesie. Daniel crawling. Daniel dressed in a small blue-and-gold Korean gown, in front of an ornate display of rice cakes, flowers, and oranges.

DANIEL

(voiceover)

My parents divorced when I was three. I grew up with my umma and halmeoni. I never saw my parents together. I only heard them argue over the phone. I didn't know what a good relationship looked like. When it came to dating, I was hopeless.

REBOUNDS slideshow plays.

Daniel's selfie in Yogurtland with a couple making out in the background.

Daniel at Runyon Canyon with a girl sitting on a rock away from him.

Daniel in the back seat of a limo, giving a peace sign. The limo driver is next to him.

DANIEL

(voiceover)

Every girl I dated ditched me to get back with their ex. It seemed like love skipped over me, so I gave up. I stopped looking. Then, I met this girl.

FREEZE FRAME FLASHBACK: *Chloe at the first* Heartifacts *exhibit, approaching Vincent and Daniel.*

DANIEL

You might recognize her from earlier. I fell for her the moment we met.

(beat)

Except, she had an ex-boyfriend who'd broken her heart. I convinced myself I'd get over her. When she asked me out, I said no.

PHOTO: *Black-and-white still from Daniel and Chloe's movie night. Daniel and Chloe laughing.*

DANIEL

I made a serious documentary about romance being manufactured by big corporations to make money on

Valentine's Day. But the truth is, I'm afraid to tell her I want to be her boyfriend. It's easier to hide behind a no.

INT. DANCE STUDIO STAGE—DAY

Vincent stretches on the dance floor with his back facing the camera.

DANIEL

What would you tell someone about heartbreak?

VINCENT

(laughs)

Do it. Then do it again. Some people might think I'm too young to have an opinion on love. I've had exactly one and a half relationships in my life, but Connor breaking up with me inspired me to choreograph this new piece.

Vincent moves close to the mirror and barre.

Instrumental piano music plays.

CLOSE ON: *Vincent's face in the mirror.*

Vincent backs away from the mirror in long strides.

He curls into a ball in the middle of the floor.

Music changes to thumping rhythm.

Vincent rises, stands up straight with his arms stretched to the ceiling. As the music crescendos to a steady beat, Vincent spins and leaps into the air. When he lands on his feet, he flops back like he's snapped in half.

Music stops.
Vincent breathes heavily on the floor.
FADE OUT.
INT. DANCE STUDIO STAGE—DAY
Vincent sits in a chair, composed.

DANIEL
(off-camera)
How did choreographing that new piece help you get
over your breakup?

VINCENT
(smiles)
I spent days and nights alone in the studio, working it
out. Some days, I was on the floor, bawling my eyes
out. Other days, I was so angry I stomped all over the
studio. The physicality of dance allowed my feelings
to come out.
CUT TO:
INT. DANCE STUDIO STAGE—DAY
Vincent dances alone in the studio.

VINCENT
(voiceover)
This piece reminded me I have a great love in my life.
(pause)
Dance. I put my hurt there and it gave me life again.
FREEZE FRAME: *The silhouette of Vincent's body.*

CUT TO:

INT. DANIEL'S BEDROOM—DAY

A few beats of silence. Daniel smiles at the camera.

DANIEL

I started this documentary to prove Valentine's Day is a
manufactured money-making scheme. But now that
I'm done, I realize all I've ever wanted is to be more
than just some guy. I want to be someone to love.

FADE TO BLACK.

I can't help myself. I clap loudly. Francesca whistles from
her seat. The audience joins in with loud applause. Vincent
leads Daniel to the front of the room, right in front of the
screen. Daniel takes a bow.

Vincent and another friend set up two black director
chairs. Daniel takes one. Vincent takes a seat with a microphone in hand. Vincent waits until the noise dies down.

"Let's hear it one more time for the director of *V-Day!*"

A rousing round of applause. Daniel smiles. Vincent leads
the discussion, and I enjoy listening to Daniel answer about
his creative process and how he worked on the film.

Vincent says, "When you asked me to participate, I was
floored. I knew you originally had a different vision for the
story. Why did you decide to include more of yourself and
your friends into your final cut?"

Daniel says, "A friend gave me feedback after I showed
her an early cut. At first, I was so pissed about what she said.
But she was right. For a documentary about love, it missed a

lot of the humanity in it. I realized our collective stories are more powerful than hearing CEOs talk about profits from Valentine's Day."

I feel myself beaming like I'm covered in glitter. I'm sweating. Vincent's next question will be my cue for my *big romantic gesture*. Here goes nothing.

"Now, let's take questions from the audience. The girl in silver sequins. What's your question for Daniel?"

My ass is stuck to the seat. Daniel perks up when his eyes connect with mine. Cool. I look around. Francesca mouths, *Ready?*

I stand up. My knees knock together so loud I swear they are stereo speakers with my heart as the bass. I stare at my yellow Post-it Note like it'll give me courage. Every eye is on me.

You've got this, Chloe.

I say, "Daniel, I want to see."

Francesca stands and reads her Post-it: "The world through your eyes."

Tasty D says, "I want to be the one who makes you believe."

Jujube chimes in, "In love and in yourself."

When Mrs. Haefelein stands up, Daniel's jaw drops open.

Mrs. Haefelein ends, "I want to be your girlfriend." She chuckles. "To be clear, the young lady over there is asking. Not me."

The entire audience laughs as I turn so bright red that beets would pale in comparison.

Damn it. I got the Post-it Note order way wrong. I should've ended with me saying what Daniel's teacher said. *Oh, Chloe.* I stare at the ground, hoping the floor can swallow me whole.

I don't notice the room is quiet again.

I don't notice Daniel has gotten out of his director's chair.

Or that he's walking down the theater aisle to me.

I do hear him when he says, "I'd love to be your boyfriend, Chloe Chang."

I feel him when he kisses me on the lips and wraps me in an embrace that knocks me off my feet in a different way.

Our first real kiss. Francesca whistles loudly, then Vincent. The whole screening room cheers.

When we pull apart, I whisper in his ear, "I loved the final cut. The flashbacks and voiceovers were so heartfelt and endearing."

"Thanks to you," he says back.

I glance out into the audience. I make eye contact with Francesca who gives me a huge wink and thumbs-up. I smile.

Daniel returns to the stage to finish his Q&A. I'll be honest. I don't remember a single word. Afterward, Daniel is surrounded by his supporters. He and his former English teacher are laughing and talking closely. I rush over to Francesca. My cheeks are flushed and warm. She grips my face and plants a big kiss on my cheek.

"You did it!"

"I almost died."

"I'm talking to a ghost?"

"Yup," I say.

She wraps her arm around my shoulders. I lean against her for a second.

"Thank you. If you weren't second, I would've chickened out."

She squeezes my arm. "Come. Let's go out and celebrate."

Francesca purses her lips together and emits such an ear-piercing whistle that the entire room freezes. She hollers out, "Nerds, see you at Highland Bowl for the after-party!"

She turns to me and says, "See you there, girl."

She takes off with her crew. Daniel waves me over. He and his teacher are still talking.

"Mrs. H, I'd like you to meet my girlfriend, Chloe."

"We met." She smiles warmly at me. "Daniel told me all about your gallery exhibit. I'm interested in bringing my freshman English class."

"I'm happy to talk to Lourdes, the owner of Ruby Street, and set that up," I say. "If we can work it out, I can lead a personal tour."

She turns to Daniel and says, "I'm so proud of you. Keep me posted on what happens next with the film."

She smiles at me. "It was so nice to meet you."

We talk to a few more people. Daniel introduces me as his girlfriend each time.

When we're finally alone, Daniel kisses me. This time, it's slow, deliberate, and hot. I am floating away in a cloud of happiness. His full lips are gentle against mine.

"Excuse me," calls out Vincent. "When you two are done lip-locking, head over to the Bowl. We'll see you sickening lovers over there."

"Thanks, Vee," says Daniel. His eyes are on me. "I can't believe all of this happened tonight. Am I in a dream?"

"You were adamant that we were better as friends. You insisted. In fact, you turned me down twice before. What changed your mind?"

Daniel tilts my chin until I look up into his beautiful brown eyes.

"Editing my doc. I'd see something in a scene and want to text you. Or I'd finish a two-hour edit and wish for a doughnut date with you. It felt like torture to know you existed in the world and I wasn't your boyfriend. My brain knew before my heart that you are the one for me."

I jump up to kiss the side of his head. "Thank you, Daniel's brain." I rain kisses from his ear to his lips. "Your documentary turned out amazing. Now I want to watch more docs."

Daniel grins. "Stop. I'm already in love with you." He pauses as his eyes run over my body. "You look beautiful in this silver jumpsuit."

"You should wear this suit every single day."

He leans down to kiss me. My hands run through his thick black hair. His hand is on my butt. I cup his. Suddenly, I can't remember not touching Daniel's body. We are electric, buzzing from the high of being alone and finally being honest. Words are gone, replaced with hot kisses along my neck. My hands hunger for underneath his white button-down shirt. He touches my stomach and now my hip. I return the gesture. Daniel stops kissing me for a minute.

"We really should leave for the after-party," says Daniel.

I nod. "Totally."

I tug the edge of his shirt to pull him closer to me. His hand is on my thigh. I am breathless.

Daniel whispers in my ear, thrilling me, "Never stop kissing me."

I reply by kissing his ear, raining kisses along his jawline until I reach his full lips.

"I intend to never stop kissing you, Daniel Kwak."

"Stop talking, Chloe."

I don't talk for a deliciously long time.

have three weeks left to pull off this major revamp of *Heartifacts,* set to open on Valentine's Day, which sounded like a lot of time twenty-one days ago. Today, I'm staring at five to-do lists, twenty-eight reminders on my phone, and 251 unanswered emails. Daniel is busy editing a final cut of his documentary for the festival submission deadline. Our relationship is strictly text messages for now.

On a Saturday, I'm sorting through sixty-two shoeboxes at Ruby Street. T-minus fourteen days! My *Plan It Girl* community came through, and now I'm drowning in people's breakup stuff. Francesca arrives, surveys the room, then hands me a Sweet Yen cup.

"Wow," says Francesca. "Your dad sent this along. He knew you'd need it."

I take a generous sip. Dad's mochas are smooth electric energy. I wander over to the wall where we will display the *What Love Is and What Love Isn't* pieces.

"You're doing that thing in your head," says Francesca.

"What thing?" I ask.

"Silently freaking out. Your eyebrows shoot up to the ceiling."

"The wall isn't ready!"

Francesca takes out her phone. "You texted me some font

ideas. I'll start sketching." She grabs a ladder and climbs up to the top of the wall. "Hand me a pencil."

"You can just look at a font and re-create it?"

"Yeah."

"That's badass," I say.

"I know." Francesca glances at her watch. "Arte Para La Gente is coming in ten minutes. We'll sort through the boxes and organize them."

"You are a lifesaver."

"You asked me to co-curate. You think I'm gonna leave you out to dry? We're in this together," says Francesca.

While she draws on the wall, I hand out log sheets to Francesca's club so they can write down the contents of each box. I distribute the boxes, then sit down with my own stack.

The first one: stacks of notebooks, half-used pencils embossed with *But First, Coffee,* and movie tickets. *Why we broke up: he left for college. I left for college. We decided it was best to start fresh. It sucks, but we're only eighteen. I want to be on my own, even though it hurts to say that.*

The next one: love letters between two people named Peter and LJ. It would be cool to stack up the letters in two piles so viewers could see the many letters in here without opening them.

The third box: small superhero LEGOs. An anonymous letter includes a specific list of how the toys should be placed in the display. They even included a blue LEGO base. I follow the detailed instructions on the note. When I'm done, all the superheroes are lined up like chess pieces. At the bottom of the instructions, there's one line: *If you see this, I hope you know you will always be my superhero.*

Wow. Intense.

When we're all done sorting and logging, I drag over a huge rolling dry-erase board. I write down themes as the group shares what they found—letters, toys, drawings, music.

I write down a theme on each Post-it Note and stick it to the floor. The group and I look up and down the long line of boxes we have.

"Chloe, I have an idea," says Monica.

I nod.

"I'd put Peter and LJ next to the coffee couple. They flow naturally to me," says Monica.

"Yes!" I say.

An hour later, we've organized all the boxes. One step done. A million more to go.

"Thanks so much, everyone! I really appreciate your help."

I slap high fives to the group and follow them out to the front door. Daniel is there, holding two Mochinut boxes.

"I thought you could use these."

I kiss him on the cheek and snag my doughnut. "You read my mind."

He leans in and nuzzles my neck. I temporarily forget whatever random problem popped into my head earlier. I lead him back inside the studio space and we sit down on top of brown boxes.

I point to Francesca, who has on headphones and is focused entirely on the wall. Shapes of words appear under her hands.

"She is freehand-drawing a font I like on the wall. She amazes me," I say. I bite into the Nutella doughnut. "Oh my god. This is heaven."

A twinkle in Daniel's eye. "Did you proclaim food from Los Angeles as amazing?"

I lightly smack his arm. "Don't tell anyone in New York. I don't want to lose my cred."

Daniel wraps his arms around me in a hug. "I won't tell a soul."

We make out for a few good minutes, until the panic sets in. I hop up.

"You are distracting me. I am super-duper behind on my to-do list."

He pulls me close. "I'll go. My documentary is still not working."

"Your last cut looked great to me."

"I need it to be—"

"Fantastic," I say, finishing his sentence.

"Exactly. You know how it goes. I'll stop distracting you. Come by later?"

"Definitely," I say.

I stare at Daniel's butt as he walks out. I smile to myself, then get back to work.

Francesca and I keep hustling through the night until a pizza arrives. Francesca offers the delivery guy some cash. He waves it off.

"It's all been taken care of," he says.

We sit down with paper plates and hungrily devour our slices. It's not New York pizza quality, but it's halfway decent. I look up at the wall space where Francesca has outlined *What Love Is and What Love Isn't*. Her version of the Opulent font is even better than I could've imagined.

"You're wildly talented," I say.

She smiles widely. "Wait until you see it all colored in. It's gonna be popping. You know, if you like that, what if we did the same for the front entrance? Like, a bold, hand-lettered font."

I glance over at the entrance with my butcher-paper mission statement. I've never really loved it because it seemed too simple. With Francesca's design, it'll look 1,000 percent better.

"What would I do without you?"

"I don't know. Probably not have a cool boyfriend or the amazing finishing touches that you do," says Francesca.

We laugh.

"But for real, you helped me. I was down in the dumps about this breakup, and I feel like we both got to channel sadness into some kickass art."

A buzz comes through on my phone.

Daniel: How's the not-as-good-as-NY pizza?
Me: Haha. Thank you for sending it. We were starving. I'll
    save you a slice.

I slip my phone back into my pocket.

"I remember that look," says Francesca. "Every time their name shows up, it's like you remember how cute they are."

"Jake never did stuff like this. Order me pizza or check on me. He was cool, but he was focused on his art. I feel so lucky to be Daniel's first real girlfriend. And also terrified."

"Terrified?"

"What if I screw everything up?"

We toss out our plates. Francesca climbs the ladder to continue working on her lettering.

"You *are* going to screw up something. Relationships aren't about being perfect. You know that."

"I'm his first everything."

"Including?" Her eyebrows raise up. I nod.

"Well, that's different."

"I know!" I say, throwing up my hands. "Jake was my first. I wasn't his. It felt easier. Like driving in a car with someone who already had their license."

"I gotcha. It's a big responsibility, for sure, but you two will figure it out. I've found every couple has trouble figuring out that stuff, even if they've driven lots of cars. Look at you making car metaphors. Los Angeles has got its hold on you, girl."

I stick out my tongue. "It's happening. I'm being converted. I might even complain that fifty degrees is cold."

Francesca laughs. "Fifty degrees is the Arctic. Better not tell Selena that. She'll yell at you so loud that the entire island of Manhattan will hear it."

I pause from looking at the canvases against the wall for a sec. "Have you and Selena been talking?"

Francesca shrugs her shoulders. "She's cool. That's all."

"I didn't figure you for a long-distance relationship."

"We're just talking," says Francesca.

"That's what she said too."

Francesca tosses a dry cloth at me. "You knew? Why are you playing like you didn't know?"

I wiggle my eyebrows. "It's totes obvi from how your face lights up when a text from Selena comes through in our group chat. It's awesome that my two amazing, wonderful friends dig each other."

Francesca smiles, then slips on her headphones. I let her continue drawing without teasing her further.

I lay out the canvases in a row along the wall, examining each one. When art comes in, I like to glance over it and go with my gut. What feels like a natural progression for my eye to see. I rearrange them over and over until it finally feels right.

I bend down and study Sam's painting up close. I don't put on the song that goes with it. I want to see what it feels like without the music, in case it doesn't work.

They've changed the original piece, adding more layers. They created two other paintings and the series is titled *Coming Out*. I run my hands along the bumps and ridges. They've embedded found objects in the paint. Some you can see. A bottle cap. Others you can't. Like a handwritten note. I move to the second painting and the landscape changes to brighter colors. The center is a yellow heart with tiny little hearts inside. I touch the tiny, heart-shaped beads that glitter and sparkle in the light. They have a trail of hearts coming out of the main one. The trail turns into candy hearts—the ones that taste like chalk and are everywhere on Valentine's Day with silly messages on them like *True Love*. The third painting continues the candy hearts, and all the colors from the previous two are melded together in the last one. A mixture of bright colors, dull ones, and rainbow glitter is rubbed into the canvas, almost aggressively.

I touch the edge of glitter. Some flakes off. Oops. Under the glitter, I see in black Sharpie words that Sam has written underneath. *L-O* starts the phrase.

I can't help myself. I scratch the rest of the surface like a cheap lottery ticket until three words reveal themselves in the center of the last painting.

Love yourself first.

I stare at the words and let them wash over me. After Jake broke up with me, I thought I would never be back here. I chalked up my failures at a relationship and my first big solo show to mean I wasn't any good at either.

Before I leave for the night, I hang the three pieces together, leaving my imprint in the piece—the reveal of the words—as part of the final story. A nod to how far I've come.

t's opening night for *Heartifacts* version 3.0. I'm outside Ruby Street in a red wrap dress, and I've been standing here for twenty minutes, frozen like a snowman. The exhibit doesn't open for another hour. I feel a buzz from my phone.

Jake: Break a leg tonight, C-Lo.

I stare at the text, unsure how to respond, as Daniel arrives with his Smoko boba tea box wrapped with a red bow. He kisses my cheek. I slip my phone in my pocket and focus on the warmth of Daniel's body next to mine.

"For opening night," he whispers.

I unwrap the bow. Nestled inside are the index cards from our first brainstorm. His name tag from the Melissa Mercado performance. An empty Choco Pie wrapper. I laugh, holding up the wrapper.

"Did you save this from our movie night?"

"Maybe."

He taps the box. "It's yours."

"What? No."

"Yes," says Daniel. "It's my Valentine's Day gift for you so you have to take it."

I hold the boba tea storage box against my heart. "Thank you. I love it."

I turn to the doors of Ruby Street. I say to myself, "You can do this, Chloe."

"You can," says Daniel, squeezing my cold hand.

Together, we step into the gallery space. Daniel hasn't seen the absolute final version. Even when he met me here last night, I didn't let him see anything. I made him put on a blindfold.

I want his unfiltered reaction. He steps into the space. Completely silent as he wanders through. My hands turn clammy. I stand at the edge, waiting to hear. My stomach somersaults. He turns to me.

"Chloe, it's amazing. Actually, amazing doesn't even cover it. It's stupendous. Is that a word? It sounds like a made-up word."

My nervousness breaks up as I laugh. "*Stupendous* is a real word."

He gestures around him. "Look at what you did."

"What Francesca and I did. The artists. My planner community. We did this," I say. I reach for his hand. "I want to show you something."

I walk him over to Jake's and my box, pointing to the *why we broke up* placard.

"I rewrote it," I say.

He reads it silently.

Why we broke up: I moved to Los Angeles. He's in NYC. He dumped me with this box. He said he couldn't do long-distance. As weird as it sounds, I'm grateful he broke up with me so we could both move on to what's best for each of us.

Daniel pulls me in for a hug and I melt into him.

"I love this new version," he says, his lips brushing against my ear. "Now, I want an exclusive private tour with the curator."

"Right this way," I say.

He keeps his arm wrapped around my waist, asking me about each part, sharing what he loves, and when he talks a mile a minute, I know he really loves it. It's not an act to be nice. He genuinely loves it. The icicles in my hands defrost as I realize he's right. It's better than the original idea. The original idea was a start. This version is the finish line.

"Ready to launch this baby?" asks Francesca.

Vincent is right behind her. He holds two giant bouquets of red roses. He presents one to me and another to Francesca. Then he gives Daniel a single red rose and starts clapping for him.

I turn to Daniel. "Did you turn in your submission?"

He blushes.

"Oh my god!" I shout, then smack Daniel's arm. "Why didn't you say anything!"

"You have your show."

Vincent hugs Daniel. "His final cut is amazing."

Francesca bonks Daniel over the head with her bouquet. "I would shout the news from the rooftops. You wouldn't be able to shut me up about it."

Vincent points at Francesca. "Take a page out of that girl's book, D."

He waves his best friend away, but Daniel's smile is pure sunshine. My bashful, amazing boyfriend.

I hug him tightly, whispering, "I'm proud of you. You've worked hard to finish it."

I kiss him right on the lips, then pull away, remembering we have a lot to do before the doors open.

"Right, we have to get rolling. Vincent, you're on press duty. Here's my clipboard with who RSVPed. Anyone on this list should get a special tour with me," I say. "Please set up the press kits on the front table, including the name tags."

I hand over my floral clipboard. Vincent salutes me.

"Daniel, please make sure all the tech is in working order. Your slideshow, film, the music for the specific pieces."

He kisses my cheek then goes to start checking all the equipment.

Francesca comes over. "I'll head over to pick up the food. Your dad texted that they're ready."

"I'll go. You stay. I could use some fresh air."

"You sure?"

"Definitely."

As I step out, I take a long look at the final exhibit. It's so different than anything I've done before. It's not as picture perfect as previous shows.

I walk down the street to my parents' shop. I check my reflection in random storefront windows and notice I'm actually smiling.

When I get to the shop, I see Ahma, dressed in a long silver dress with her pearl necklace she only wears for special occasions. Dad is packing the last pineapple cakes and heart-shaped mochi into pink boxes. Mom is dressed up too.

"What's going on here?" I ask.

"Big art show," says Ahma in Hokkien.

I look at my parents with wide eyes. I never invited Ahma because I didn't think she'd remember or understand. The last time she came to see a show I produced, I was in eighth grade. Ahma came as my date to my art club fundraiser. After that, her health started to go downhill, so she hasn't seen anything I've done since then.

"I got the food. I'll load it all in the truck. You take Ahma," says Dad, winking at me.

I oblige and hold out my arm to her. She slips her hand through my arm, gripping me as she walks forward slowly. Mom follows. Together, the three of us make our entrance to *Heartifacts*.

When the doors open at 8 P.M., I see a small crowd, and two people in the press line. We let the reporters in early. Vincent is perfect at talking to the media. When he escorts the journalists to me, they are laughing along with whatever joke he's told. I quickly glance at their name tags and publications. *Angeleno Art Now* and Mia Vasquez. Oh my god. I recognize her name! She runs the teen program at the Museum of Contemporary Art. I recover from my momentary shock and lead them through the exhibit.

"What inspired you to relaunch the exhibit? From my understanding, it was quite successful as an immersive Instagram experience," asks Jean Trinh, the writer for *Angeleno Art Now*.

"Great question. I'm a fan of your writing by the way," I say.

"Thank you," says Jean with a smile.

"Basically, I realized my previous format didn't honor my

original vision for the show. It became more of a spectacle than a thoughtful examination of love and heartbreak. Working with local artists, like my co-curator Francesca Cruz, brought to my attention the many ways we can interpret what *Heart-ifacts* means. Relationships imprint on us, and I thought asking artists to add their voices to my basic concept could elevate the show to another level," I say.

Jean jots notes in her notepad. I lead the group to Francesca who is commanding quite an audience. We make eye contact. I raise my eyebrows three times as our secret code. Francesca joins me, shaking hands with each person.

"Francesca, as co-curator, how did you contribute to taking *Heartifacts* into a new direction?" asks Mia Vasquez.

We rehearsed some key phrases earlier today. Vincent played the reporter, drilling us on questions we might be asked. Lucky for us, he asked this very question, so Francesca answers with a huge smile, radiating confidence.

"When Chloe presented the idea to me of *What Love Is and What Love Isn't*, I asked Arte Para La Gente to contribute individual pieces. I think it's important that stories include diverse voices so romance isn't entirely defined by one voice. Working with my collective, we discussed ways we could express what it means to fall in love," says Francesca.

We time it well and arrive in front of the *What Love Is and What Love Isn't* wall. In fifteen minutes, the doors will open for the general public. The reporters examine the pieces. Mia Vasquez points at the sign on the wall that says PLEASE TOUCH.

"Are you really inviting viewers to touch a piece of painted art?"

Francesca and I nod enthusiastically. I gently touch the canvas. Mia and Jean are intrigued.

"The piece is meant to be interacted with and I invite you all to take some time with it."

I look over at Daniel who waits for my signal. I give him a thumbs-up and the song pumps in on cue. We set up two Bluetooth speakers so it would give a surround-sound effect, and it works beautifully. Phew.

"The artist chose this specific song to be played when viewers examine the three canvases. They wanted viewers to have a unique experience of matching the love song with how they interpret what love is," says Francesca.

"What if the canvases get damaged?" asks Jean.

"Sam, the artist, will be repainting them every few days. They had this idea that when we're in a relationship, our lives change. The canvas within us changes. They wanted to have an ongoing conversation with viewers," I say.

Mia, the MOCA teen program director, comes forward first and touches the canvases. She presses her hands deeply into the dried paints. Jean joins her. In the distance, I see Vincent snap a photo. I give him a quick thumbs-up. It's an amazing moment. I can't wait for Sam to see people interacting with the piece.

The doors open. More people come in. I let Francesca take over the chatting as I rush over to Ahma's side. Daniel is already there, holding her arm and talking softly with her.

When Ahma sees me, she grabs my face and sucks in my cheeks like she's inhaling me whole, and I know she loves it. Tears spring in my eyes. Her frail arms engulf me in a hug.

"So smart," she whispers.

"Thank you, Ahma."

Together, Daniel, Ahma, and I stroll through the exhibit. It's not jam-packed. Instead, viewers read through the placards and study the objects in front of them. Mom and Dad pass out heart-shaped mochi and egg tarts as fast as they can.

Out of the corner of my eye, I see someone who looks exactly like Selena. Wait. It is her. What?

When Daniel sees my face, he kisses my cheek. "Go. I've got your ahma."

I weave through the space until I reach Selena who is dressed in a long, sleek black blazer, with nothing underneath, and heels. I hug her tightly before shrieking.

"What are you doing here?"

"Isn't it the opening night of my best friend's exhibit?"

"Yes, but New York. Los Angeles."

"It's called my parents' credit card airline miles. And you can't hog all this sunshine for yourself. Now, introduce me to your filmmaker boyfriend."

We're arm in arm. Ahma recognizes Selena, which is amazing, because she hasn't seen her in three years.

"This is Daniel," I say.

"Nice to meet you finally," says Daniel.

Selena wags her finger over Daniel's face. "I've heard good things about you, but I had my doubts. Who turns down my girl twice?"

"Selena!"

"She has a point. I was a fool before. It'll never happen again," says Daniel.

"Good," says Selena, smiling.

Then she glances around the room, trying to act all slick about it, but I know she's searching for Francesca.

I smile. "If you want to meet my co-curator, I'm happy to introduce you."

I lead her over to Francesca, who is in the middle of talking with Mia Vasquez. We wait off to the side. Selena looks around.

"Wow, Chloe. You've done it again. It's stunning."

"I'm still in shock that you're here."

"Mid-winter recess. Something I doubt you have here," says Selena. "How am I seeing people bundled up like it's a snowstorm when it's sixty-nine degrees in February? Oh my god. I would be wearing all my shortest skirts on a loop."

I laugh. "Move here, then."

Francesca's finally done talking and is by my side like glue.

"I think you know who this is," I say, gesturing to Selena.

Francesca goes in for the hug. "Our plan worked," she says.

"Excuse me," I say. "What plan?"

Selena thrusts her hands on her hips. "You're not the only one who can make plans, you know?"

"What other plans do you have in store?" I ask.

"You'll have to wait and see," says Selena.

I can see she's itching to talk to Francesca alone from the way she inches closer to her. I take the hint.

"Go. Show Selena around. I've got it from here."

"You sure?" asks Francesca.

"Definitely. Get out of here."

The two of them talk closely. I walk to the front table where Vincent is gabbing away with a good-looking dude. The way they are touching each other's arms, it's clear there's bubbling interest. I decide to give them time alone and step outside.

Lourdes is outside, smoking. She sees me and waves away the smoke.

"Bad habit, I know. I let myself have one cigarette a week."

I stand next to her as she puffs. She gestures toward the studio space.

"You and Francesca really turned it out," says Lourdes.

"Thank you. Thanks for the space. Not many people would give a teenager an entire studio space to transform," I say.

Lourdes stamps out her cigarette on the ground. "I was a teenager when I started these salon events, gathering musicians, artists, writers for these collaborations. People looked at me sideways, like, *who is she,* but in the back of my head, I knew I'd make something out of it. You will too. This is just the start."

She peers in through the glass. "Ooh. Looks like your mom's egg tarts are flying. I better snag one before I lose out."

Lourdes touches my arm before she leaves. "Let's talk next week."

"Cool," I say.

I am anything but cool. My heart leaps up in my throat. She waves goodbye then heads back in.

"What's going on?" asks Daniel.

He slips his arms around my waist and turns me around

to face him. I kiss him hard, like my excitement can be passed on.

"Lourdes wants to talk to me next week."

He extends his palm out and we high-five. He spins me one more time. I am dizzy with excitement.

"Vincent said Mia Vasquez wanted to speak to you," says Daniel.

My eyes go wide, and I dash back into the space. Vincent and Mia are laughing hard. That's a good sign. I make my way over to them. Vincent raises his eyebrows.

"The girl of the hour," says Vincent. "You mentioned wanting to chat with Chloe about an opportunity."

I wait, all ears, until she stops laughing. She dabs tears from her eyes.

"Yes. I have to catch my breath. You're too funny, Vincent, Vincent. So, Chloe, I spoke with Francesca earlier and wanted to share this information with you too. I don't know if you're aware, but the Museum of Contemporary Art offers a fully funded youth fellowship program for young artists. I'm convinced we need to expand the fellowship for future curators. I need to speak to my board members first, but you two would be ideal candidates." She pulls out her business card. "Email me."

"Of course. Yes. Thank you. I'd love that," I say.

"And Vincent, you *must* apply to be a docent at our museum. We have to snap you up," says Mia Vasquez.

"Will do, Mia!"

She leaves, and Vincent and I wait until she's completely

out of earshot to shriek in delight. We hug tightly. Across the room, I see Selena and Francesca sharing a seat and cozied up. I smile.

"Thank you, Vincent! I appreciate you so much."

He waves away my words. "If I land a side hustle, it's all thanks to you. Now, excuse me while I get the number of that hottie before he hightails it out of here. After-party at the Bowl?"

"Definitely."

I find Daniel sitting with Ahma. She talks softly to him. As I approach, I hear my uncle's name as she looks at Daniel. It's time for her to head back home.

"I'll take her home," I say.

Mom and Dad swoop in.

"We're all out of goods. We'll take Ahma home. You enjoy, sweetheart," says Dad.

After they leave, Daniel nuzzles my neck. His warm, full lips are on my collarbone. Our hands touch. We briefly kiss before Daniel pulls away.

"Can we do one more lap through the exhibit? Just the two of us?"

"Definitely," I say.

We slowly stroll through the exhibit. Now that the pressure is off, I can finally enjoy what Francesca and I put together. Daniel stops in front of the three paintings. He brings my hand over his, and we place our hands together on the canvas. He traces the paint with my palm. I am electric with a different kind of excitement.

"Does it look different to you now?" he asks.

"Very," I say.

As the song plays on a loop, with Daniel by my side, I see the colors as separate parts of a whole coming together. The first time I saw it, it seemed like a clash of colors. But suddenly, it all makes sense.

I see the connecting lines Sam put from the first canvas through to the second and how they end in the third. The lines all end on *Love yourself first*.

"How is it different?" asks Daniel.

"I never saw the connections between the three canvases. I always thought they were stages of falling in love, heartbreak, and being alone, but the way this thick black line runs through the three paintings makes me see how all parts of the process are connected. You can't have one without the other."

I turn and kiss Daniel, whispering, "I couldn't have fallen for you without getting over Jake first. You were right about that."

He kisses the tip of my nose. "I'm glad I'm right about something."

We move away from the painting, holding hands. We stay until every last visitor is gone. I urge Selena and Francesca to join Vincent who is singlehandedly starting the after-party. Daniel helps me shut off lights and lock up.

We stand outside of Ruby Street with the warm orange glow of a streetlight above us.

"Ready?" asks Daniel.

"Not yet," I say. I pull him close. "Let's be late."

Daniel's eyebrows shoot up. "What happened to my beautiful girlfriend?"

"She wants to make out with her handsome boyfriend," I say.

We arrive Daniel-style late to the after-party.

ACKNOWLEDGMENTS

I always love reading the acknowledgments in a book because as any writer knows, a book is built with the support of a huge team. I am grateful to have the most amazing people in my life to cheer me on through the ten-plus-year journey to get here.

Thank you to my brilliant agent, Caitie Flum, who gives the best feedback, calms my writer worries, and suggests great books to read. I love working with you. To my fantastic editor, Vicki Lame, I am incredibly lucky to collaborate with you. It's been an absolute dream come true from the moment we first talked. Thank you to Vanessa Aguirre for your kind comments and for making it easy to move this book along. Many thanks to the incredible team at Wednesday Books: Sara Goodman, Eileen Rothschild, Eric Meyer, Lena Shekhter, Carla Benton, Cassie Gutman, Sara Thwaite—for her eagle-eyed copy edits—Susan Walsh, Rivka Holler, Brant Janeway, Meghan Harrington, and Lauren Ablondi-Olivo. Thank you forever to Kerri Resnick and illustrator Leni Kauffman for the best pink book cover a girl could ask for!

Thank you to my sensitivity readers, Melissa Vera, Elizabeth Park, and Akilah White, for helping me make my characters authentic. Thank you to my early beta readers who helped me revise this book for the better: Nia Davenport and

Felice Keller Becker. Thanks to David Licata for your filmmaker knowledge and your support since the beginning. A million thanks to Sutton Long, my best friend, my shoulder to cry on, my dogs-are-the-best fan club copresident, for reading, encouraging me, and for our Saturday morning chats.

A few amazing authors wrote the kindest blurbs for my debut book, so thank you to Brian D. Kennedy, Lyla Lee, Laura Taylor Namey, Suzanne Park, Eric Smith, and Ashley Schumacher. Thanks to Team Vicki for our monthly Zoom meetings that helped me get through my debut year.

I would not be where I am today without the support of my friends: Jessica Lipps, Melissa Sarno, Celena Cipriaso, Laura Beck, Yin Chang, Moonlynn Tsai, Bernadette Guckin, Nikki Santacroce, Alina Kwak, Mike Chen, and Lauren Gibaldi Mathur. Thank you for always having hope.

To my mom friends: Francisca Coombs de Arend, Lisa Bay Santiago, Margaret Nielson, Robin Faerber, and Caitlin Brady-Bell, thank you for listening and helping my family.

To my UPOD family: Tre Johnson, Debby Waldman, Claire Sibonney, Lydia Kan, Jean Trinh, Tara Ellison, and many others for the constant cheerleading that led to this publication. Thank you to David Hochman for the pep talks, coaching, and "write for fifteen minutes a day" advice. Thanks to Jenni Gritters for helping me see the big picture.

To my Pennacook Wonder Women: Alise Alousi, Jen Garfield, Katie Patterson, Katherine Brown, Sabina Khan-Ibarra, and Rena Potok, thank you for lifting me up when I needed it and sending the absolute best group text messages. Special thanks to Rena for our inspiring weekly chats.

To my high school creative writing teacher, Karen Haefelein, thank you for teaching me how to become a writer and seeing who I was before I did.

Thanks to the WriteGirl mentees, staff, and fellow volunteers for inspiring me to have fun while writing.

I saved my family for last because there's so much I want to say. To my husband, Brendan Hay, for taking care of our kids, reading drafts, holding my hand, and helping me add more comedy to this book. You've cheered me on since the day we met. Thanks to my mom, who gifted me books and dropped me off at the Monmouth County Library so I could check out all the books. Thank you to my in-laws, Maureen and John Hay, for reading everything I've ever written. A special thanks to my ahma for watching pro wrestling with me, making me food, and showing me how to have strength. I miss you always. To my twins, Chloe and Clark, thank you for understanding when Mommy had to take time away to write. I love you both so much. I must thank my sweet departed pug, Chewie, who was with me when I got the news of this book deal. To my current cuddle companions, Ziggy, Zoey, and Gremmy, thank you for making each day so cute.

Lastly, thank you, dear reader, for spending your time reading my book. I wrote it during a time when the world felt joyless. I hope it makes you smile and brings you as much joy as I had writing it.